MOURNING
OF THE DOVE

Mourning
of the Dove

Sandra Fox Murphy

atmosphere press

*This novel is dedicated to all the men,
women, children, and creatures,
regardless of North or South, who were forever lost
or harmed by the ferocity of the Civil War—
a war that was both necessary to grant the value of a free life
and unnecessary in its brutality
when changing hearts is always the better path.*

Mourning of the Dove

May you see God's light on the path ahead
when the road you walk is dark.
May you always hear even in your hour of sorrow
the gentle singing of the lark.
When times are hard
May hardness never turn your heart to stone.
may you always remember when the shadows fall
you do not walk alone.

~ An Irish Blessing

Prologue

November 1860

The feeble light of late fall seeped in the windowpanes at the Hughes' home in Austin. Its shrouded brilliance fell across the bride's face and laid bare the gravity held in her father's expression. Beads of autumn sunlight fluttered about the room like playful fireflies on a summer night, yet it was the same week the country had elected a new president, Abraham Lincoln, and now Fidelia stood beside her Pa, ready to be joined forever in wedlock. Each a sober pledge. Yet a sadness troubled Fidelia's pale eyes and held a burden of regret, for she knew this wasn't the wedding she'd dreamt of.

Her dreams had been filled with the spirited love between her and Miles Maloney. Dreams of a wedding to the young man who'd stolen her heart, perhaps a ceremony in the meadow near Grandpa's farm, where sunlight would splay the colors of spring's wildflowers with the bond that had drawn her to the man from North Carolina. He'd held a confidence that had enfolded her like the comfort of a winter blanket, a confidence that came carefree and full of easy laughter binding their shared desire to feel the nearness of each other. That was the wedding day she'd dreamed of even after she'd succumbed to James' persistent proposals.

For months, her resistance had remained firm. She knew she would hear from Miles, or better, see him riding his gelding Marco up the path to the McCord farm. She'd had no doubt that their bond was genuine, mutual in their devotion to each other.

But now she stood elegant in the silk gown of the palest of blues, the gown her ma and aunt, Matilda, had sewn for her. Her hand, dressed in crocheted lace at her wrist, rested on her pa's arm, and she took the first steps through the room where her betrothed stood in front of the reverend. Suddenly there was a spasm in her belly. It came with an ache that made her want to double over, made her want to run, but she resisted the palsied anguish and straightened her spine. Her hand tightened on Pa's arm, and he turned a questioning look toward his daughter when, at the same moment, Fidelia suddenly became aware that he appeared a stranger to her. He'd always been distant from his girls, and now she was his only daughter. An ache for her father's love poured through her as the spasm in her gut faded. Fidelia's eyes turned to find James, the man across the room who would soon be her husband, and the adoration she saw in his eyes rallied her. She pushed back her shoulders and took in a slow, deep breath to calm herself.

When she saw James smile at her approach, she averted her eyes to find the face of her mother watching her only daughter. Next to Ma sat Grandma and Grandpa, their faces lit with love and pride in their granddaughter. *Why were they smiling?* They knew her heart was consumed by love for another, yet they'd all told her she was foolish and pining for someone not worthy of her.

"Delia, he's not coming back," they'd said. "You would have heard from him," they'd said. And, each time, she had looked right through them, her heart aflutter with sorrow and yearning, a yearning that had choked her. Their ceaseless counsel had made her dizzy with uncertainty, and, finally, she'd faltered.

Now, as she followed her Pa's lead and took the third step forward, her eyes rose to meet James' gaze. He was her friend, her confidante, her advocate. She loved him, but not in the way she'd loved Miles. She held the gaze of James' eyes until she stood by his side, as the buzz of the reverend's words surrounded her. All she felt was the flush of her face from the warmth that seeped through the room as if grace had sought her and could not find her.

Reverend Gillette spoke the words of their marriage covenant, and Fidelia heard words fall from her mouth as if they were spoken by another. Practiced words of obeyance and sickness, and as she looked once more into James' eyes when they'd been deemed man and wife, the love she saw there brought her back to the moment.

The noise and the savory smells of celebration filled the day until night fell into Austin, and the deed was done.

CHAPTER 1

1861, Austin, Texas

Fidelia found no comfort as she sat at the window of her home in Austin. Her tears dropped slowly as the rain muddied the street outside. She usually loved the comfort of a steady rain, but her husband James had left in the morning. His horse outfitted for travel to join up with the 8th Texas Cavalry Regiment in Bastrop, his musket stowed in his scabbard, James had pulled his wife tight against him and kissed her as if he might never see her again, and that very fear had made her tremble. He'd then squeezed her before he mounted his gray mare, tipping his hat toward her before he rode off with his friend Wayne Hamilton. Only minutes later, the rain fell heavily from the skies as if a proper farewell and then waned to a drizzle as the day wore on.

Leona set a cup of hot tea beside Fidelia. In a comforting gesture, she gently brushed Fidelia's shoulder as she walked away. Leona was the daughter of Mary, the woman who had long worked for the family and who'd stayed with James' late mother through her short illness. His mother had died only a month after her son's wedding, and Fidelia had spent a week tending to the sweet lady. Those days had reminded her of how swiftly a fever could take away a loved one as it had her young sisters.

Leona's footsteps echoed on the wooden floors as she left the room, and the new emptiness of the house rang pro-foundly. Fidelia put her handkerchief to her face and dried her eyes and nose. As the rain fell to a drizzle, activity hummed in the muddied streets as men busied themselves with tasks and small groups mustered to speak of war. The commotion was an odd mixture of hoots of war and glory and, like this morning in front of her own home, the dismay and fear of what was to come. The air outside hung with uncommon disquiet as wagons splashed down the road, wagons carrying the sustenance of war. Many headed toward the coast, toward Galveston, and some rode west and north to thwart the surge of Indian attacks.

Fidelia thought of the McCord farm to the north of the city, where her grandparents lived, where she'd grown up. And then, she thought of her ma. Ma and Pa now lived alone in the cabin to the northwest near the river, and Fidelia could not fathom the isolation her ma endured. The life she, herself, had feared when she was a girl, when Pa was building the cabin amidst his fields.

Now, a sense of guilt wove through her mind as she sat in the comfort of her home. She had a servant to prepare meals and lived amidst the bustle of people. And Fidelia wished she could bring her ma to stay with her, yet she knew full well her mother would never leave Pa. *But she could invite her mother for a visit, and what about Pa? Would he volunteer to join a regiment as had James? Or had he already done so?* She'd received no word from them.

Texas had voted to secede from the United States in February, overwhelmingly and contrary to the governor's counsel. Now, Governor Houston was gone and replaced by a new man, Edward Clark, an advocate of the secession. Word spread that Sam Houston had resigned at the convention's decision to secede, and the lawyer Tom Hughes, in

Georgetown, had supported the governor, had convinced the county to support the Union. But fears of the unknown spilled through the market and into dining rooms. Heads shook, for the folly of it all was beyond the grasp of a state with such a painstaking history in seeking statehood. James had continued to work and worry each day at his print shop, knowing its very future was in jeopardy, though the printing calls kept the machines running all day. The staff began leaving one by one, relocating their families or enlisting with a regiment, and James knew he'd soon be out there inking the plates himself, if not finding himself on battle lines. He'd worked hard for the success of his print shop, and though he knew his time to take up arms would come, what would become of his business? How long could his man, George, keep things running? George was a master of the books, a magician with the monies, but he had no inkling how to lay out a job or run the presses.

Summer had arrived with its relentless sun and endured into August, and a day after James had told his wife that, at the urging of John Wharton, he'd joined the cavalry, she'd revealed her suspicion that she was with child. She hadn't needed her mother to confirm her condition. She knew the signs of an absent bleed and retching in the mornings. She'd seen her uncle's wife, Matilda, go through the daily agonies.

"I pray I'll be home before the birth, Fidelia. I pray," said James when he'd bid her goodbye in the parlor before they'd walked outside together. The unspoken sentiments and fears in between the uttered words were heard clearly by Fidelia, though the rumors had been that the war would be speedily won. The unknown had brought Fidelia to cling to her husband before he'd mounted his horse that morning to ride east. From his horse, he looked down into her eyes, looking taller than he was, his hair, the color of wheat, beginning to curl in the mist.

But it was his words, *may it be a daughter as beautiful as her mother,* that settled in her thoughts, in her heart. Despite how they'd come to marry, she did love this man. This man who'd both wooed her and been her friend. His words about a daughter rang with such a tenderness that diverged from the constant dismissal by her own father, who'd almost daily bemoaned the absence of sons.

Now, sitting alone in Austin, her thoughts turned back to her wedding day only months before in the autumn of last year. How such melancholy had filled her on that day as she'd thought of Miles. Miles. It was as if he'd vanished from the world, as if the Indians might have captured him near San Saba, but Indians took only women and children They would have killed a young, strong man like Miles. And, had they done so, the buzzards near a Lampasas trail would have picked him clean. Fidelia shuddered at her own thoughts and then remembered her aunt, Audrey, all those years before. A young beauty, smitten by the captivating trapper, Edmund Chouteau, from Kansas City. Fidelia remembered how her aunt had run off with him and Pa had gone after her, how Pa had ripped his sister from the only chance she'd had of a devoted love. *Had they only known God's plan.* How she'd lost Edmund, and then, how he'd lost her to scarlet fever. Suddenly, Fidelia felt as if she walked her aunt's path. *What had happened to sweet Miles?* He was younger than her husband, and she'd fallen in love with his carefree spirit and smiling eyes, and she could still envision him, tall and lean, his brown hair often tousled. When he wasn't solemn, he appeared younger than his years. *What would become of her husband James, now riding into war?* Aunt Audrey's early death had made such an impression on young Fidelia of the impact of life's choices. *Had she chosen the wrong path by marrying James?* All those choices were snatched from her, just as life had been stolen from Aunt Audrey, and the thoughts carried her back even farther, so many years ago, to the day her family had loaded the covered wagons in Indiana, not far from Lake Erie. How she and her sister Emily, just young girls then, had stuffed their chemises and dresses into chintz sacks for the long and treacherous journey to Texas. She thought of all the years since that day and the losses that befell the family. But there had been joy and laughter as well, held so merciful midst the sorrows.

A rumble of thunder brought Fidelia back to the present moment. Rather than getting lost in idle nostalgia, she shook off the distraction and went to the kitchen to help Leona prepare dinner.

"Will there be fighting in the streets, ma'am?" asked Leona, her voice unsteady. Leona was a young woman of only sixteen, and when her mother Mary, who'd only worked at the home during daylight, had died, James and his mother had decided to provide Leona a stipend and shelter in their home in return for her services.

"I don't think so, Leona. I hope not," Fidelia said. "I imagine it will be more to the east of Texas, far east I would assume. Time will tell."

But her spoken words quelled none of the uncertainty hanging over the two women, and they prepared the meal and sat together, speaking only of the weather as they ate.

"Leona, I am tired," said Fidelia, after the meal was done. "I am going upstairs to lay down."

Upstairs, she pulled her tapestry bag from beneath the armoire and set it on the window seat. She would pack it another day for travel to Grandpa's farm when the roads had dried, but looking about the room, she realized she was alone. *James was gone, and who would ensure her safety?* A woman alone should not likely be taking a buggy north of the city, but the realization of altered circumstances set her mind spinning. So many of the men had left, and the city was full of women suddenly alone and leading households. *How would the women conquer this new world still so untamed?*

She caught her reflection in the mirror of the dressing table and stopped. Fidelia looked at herself and swiftly recognized the farm girl she used to be. Her dress was fancier and her hem not soiled, but her hair was askew, and there was that set to her jaw that revealed her willfulness. She'd loved her life on the farm, sneaking off to Brushy Creek with her friend. She'd never let fear of dangers keep her from pacing her horse, Trapper, now stabled at Grandpa's barn, yet she knew well the dangers and tragedies of working the frontier land. She looked once more at her reflected image. She'd be fine and would do what needed doing.

CHAPTER 2

Mount Vernon, Ohio

The gas lights of Mount Vernon had been dimmed, and the leaves of the linden and elm trees along the street were barely rustling in the morning light as the young man walked down Mulberry Street. He heard nothing but the cadence of his own steps, and anticipation stirred within at meeting with Tony Norton after over a year, a year of unsettled times. There was much to share.

Anthony Banning Norton had arrived in Mount Vernon on the eve before, and Miles Maloney walked down the street with thoughts churning with all the information he'd gleaned over time and full of curiosity to learn of conditions in Texas. He looked up to see the elm leaves turning shades of yellow and brown and realized, abruptly, how fast seasons had passed since he'd left Texas. He winced at the awareness, at how much times had changed, and then, with sudden insight, at how much he'd changed. Now, he was a man driven, spurred to get the story at the cost of himself.

The two men had seen each other only once, fleetingly in Washington, since Norton, editor and owner of the *Southern Intelligencer*, had sent Miles on missions into the Northern states, forcing Miles to part from home and family. There'd been nights, sleepless nights, when Miles had wondered if his position at the newspaper had been worth the cost of his private life, but the issues separating the country were daunting, and Miles held great respect for his boss. He was keen to share the information he'd garnered from his time with the Pinkertons, his forays into the Confederacy, and from his time in Washington, the Columbia Territory.

As clouds hung heavy in the sky, predicting a drenching, Miles turned right onto High Street and remembered the big skies of Texas. The prairie was harsh in winter and flowered in spring, and there were gray clouds on that misty day he rode over an embankment and saw John McCord's fields and then the intense stare of a striking woman. That moment he fell in love. Now, on an autumn day in Ohio, the man of only twenty-four felt older than his years and thought on how he'd seen more of his country than most men three times older.

He steadied himself on the stoop of the Norton home and straightened his shoulders as he breathed in the morning air. Miles had thought of Texas every single day since he'd left. Of Fidelia, the only woman he'd loved yet been foolish enough to leave behind. He thought of the creeks and grassland of San Saba and the white Indian—the boy he had met who'd been captured and held by the Comanche and could never return to his white ways. But last night, he'd laid on a cot in a boarding house, wrapped in sheets that had held no warmth. His memories of Fidelia had filled his head, and he'd tossed and turned for hours. She held a passion and ease in life he'd not encountered in any other woman.

He knocked on the door of the shingled house on High Street and waited, unsure if his friend would yet be awake but remembering his boss was an early riser. In the past, he'd often wondered if the old man ever went to bed.

The heavy snows in Michigan had been a hindrance to his work and travel, sometimes delaying a story to Tony Norton, and they kept the winter trains to Washington stalled more often than not. Even the years he'd spent in Arkansas had not prepared him for the unrelenting winters of the Great Lakes. Tony had sent him north to dig for stories before the war even started, but it was already stewing, and Miles became immersed in covert actions at great risk to himself as well as those dear to him, all of whom he now kept at a distance.

He knocked on the door more forcefully. He waited, removed his hat, and ran his fingers through his hair, and, as he did so, he thought of Jackson, his brother in North Carolina, now married and a father. *Had Jackson enlisted in the war effort?* He surely would have been expected to do so, and now the two brothers may be at odds on the politics of war.

The door opened and gripped Miles in the present.

"Sir," she said. "May I help you?"

Miles did not recognize the woman. It was not his friend's wife.

"Yes, I'm expected by Mister Norton. The name is Miles Maloney."

"Aye, my brother said you would be coming." She beckoned him inside.

Tony came sprinting down the stairway, dressed, but Miles saw his hair was uncombed, and his unruly beard seemed to have grown even longer than last Miles had seen him, as if that were even possible. The man, small in stature and tall in confidence, came straight toward Miles and embraced him in a firm hug, the unexpected gesture startling the young man.

"Maloney," he said, grabbing Miles' hand and shaking it vigorously. "Get some hot tea for us, Melanie."

Norton's sister turned and walked away.

"Come, sit down in here," he said, walking into a sitting room with a large desk and worn, overstuffed chairs. Miles took a seat, the one nearest the hearth.

"Maria is still sleeping, but she will be glad to see you again. Our journey tired her," he said as he sat in a straight-backed chair. "I believe I got out of Austin before the politicians turned on me. My old friend Barrett from Indiana has already shut down his paper in Houston, but I've heard it rumored he's ill. Once they've discovered I'm gone to Ohio, I'll likely not be able to return. But we shall manage the newspaper from here, for as long as we can. And from here, we can publish anywhere. Can you believe they have stricken old Sam Houston from office?"

"No, sir," said Miles. "After all Houston has done for Texas. But I admire him standing ground."

Miles squirmed in his seat before continuing. "Sir, I know the risks, but I am eager to return to Austin. Can I be of any service in the city? Garnering information from the South for your benefit?"

Norton sat silent. He lit his pipe and stroked his beard, a scraggly beard he refused to trim. "Not until Henry Clay is President," he'd declared to everyone who suggested a trip to the barber. Norton was known for his appearance, and, equally, for his opinions. The old man had sent Miles north on assignment, just prior to the most bizarre incident in Austin. Norton, who had purchased the *Intelligencer* in 1860, and John Marshall, the editor of the *Texas Gazette*, constantly argued when in each other's presence and often in the print of their newspapers, and harsh words had carried them to the declaration of a duel. Duels were unlawful in Texas, so Norton, fearless and as bullheaded as they come, said he would meet Marshall beyond the boundary in Indian territory. To Norton's surprise, Marshall accepted the challenge. Though both traveled to Sherman, circumstances and, likely, self-preservation spared their meeting and doable harm, but the enduring harsh words between the two men continued. In Texas, Norton was known in political circles as "Houston's bugle."

Miles had been grateful that the news of the duel had reached him two months after the ordeal, for he would have been terrified for his editor, who had truly become a friend and mentor.

"Son, I suspect I know your motivation to return to Texas, but the risks are too great. They are hanging anyone in Texas speaking against the Confederacy. A fella who boarded the train in Dallas told me of an old man called Josiah hanged by a group of men when he said the South couldn't win. I had to chuckle at hearing the tale, knowing the man spoke the truth and hoping that old Josiah found repentance on his way to the Lord. Just remember, Son, the risks, should your endeavors be discovered, would extend to family and friends."

Norton's response was not unexpected, but, still, the spoken words sat heavy with Miles. Norton continued.

"Miles, it appears to me that you may not be aware, but James Hughes wed your Miss McCord. In November. I believe you know Mister Hughes, of the print shop. And, by the way, I expect the shop will likely shut down soon as a result of Hughes joining up with the cavalry. Sorry to bear this news, particularly if you did not already know."

Now it was Miles who sat speechless. He had not heard of the wedding, for he had cut his ties in the city due to the nature of his work. He had written but one letter to Fidelia, the letter warning her of the onslaught of a coming war and asking her to wait for him. He had declared his love for her and his intent to return to marry her when the war ended.

Norton placed a glass of whiskey in Miles' hand but held onto the glass until the young man's fingers gripped it and their eyes met. Miles took a sip. Shook his head. Shook off the shock of the news he'd just heard. Norton returned to his seat.

"It's early in the day, Son, but down the elixir," said Norton.

"I'm sorry, Mister Norton," said Miles. "The frankness of your words, the news, did take me by surprise."

"Good God, boy," said Norton, his eyes full of their familiar mischievous glint. "A woman is the least of our worries. The nation's at stake, and, in the wrong place, we could be hung."

The outburst startled Miles, and Norton paused a moment.

"Let me add, much inappropriately, that James Hughes may not survive the swash of a saber on a battlefield. Life is day by day. As for your return to Austin, I can tell you that the goddamned rabble-rousers were hanging free-staters before I left. You don't want to view Texas from the end of a rope, do ya? Or, for that matter, your Missus Hughes, should she be caught with a letter from you."

The shock of hearing her called Missus Hughes startled Miles again, but Norton, oblivious, sipped his tea, now lukewarm, and yelled for his sister and a fresh pot.

"Make it hot this time," he growled at her when she took the teapot. She pulled a face and then looked toward Miles with a smile, as if she were accustomed to the demands of her brother. Norton turned back to Miles.

"After all you've done at my behest, Son, you best call me Tony and stop calling me mister. We'll keep this briefing short today. I will have plenty of time here in Mount Vernon."

In July of the previous year, Tony Norton had sent Miles to the Territory of Columbia, right into the chaos of Washington. He'd made accommodations and helped him gain access to politicians and military officials so information could be fed back to the newspaper in Austin. He'd warned Miles to cut his Austin ties, for animosity was building between abolitionists and the secessionists defending slavery.

Miles had struggled with his mission. In spite of his

southern roots, he did not support the ownership of slaves, a belief that fell in line with that of Tony Norton from Ohio. But, on the other hand, in addition to family in the Appalachian Mountains of North Carolina, Miles was leaving behind Fidelia, who meant everything to him, and his aunt in San Saba who'd come to rely on her nephew's help. The choice before him had kept him awake at night, and it took him almost a month to compose the concise but beseeching letter to Fidelia, which he later mailed from Maryland, a state still undecided.

What was ironic was that Fidelia's family would have supported his mission, since they were free-staters from Indiana, but he knew any knowledge of his work, as well as mail from the North, could compromise them in the eyes of the state or, even, their neighbors. He held firm in his belief, and from all that he'd heard, that this conflict would be short-lived. He could return in a year or less. But now, as he sat in Norton's home with his friend and editor, it was not lost on him that he'd left Texas over a year ago.

"Tony, my two months with the Pinkerton Agency were enlightening, but, at present, the Pinkertons are engrossed in protecting the President, and, before that, they seemed to be chasing trains, guarding the money loads."

Miles had pursued the Pinkertons based on information he'd uncovered in the East. The agency had been protecting Lincoln even before he'd won the presidency.

"They're an odd bunch, disordered, in my opinion," Miles continued, "but I had the occasion to go on a few jaunts looking for bandits. What can I say? They like to live on that feeble line in life where death doesn't frighten them, and in the midst of their raids, I would find a thrill traveling that daring line with them. I did use some of their techniques this year to venture into political meetings where my very own allegiance was never suspected. Sir, I was amazed, myself, at the ease with which this could be done."

"Really? Explain," said Norton as he leaned forward and rested his elbows on his knees, holding his face in his hands. His eyes lit with curiosity.

"In May, I took the train from the District down to Richmond, Virginia, hoping to interview some of the secessionist politicians. Billy Smith, for example, is now with the Congress of the Confederacy. I hoped to get some feel for their strategies.

"'Boy, I heard you're from Cherokee County,' Smith said to me. 'Come join us for a drink. I've heard your old man is a moonshiner back home.' I acknowledged my pa's tendencies and that I'd grown up in the hollers, but then I told him I'd been working in Texas, further warranting my ties to the Confederacy, striving to loosen his lips. Said I was searching for information for our newspaper in Austin, and the old man seemed surprised there even were newspapers in Texas," said Miles, sending Tony Norton into laughter. "He willingly let me interview him, but there was little revelation of military maneuvers. He even asked me of McClellan's plans to attack Richmond, and I laughed and told him such intelligence would not be shared with the likes of me, though I knew McClellan was training the Union's army near the capital and would likely lead troops south soon enough. Mostly, I sensed disorder in the Confederate's Richmond, peppered with a bold hunger to go forth to battle. Gratuitous confidence."

"Well, I'd best not print that in the paper down in Austin," said Norton as he extinguished his pipe. "I just wonder how long before they burn down our office."

"Old Smith told me plenty of their politics, but much of it useless as to war schemes. Yet, I took notes on everything," said Miles as he caught sight of Norton's old familiar buckhorn cane leaning near his desk.

Norton shook his head.

"It's the same as the rabble-rousing I saw in Austin and heard of throughout the state. Cries for war," said Norton, his head hung in anguish. He looked like the silhouette of a Quaker in sorrowful prayer. But Norton was no Quaker.

"I'm staying here, Son. In Ohio," he said. "Old Marshall at the *Gazette* will not stop me. We'll work from here."

The fire in Norton's eyes heartened young Miles, but deep in the pit of his stomach, he still ached for Texas.

Chapter 3

Bastrop, Texas

James had been at the camp in Bastrop for over a week, where he shared a tent with a fellow called Pete Mullen from near Caldwell. The man said he'd left his wife and child behind at his pa's farm. Said he and his pa had been raising sheep, and with the field harvest behind him, his father had encouraged him to join the cavalry. "Join up," his father had said, "before the Confederacy gets ya carrying a rifle on foot, make you naught but a bullseye on the first line into fightin'."

In the darkness of their shared tent, midst the calls of an owl, James lay on his rickety cot and remembered the softness of his Fidelia and the warmth of their bed in Austin. He held little doubt in his mind that, in the cot beside him, Pete was having the same thoughts and wondering if he would live to return to the arms of his own family. It was said the war would be short-lived, but those words came mostly from the Union. The determination of the South would be more than they would expect, and James wondered if Texas should have stood on its own, either as the republic it had once been or, at least, against this war. Yet, the plantation owners in east Texas and their politicians would only abide secession and a fight.

James rolled over to face away from Mullen and remembered when, back in Austin, he'd met John Wharton, a delegate at the secession convention who'd come into the print shop, and the two men had struck up a conversation about the war. James knew even then that there would be expectations to defend the state and, now, the Confederacy. As Wharton waited for posters to be printed, he advised James to join the cavalry.

"They'll be filling positions for artillery and infantrymen soon enough," Wharton had said. James now remembered the man's words clear as the chime of a bell. "We're Texans, Son. Cavalrymen. We're at one with our horse, so you'd best get in now."

By July of 1861, James had heard the calls to muster, seen the posters for Benjamin Terry's Rangers, and remembered Wharton's advice. He signed up.

His shop would likely be lost if the fight lasted too long, a fate he feared, yet he held hope that old George could keep the business afloat. He knew getting help to run the presses would fade if the war persisted. Farms would fail, and it was already clear that the Indian tribes were taking advantage of the chaos. The future looked dim, but he knew he wasn't alone, and he knew his Fidelia would be the grace he could come home to.

Then, as he lay there in his tent, his thoughts turned dark like the veil of night in the piney woods. *What had become of that Miles Maloney?* Though he'd taken advantage of the young man's absence, James did not believe Miles was the sort to vanish—not without a word. James knew well the man from North Carolina was smitten with Fidelia and had formed a bond with the McCord family. There'd been no report of his death, though he'd often traveled alone on the trail to San Saba. James' thoughts persisted. *Would he show up again? And, if he did, how would his own wife react to the young man's return? And the war. How might that complicate the absence or return of Miles?*

James had not been passive in the matter. He had visited the newspaper and asked about Mister Maloney, and he was certain that Fidelia or a member of her family would have done the same when Maloney seemed to disappear. James had spoken with the editor, Norton, but the old man's only response was that the boy had been sent on assignment and Norton would say no more. Just shook his head. It was mysterious in a time when everyone had been on edge, and James was suspect of the editor's candor or, likely, the lack thereof. Maybe Miles had gone home to the Carolinas as had his brother. Finally, in the midst of the night, sleep found James and quelled his troubled thoughts.

"Hey, Hughes, get your ass out of bed," came the wake-up call from Lieutenant Burdett, a tall fellow sporting a red beard. James had heard the lieutenant was from Austin but had never seen him in the city, not that he recalled.

"We're heading east in a couple days, and you don't appear ready. You've likely missed your vittles."

James pulled on his pants and socks, dressing hurriedly, and walked over toward the mess tent, splashing trough water onto his face on the way. The mess was about half empty, and he filled his plate and sat down next to Pete Mullen and Paul Watkins, both about done eating.

"Didn't sleep much last night. You?" asked James, downing lukewarm coffee. He pulled his warmed hands from his pockets to each side of his head, smoothing down his hair.

"Not much," said Watkins without looking up from his plate. He was a farmer from south of Austin.

"Tried to wake you, but you was sleepin' like a log. Me—I slept like a babe," Pete said, proving James' nighttime reckonings to be flawed. He figured the fellow slept peacefully because his infant was back home. Maybe it was the first good sleep he'd had in months. James gobbled down cooled eggs and biscuits before heading over to the barn.

James knew his shooting abilities were excellent but fretted that his riding skills were lacking the confidence that he would soon need on a battlefield. He'd grown up in Alabama, on a farm just east of Muscle Shoals where his father had an old printing machine in the barn. When someone had needed a poster or such, Pa Hughes would go out in the barn and set the letters, ink the press, and charge customers for things such as horse bills and contracts. James never did find how his pa came to own that old iron press.

In Alabama, James had learned to shoot and turned out to be a swift marksman. When he turned seventeen, he attended LaGrange College for two years, but he left for Austin when the school moved to Florence and, at the same time, his father had sold the land and decided Texas held prospects. Along with his uncle, the three men headed west with the iron press stashed in the second wagon. But, in all those years, young James learned the care of horses but never became a practiced rider.

"Hey, Pete, let's take our horses out," yelled James, seeing Pete brushing his chestnut bay on the other side of the barn. "Do some drills."

"Yep, I could use some run-throughs. Ain't got much learnin' from spending my time behind a plow or shearing sheep," he yelled back. "Give me a minute."

Once their horses were saddled, the two men rode down the trail eastward on a rare misty morning in August. Some vaporous clouds hung near the ground and wove their way through the tall pines.

"Guess we'll get the mounts they give us, once we're in the field. I heard the company hired three or four local boys from near the academy to take our mounts back to Austin. You got someone to pick up yours?" asked James.

"I sent word to my pa. He'll pick up my mare."

"Well, I'm hoping to get a good steed when we get where we're going," said James.

"Luck o' the draw, sir. S'pose we're only as good as our mounts."

"Call me James. We're no different, Pete. Just two sorry souls heading out to God knows where," said James, then he whipped his horse to the right and into the pines.

"Follow me," he yelled back to his companion just as he snapped a couple of twigs with the top of his head. "Whoa." He stopped to retrieve his hat in the leaves and remounted.

With that, Pete turned and coaxed his mare to follow James, easing through the woods. When James went out of sight, Pete stilled his horse and listened for the snapped twigs or the snorts of a horse, then followed the sounds.

"Now, me," said Pete, after weaving amongst the trees for about twenty minutes. "You follow me."

After wandering through the thickets of the piney woods, the two men came upon a creek and stopped to rest and water their horses.

"Not bad," said James. "Guess we should do the drill while sighting our weapon. S'pose it'd be good we get more adept at shooting and riding at the same time."

The two of them chuckled, their laughter holding a tinge of tension.

"Ya know the way back?" asked Pete.

"Nope. But wish I had a fishing pole. Look at all those suckers swimming in the coolness of that water in the shallow down where the creek meets the river."

Pete ignored the river and looked flinty at James as the horses still watered at the creek's edge.

"Do you know how to track?" asked James.

"Not much. Only tracked the scat and prints when hunting," said Pete.

"Well, I guess it's time we learned. Suppose we could be tracking Indians or the enemy up yonder. Let's find our tracks back to the trail."

"We're fightin' Indians, too?" asked Pete.

"Ha! I do hope not. I think the Northerners have driven most of the tribes west." James rose and stood looking at the river, and then quickly turned, stepped into the stirrup, and mounted his horse.

"You lead, James. I don't wanna miss dinner," said Pete, smiling over at James and holding his reins taut.

The journey back to the trail took twice as long as it did to find the creek, and for a moment, the men lost their way. But, between the two of them, they found the snapped twigs, impressions in the moss, and tousled leaves that marked the path they'd first traveled toward the trail.

At dinner, the lieutenant told the men that Company D would leave camp the morning after next.

"Pack your gear tomorrow. Be certain you pack what y'all need, for we're going a long way," he said. "The regiment's waiting for us in Houston."

When Miles finished his meal, he walked again to the barn. He checked the saddle bag to see if it held anything but found it empty, and he tightened all the straps. He brushed down his old mare, destined back to Austin, where Herman Cannon would retrieve her and make good use of her, as James had instructed. With the strokes of the brush, he recalled how Fidelia would sit at her dressing table and brush her long, dark hair at night. The delicate turn of her neck as her arm moved back and forth. How she still carried a shyness when she turned back the blankets and lay beside him, but James knew the source of her reserve. He knew that Maloney, though absent, stood endlessly between them. She wouldn't speak of it, and sometimes James just wanted to get it all out in the open, but he was afraid of how such a conversation might end. Now, he hung up his saddle and carried his saddle bag, walking back to his tent and wondering how the story would end. Surely, raucous battles lay before him and his comrades, and he pondered if he would come home and what he would come home to.

As darkness cloaked the rows of tents, the journey before the Rangers sat heavily in the thoughts of the two men silent in their cots, where James fell into fierce nightmares of combat and young Pete lay wide-eyed in the night, fearful of what the future had in store.

CHAPTER 4

Austin, Texas

Before the roads had dried and Fidelia had packed a bag for the trip to Pond Springs, Herman Cannon showed up one morning. Leona led the man into the dining room as Fidelia sat at the table in her morning dress, her dark waves still unpinned and falling over her shoulders, as she penned a letter to her mother.

"Ma'am," said Herman, removing his hat.

Fidelia looked up to see her guest, and it took a couple of moments before she recognized him.

"Oh, dear. Good morning, Herman. It is a pleasure to see you again," said Fidelia. "It's been such a long time."

"Yes, ma'am. Was at Master Jeremy's funeral, the last I saw you. Now, my hair's a bit grayer," he said and bowed his head at Jeremy's memory. "Your Mister Hughes gave me clear instructions to see to your needs while he's away, should you need to go anywhere," he said.

Fidelia smiled, both at the old man's kindness and at the care her husband had provided. She laid down her pen.

Herman had been one of the carpenters in her Uncle Jeremy's woodworking emporium, a warehouse that was once across the street from James' print shop. Uncle Jeremy, who was much older than Fidelia, and James had been dear friends, and that is how she'd met her husband, through Jeremy. Fidelia thought highly of Herman, who had often taken the time to visit with her when she traveled to her uncle's shop.

"How is your family, Herman?" asked Fidelia.

"My wife passed last year, and my sons are both gone to the army. I do have a daughter-in-law, Ida, and her tot, Isaac, living with me. It sure is good ta have some company at the house again," he said.

"I'm sorry to hear of your wife. And all these men gone off to war are in my prayers every night," said Fidelia.

Herman shifted his weight to his right foot, and Fidelia noticed how her old friend had aged. The man, his hair grayed at the hairline, had been grateful for the job at Jeremy's shop after his farm to the west of Austin had failed. He'd been a hard worker, and she recalled how the man had always talked of his wife and his sons who, back then, were working cattle drives from Abilene up to Baxter Springs. Uncle Jeremy had always relied on Herman to get things done for him, to make sure deadlines were met.

"Thank ya, ma'am," said Herman. "I's praying, too, that my boys come back home."

"Sit down. Here, with me," she said and called to Leona to bring a pot of tea and two cups.

"Ya need anything, Missus Hughes?" he asked. "I can take ya anywhere. Got all the time in the world now."

Fidelia was certain that James had paid and promised compensation to Herman Cannon to watch over her. She knew her husband well enough to hold no surprise at these arrangements. She suddenly realized that after her uncle had been murdered and the warehouse shut down, she'd had no knowledge of what had happened to his employees.

Leona walked into the room and set two cups at the table with a steaming teapot and a plate of freshly baked biscuits, still warm.

"And I'll bring some strawberry jam."

"Thank you, Leona," said Fidelia. "Please join us if you'd like."

"Thank you, ma'am," she answered. "But I do have some

bread at the stove, ready for the oven."

"Herman," she continued, "what have you been doing since the woodworking shop closed? Did you find a position?"

"I've worked a bit for a smaller shop, a few hours a week, and I've been doing some carpentry through word of mouth. Repairs, a few pieces of furniture. Been enough to pay my bills," he said.

"That's good to hear. I imagine things have changed since the war's begun. I now have the printing shop to worry over, but, for now, I rely upon George to see to things," said Fidelia. She looked toward the window. "I can ride a horse and take out a wagon, but I have planned a trip up to Pond Springs and likely on out to the river to my Pa's cabin. I was worried about traveling alone in these times."

She did not mention her suspected pregnancy. It was too early, she thought, as Leona set the jam on the table.

"If you are available to take me and Leona out to my grandpa's home, it would be a blessing. I can compensate you."

"Yes, ma'am. No compensation is needed," he replied.

"Oh, yes, it is, Herman," she said. "Or has my husband already taken care of that?"

Herman saw the twinkle in Fidelia's eyes as she looked toward him, and he nodded and smiled widely.

"Well, you let me know when you're ready, ma'am, and we'll be going. And, before I leave you there, let me know the date I need to return to retrieve you and Miss Leona."

"That will work," said Fidelia.

He rose to leave, and Fidelia told him to sit back down.

"Finish your tea, Herman," she said, "and tell me all about little Isaac."

James had been gone three weeks when Herman tied the satchels to the buggy and Fidelia and Leona climbed in. Fidelia sat next to Herman for the ride north to Pond Springs. She had not seen her grandparents since she and James had visited in the spring, though there had been letters between them. She knew that Grandpa struggled with the absence of family. It wasn't the work that overwhelmed him, but the absence of conversations, the absence of children and grandchildren.

"Thank the Lord that your grandpa doesn't have a fondness for saloons," Grandma had written in her last letter, and the words had made Fidelia laugh. Yet there was a tinge of sadness that lingered, sadness for both Grandpa's loneliness and the unspoken words about her own father's weakness for wagers and the drink.

It was still warm in October, and the sky held a stillness as if the heavens were loath to find winter. Though the ride was bumpy, fresh air and sun lifted the spirits of the women. Young Leona rarely left the Hughes' house except for forays to the market, and, on their journey, she remarked often to Fidelia about the sights revealed as they traveled north through the city and beyond.

"Oh, Missus Hughes, look at the vast fields. Why is that man plowing so near to winter coming?" Leona asked.

Leona's childhood had not included travel in the country. Her mother was widowed when young, and the two had been tied to the city, where Leona attended school until learning her letters. After she'd learned to read, she would help her mother at home and at the Hughes' house. The young woman, her youthful features screened from the sun by her bonnet, was mesmerized by farms and the largeness of life beyond the captivity of the city.

"Leona, he's likely turning the loam after harvest to ready it for spring, though there are some winter crops grown here in Texas," said Fidelia. She turned to look at young Leona.

"You are going to have a rousing time at the farm. The

both of us will. I don't imagine you know how to ride a horse, do you? We'll get you some bloomers and up on a horse tomorrow. By the end of the week, we can ride out to the creek," said Fidelia, filled with new delight at the prospect.

"Oh, missus, I wear bloomers," said the girl, her face flushing. "And I'm not sure I can ride a horse."

Fidelia laughed.

"Oh, yes, you can. And I should have said breeches. They are pants to wear under your skirt so you can ride astride the horse. Grandma let me ride astride when I was a girl, and now I prefer riding as a man does. Except in the city. We do have a side saddle in the barn if that be your preference. We'll broaden your horizons, Leona." Fidelia paused and pondered her own thoughts. "Goodness, I yearn to broaden my own horizons. You know, one day, I would like to ride a train. And see the ocean."

Leona stared at Fidelia, and Fidelia saw how the girl's eyes lit up at her mistress's folly.

"Well, maybe these things should wait till the war's behind us," said Fidelia as she retied the ribbon of her bonnet. "Being here in the countryside makes one forget our country's woes."

"Yes, ma'am," said Herman, his voice startling the two women as if they'd forgotten he was there, and they all laughed.

When they neared the farm in Pond Springs, Fidelia noticed how quiet it seemed. No one was about, and this was not how she remembered it. As the women stepped down from the buggy, Grandma came out the back door, drying her hands on her apron.

"Oh, Fidelia. How delightful to see you. And Leona," said Grandma as she hugged them both.

"Grandma, this is Herman Cannon. Remember? He used to work for Uncle Jeremy. Herman, this is my grandma, Mary McCord."

"Glad to meet you, Herman. I think I met you at the funeral, but there were so many people come to give their respects, I couldn't remember 'em all. You knew my dear Jeremy," said Grandma as Herman reached to shake her hand. Grandma took it in both her hands and held it a moment, smiling.

"A fine man he was, Missus McCord," said Herman. "We all miss him and his fine work." Grandma finally let go of his hand.

"Come in. Come in, and I'll heat the coffee. I'd make a fresh pot, but these days we have ta stretch it as far as we can, so I'm sorry if it's feeble."

"The farm seems so quiet, Grandma," said Fidelia as they walked into the house.

"Well, yes, dear." Grandma lit the fire beneath the old pot. "Your grandpa is in his eighties, so he's slowed a bit. He's out in the barn right now. Must not have heard you come in," she said as she pointed to her ear and rolled her eyes. "He's not hearing as well or, perchance, just ignoring me as he always has. Abe is out in the field, finishing up the last of the cotton harvest. We only have one now. One field in cotton, but that does bring more money in than the vegetables."

Fidelia pulled cups from the shelf for the coffee as Leona and Herman stood near the table.

"Sit down, both of you," said Fidelia as she looked up.

"Ma'am, I'll get our bags," said Leona, and Herman followed her outside.

Fidelia's thoughts went to Grandpa. How had she not noticed that he'd become so old? And Grandma. She did not look as robust as she had in December, as if winter had dimmed her light, though she was almost ten years younger than Grandpa. *Now that Pa and Ma were no longer here at the farm to help, why had she not thought of such things before?*

"Where's Matilda?" asked Fidelia. Matilda, a beautiful red-haired girl, had married Fidelia's Uncle Jeremy, and they'd had a daughter before Jeremy was killed by a scoundrel.

"She and Lucy are at the Inn in Round Rock, helping out the Harris family while Missus Harris is laid up."

"She's ill?

"Yes," said Grandma. "We're praying for her. She's been poorly, and Matilda's been a godsend, but she insisted on taking her daughter with her. Now I worry about Lucy. What about you and James? Did James sign up with the army like all the other young men?"

Fidelia knew she'd sent a letter to them about James joining Terry's Texas Cavalry, but she thought it may have been lost or, maybe, Grandma forgot.

"Oh, Grandma. He did—joined the cavalry. Left three weeks ago, first over to Bastrop, then he's going to Houston. He told me they'll head east from there."

"Oh, dear, sweet girl. All the men going. So many at the church have left. You and Leona should stay here. With us."

'That's why I've come, but only to visit—to check on you and Grandpa, and then I'm going out to check on Ma and Pa. I've worried about Ma. Did Pa join up to fight?"

"No, not yet. Your grandpa and Abe rode out there a couple of weeks ago. The journey is getting harder for your grandpa, but they found all well at Cypress Creek, and Abe helped John finish his harvest and plowing. John did hire a farmhand who, I'm told, has been a great help to your pa. I'm certain your ma will be overjoyed to see you."

Fidelia sat at the table as Grandma waited for the coffee to boil. The squeals and giggles of children flowed into the house, and Fidelia was certain it was Abe's little ones. Abe lived with his wife Reka in the cottage behind the barn. Grandpa had purchased Abe and Reka and then freed them both. He bought them from her friend Rosa's brother, Hans. The two slaves had been freed on paper secretly, for such a deed was still illegal in Texas. Fidelia had first met Rosa when they were just girls, and then she'd met Abe's grandmother, Abby. She'd befriended them both, and now both were gone from the earth—sweet Abby passed after a long-lived life, and her friend Rosa's youth was stolen when her family was attacked and killed by Indian renegades on the trail near Fredericksburg as they traveled to Mexico.

Leona and Herman walked in the door with the satchels, set them near the stairs, and joined the women at the table.

Fidelia sipped the bitter coffee, softened with a drop of cream, as Grandma filled cups for Leona and Herman. She remembered a conversation with her grandpa about his fears of protecting the two freed slaves; without ownership, what would happen to them upon his own demise? These thoughts tumbled through her mind and troubled her in light of the war and Grandpa's age.

"How does Grandpa manage the farm? With Pa gone?" asked Fidelia.

"Oh, mostly from his rocker, Delia." Grandma laughed. "We might be gettin' old, but your grandpa does get around. He sold off one of the fields he'd bought all those years ago from Hans, and Abe is able to keep up with most of the work. When he needs help in harvest season, your grandpa sometimes hires someone, but now, in this war, there's few to hire. He does repairs, and now he's the one milking the cow every morning, or when he's busy or under the weather, Reka will do it."

At those words, Fidelia laughed. She'd once been the one milking those two cows in the early hours before dawn for as long as she could remember. The memories of her daily chore were happy ones, for the task had been the ritual that lulled her into each new day as the wrens cheered the rising sun. At least it had until that awful dawn when Jeremy answered her screams for help and was killed by the rogue whose name she pledged never to utter again. Uncle Jeremy, not much older than Fidelia, had found his niche in building furniture. He had opened a shop in Austin, married sweet Matilda, and the two had a daughter before that day when the scoundrel, once a farmhand hired by Grandpa, attacked Fidelia in the barn. The sight of life seeping out of her uncle's body robbed her of the serenity of her early morning ritual with the dairy cows. Robbed her of her uncle, like a brother to her.

Fidelia decided she would wait to tell Grandma about the coming birth since she was unsure that the letter revealing her suspicions had yet reached her mother. Her inklings were now a truth, and Ma would be jubilant at the news of her first grandchild. She wasn't so sure about Grandma, who knew well life's hardships and would point out James' absence. Fidelia looked across the table at Leona and smiled.

Leona had been to the farmhouse only twice, her last visit was for the Christmas gathering, and she remembered how the family had welcomed her. She knew well her good fortune to have ended up in the care of the Hughes family, how they'd taken her in like family when her mother had died. It did not escape her notice how the McCords treated the slaves, Abe and Reka. Her own mama had been a housemaid, a paid servant, but she knew kindness was not the norm in the treatment of slaves or servants. She had seen the oft-brutal treatment of slaves in the streets and prayed the war would put an end to such atrocity, but she knew better than to voice such sentiments.

"Oh, Leona, I need to share all the stories of the years I've lived here," said Fidelia, snatching Leona back from her musings. "Sad stories and happy stories."

With those words, Herman said the horses should be rested enough and rose to say his goodbyes.

"Herman, can you return for me in about five weeks? And check on the house once each week if you can? I will want to get home before the cold comes."

"Yes, ma'am."

"Herman, we did not get a chance to visit," said Grandma. "When you return, you must sit and chat a bit. Tell me some stories about my Jeremy."

Herman smiled. "Yes, ma'am. That would be an honor. He taught me much." He nodded at the women and left the house, hoping to get home before nightfall.

Fidelia jumped up from the table and, catching up with Herman, gave him a warm hug.

"Thank you, Herman, for carrying us all the way up here. What's your daughter-in-law's name?" she asked.

"Lisbeth is what she's called," he said, his eyes wide at her question.

From the porch, Leona saw Fidelia pull some coins from her pocket and place them in Herman's hand.

"You take care of Lisbeth and little Isaac," she said, "and buy a little something special for your grandson. I'll see you on Saturday. In five weeks."

Before the old man could protest, Fidelia followed Leona back into the house to gather her cup and wash it in the basin. Leona had always held Fidelia in high esteem, for in Austin, the missus was a respected lady, but Leona's curiosity swelled as she began to see a whole new side of Fidelia Hughes.

CHAPTER 5

Bastrop, Texas

Company D marched eastward along the Colorado River as a misty rain tempered the enthusiasm the men held for the mustering of the regiment in Houston. August rain was a rarity in Texas, but the brutal heat held dampness snug, the first omen of hardships that would lay before them. These men had joined the cavalry to be in the saddle, as was the common bearing in Texas, but, at times, the men negotiated their horses through mud and tall grass while afoot. The men now belonged to the Confederacy, and in Houston, Benjamin Terry awaited them—companies of eager men traveling from near and far in Texas to join him.

James and Pete rode side by side, their clothing soaked with sweat and rain. Behind and in front, in this trail of men, an eerie silence bound the company in a somber mood broken by sporadic bursts of grumbling. Their destination was the train depot at Alleyton—sixty miserable miles in August, and the men couldn't get there fast enough.

In Alleyton, they loaded their saddles and gear on the train, relinquishing their horses to the young men who'd come to lead the mounts back home. The rails had been a boon to the transporting of cotton and, now, carrying soldiers. Company D rode the rails to Pierce Junction, where they disembarked to wait for the train into Houston. They were only nine miles from their destination, yet when the connecting train didn't come, they sought sleep in the unwelcome companionship of coastal mosquitoes through the night. At sunrise, there was still no train, so the group of weary men trudged the distance into the city, pushing the freight car that held the baggage of a cavalry.

"Hey, Hughes, my man," yelled John Wharton as the men gathered in Houston. "Glad to see you signed up with the best of us."

He remembered the conversation in James' print shop, and James found Wharton an amiable man, lean and tall and, as James came to find out, an outstanding speaker. His outspoken eloquence had, at times, brought him trouble. James had never met Benjamin Terry, but as the large man roused the muster of over a thousand volunteers, Terry's eloquence and fervor were potent. By the ninth of September, Benjamin Terry had forged a cavalry out of a thousand Texas men eager to fight the war—men full of faith that they'd return home in a matter of months, victorious.

After the cavalry's muster, a train carried the men to Beaumont, but after that, it was as if the war had begun in a skirmish with nature. Beyond Beaumont, there was the gift of a steamboat and the peaceful visions of the Neches and Sabine until the men reached Niblett's Bluff, then, once again, they found themselves afoot. With almost three hundred miles in front of them, they trudged in and out of ditches full of warm water, their pants wet and boots sodden, and they camped during nights lulled by the buzz of creepy-crawlies, before the men climbed into oxen-driven carts reined by funny-talking Creoles. The wagons had no springs, and the men followed their commanders over land and through lagoons. At Bayou Teche, the men climbed into boats. It took the horseless cavalry over a week to get to New Orleans from Houston under the direction of Benjamin Terry, a one-time sugar farmer. All these men—itching from bug bites and thorny brush, itching for a fight, yet they'd begun to think the war would be done before they found the enemy or a battlefield.

It had been those last, damned, twenty miles before the bayou when James' thoughts had turned dark and went to home, went to the edge of sanity. All he could picture was the twinkle of his wife's eyes, looking up into his, doubt oozing from her gaze as her lips held a trembled smile. And his fine home, a family home, a prospering business, all these things he'd walked away from for this. But the city of Austin had emptied as words of war waged, his friends and clients disappearing one by one. With each step he took, dripping sweat lured bugs that bit and pestered him, and he became certain that he would not find his way back home. That the journey would kill them all if the enemy did not, and then, once on the boat to New Orleans, he slept. Dreamless.

The bustle of New Orleans lifted spirits, but it wasn't long before the men fixed themselves in train cars that reeked of the recent presence of cattle, and they surged north to Nashville. Terry had told the regiment that they would rendezvous with General Johnston's army in Kentucky, and the men were elated to be joining forces with another Texan cohort. As the train rolled through Tennessee, the festive orange and yellow forests and meadows reminded James of Alabama, where he'd grown up.

"The seasons are beautiful here. Seems like Texas goes straight to winter after a parched summer," said James to Pete and another Ranger who'd come from Weatherford.

"Never seen nothing but Texas," said Pete. "I see the fields are still green but already a chill. I feel it."

"The truth, Hughes," said the other man. "Family came south from Ohio, so I feel like I'm headed home. But winter'll be comin' soon enough. I remember winters, and I ain't looking forward to it."

40

"Didn't get much winter in Alabama," said James, and he pulled his hat down and leaned back in his seat.

With those words, memories of his childhood rushed into his head. The hearty planting season on Pa's Alabama farm. He remembered no absence of rains from the Gulf or down Georgia's mountains, but he remembered hunting blackberries in the woods and fishing in the Tennessee River with his friends. Mama had told him about how the government had run off the Indians, the Cherokee, but he'd been but a toddler and remembered none of that. He missed the rich soils of Alabama that could grow anything and thought of his wife's family farming that miserable land near Austin.

The regiment arrived in Nashville quite the ragtag group they were. They'd been told to show up in Houston with their clothes, weapons, and a saddle, and that they did. Most wore a slouch hat, and some wore Mexican ponchos; few carried the same weapon, but most holstered a Bowie knife. A few even wore fringed buckskin trousers. Their only uniform was the five-pointed star that some wore on a hat, some on their collar. These weren't men who cared about uniforms, only the quality of their horse, and they still had none. They were a rowdy bunch that found a welcomed respite in Nashville as James' unit, Company D, camped and reveled at the city's fairgrounds, but the celebratory mood ended abruptly when the call to report arrived. The departure was so urgent that when the men left by train to Bowling Green, they left the chance for horses behind, and it was only in Kentucky that mounts were at last issued, along with tents and meager essentials. Upon arrival, the companies waited for the horses to be driven north and penned, and the men were ordered to each choose his own. Pete saddled a couple of horses before he found a young chestnut mare he liked, and James settled on a fox-dun gelding, gentle yet with a bit of fire. James' horse was healthy and followed directions well, and he felt certain he could trust the gelding on the field. Finally, the men began to feel like soldiers, and the regiment was structured in a formal way, naming Terry as commander and Colonel and Thomas Lubbock as Lieutenant Colonel and second-in-command. The sounds of enthusiasm echoed throughout camp, but then illness began to spread through the men, dysentery and typhoid fever. Colonel Lubbock fell ill with the fever and was sent to a hospital in Bowling Green. They'd met a foe, unexpected and fierce. A battle would soon enough loom in Woodsonville, but it was disease that would first fell many to a grave, never to lift a saber.

CHAPTER 6

Pond Springs, Texas

On a pleasant, cloudless day, Fidelia and Abe rode toward Pond Springs after spending two weeks at John McCord's cabin. Fidelia's father had finished out the upstairs bedrooms and indulged in glass for the two windows upstairs, making the house more livable for Mariah, Fidelia's mother. Fidelia slept on a cot in the second upstairs room, and Abe had stayed in the barn. Fidelia was surprised to see the finished barn so large. Pa had put a lot of effort into housing the animals, keeping tools ready, and storing feed, and he'd built a loft with two cots and some pallets to house his help.

Grandma had decided it best for Abe to travel with Fidelia to Cypress Spring, thus giving her son, John, some extra help for two weeks, and Grandma had said Leona could help her at the farm with the baking and preserving. It had not escaped Fidelia's notice that Leona was blossoming into a poised young woman.

A breeze announced a chill in the morning air, foretelling winter's approach.

"Thank you, Abe, for all the help at Pa's farm. I'm certain it lightened his load for a bit, though winter will likely do that as well," said Fidelia.

"Well, we put in a whole field of onions while I was there, so he'll be busy. Said he was letting his farmhand go until February, but we put up plenty of hay and corn for his pigs and cows, tore down the old lean-to, and sealed the cabin windows. Did you have a fine visit with your mama?"

"I did, Abe, but I think Ma seemed a bit frail. Pale, don't you think?"

"Yes, ma'am. I did see. Too much time alone out here. No womenfolk," said Abe.

Fidelia sat quietly for a spell.

"She's still a great cook, ma'am. I didn't go hungry out here," said Abe, and Fidelia laughed. Found herself grateful for the lightheartedness that quelled her worry.

"Yes. You know, Abe, I did some of the cooking." She looked at Abe and smiled. "But, yes, it was mostly Mama's doing."

The sun rose bright and warmed the morning breeze. Seasons in Texas were fickle. As the two rode in silence, Fidelia worried about her mother, Mariah, and, as had been her father's way since they'd come to Texas, he had shown little tenderness toward Mama, though he had seemed glad at his daughter's arrival.

Fidelia had revealed the coming grandchild to her mother, and Ma was giddy at the news but chastised her daughter for riding around the countryside in her delicate condition. Fidelia reminded her mother that she was not delicate. Pa had been pleased at the news, but the worry of war and uncertain futures of the men gone to fight remained unspoken.

Fidelia adjusted her bonnet as she rode beside Abe and the sun rose higher in the cloudless sky.

"James has left Houston with Benjamin Terry, and I'm so worried for him." Those words sprang from her mouth, feeling so foreign as she seldom shared her fears. She'd probably alarmed Abe and turned to see his face, where she found concern. She saw that her words had instilled sorrow on the face of this man she'd known since she was young, only eight or nine, but a man she did not know well.

"Oh, Miss McCord," he said, forgetting Fidelia's married name. "I will pray that he comes home. For you. I cannot promise 'cause it's but God's will, but I will pray every night, on my knees, that Mister James comes home."

Fidelia's eyes watered at Abe's kind words. She had not meant to trouble him. She had not even realized how much the war had troubled her, but the sudden realization that James could die, might never return home to her and their child, had brought on a trembling that surprised her.

"Abe, thank you. Prayers are all I have, and I am grateful for yours. And I will tell you the news I shared with my ma last week—that James and I are expecting a child, so, you see, he must come home to Texas. To us. I have not yet told Grandma but will tell her at supper tonight."

"Ma'am, you are kind to share this news with me. I will not tell Reka until you leave for home. Unless you tell her," Abe said and smiled. "This news will cheer your grandpa, most certain."

As the sun fell behind them, Fidelia could see the trail to the McCord farmhouse in the distance, and Grandma would likely have dinner ready. When they arrived at the house, she found Leona sitting near a window in the sitting room and stitching flowers onto linen. Grandma had clearly been expanding Leona's skills. It was good that Grandma had not found the bobbins under Fidelia's old bed, or she would have the girl tatting lace. Fidelia could not remember the last time she'd done so. *Was it for Matilda's wedding dress?*

Abe unhitched the wagon and let the horses into the barn, while Fidelia downed water cold from the well, and once in the house, Fidelia spilled all the details of her visit to Cypress Creek to her grandma, who hung on every word.

"And, Grandma, one more thing. James and I are expecting a child. To come in the spring. I'm now certain but was only suspicious of my condition when James left for Houston."

Grandma grabbed Fidelia's hand and kissed it with pure delight that lit her face.

"Oh, Delia, how grand! You must come stay here with us. So we can help you."

"Grandma, I may well do so when my confinement approaches, but I do have a home to care for in Austin. Don't you worry. You will see plenty of me. And I have Leona to help at home," said Fidelia, looking across the room at the girl, still sewing.

"Your grandpa will be so tickled to hear this news, dear," said Grandma, squeezing her granddaughter's hand before she returned to the kitchen to put biscuits in the oven.

Fidelia turned to Leona and smiled.

"Well, I see Grandma has been instructing you on proper stitching." Leona laughed.

"Yes, Missus Fidelia, and Reka showed me how to make candles, and I helped her churn some butter. I remembered once making candles with my own ma. And guess what! You have some new kittens out in the barn." Leona looked up with a twinkle in her eye that Fidelia had seldom seen.

"When you've finished your piecework, we'll have to go out to the barn and see what's new," Fidelia replied.

Supper was cornbread, pork, and potatoes cooked with onion and butter, all mixed with exuberant conversation. Fidelia shared details of her parents' farm with her grandparents, and as the window darkened with night and the room grew quieter, Grandma served spiced cake and cups of steeped herbal tea, as coffee was now rare, treasured and saved for mornings.

"Will, dear, Fidelia brought joyous news today," said

Grandma to Grandpa as she set the hot tea before him. "She's having a child. Our first great-grandchild here in Texas."

"What news did she bring? Of James?" asked Grandpa, and Grandma repeated the news a bit louder and nearer to his ear. It was at that moment that Fidelia grasped how truly old her grandpa had become, and she smiled large when Grandpa turned to look at her.

"Oh, my. Another little one. A new McCord," said Grandpa. Fidelia paused for a moment—looked at Grandma.

"Dear," said Grandma as she placed her hand over Grandpa's hand, "the baby will be one of us, but the child will be a Hughes. Just look how our families are expanding, and maybe this one will be born here, like Lucy."

"Perhaps," said Fidelia. "Come spring. When the horses foal and the cows calve." Fidelia laughed. But the lightness of the moment did nothing to sway her concerns for Grandpa. He had changed since her last visit not so long ago.

In the morning, Fidelia and Leona dressed for riding, and after Grandma's hearty breakfast, they mounted their horses and rode out through the meadow. Leona had caught on easily to leading the gray mare that Abe usually rode, and Fidelia had promised to take Leona out to Brushy Creek. It was a warm day in October with a cooling breeze. She saw Reka working beside her husband out in the field, harvesting cotton as their young children ran through the rows of cotton and around the trees, chasing each other. Fidelia waved to Abe.

"Leona, we'll ride to the creek. When it's not storming, the creek is quite serene, and I would go often as a girl. Are you enjoying your stay in the country?"

"Oh, I love it here. And helping your grandma in the kitchen. And she took me to church when you were away, where I met Molly, the same age as me, and a young man called Gilbert, from the Shuler farm he told me. Do you know him?"

"I do. He finished school about the same time I did, though he was often absent in the spring to help on his pa's farm. I remember teaching Molly in one of my classes."

"You taught school?"

"Yes, I did for a couple of years before James and I wed."

The two women rode on in silence, and the rustling of leaves reminded Fidelia of times, only two years earlier, when Miles and she would ride to the creek for picnics. Miles would talk of his adventures crossing the country with his brother, talk of his work in Little Rock, and then ponder out loud the details of their future together on their own farm. There was such joy in the anticipation of building a farm together, a family. Fidelia recalled the day among the trees when she'd taught him some dance steps after she'd told him about Rosa's parents and how they would dance round their kitchen. How Missus Hoffman was from Mexico and would sing in Spanish—such lilting melodies. And there, near the creek, Miles had kissed Fidelia—for a long time. The memory of that moment stirred her to an ache. She knew he wouldn't abandon her, but he seemingly had. Gone—just like the men who'd had disappeared off to war. Like Grandpa's spirit seemed to have now vanished. Sadness circled her, but this was no time to be weak.

CHAPTER 7

Cleveland, Ohio

In spite of the Lord looking down upon the year 1861, it had passed quickly enough and arrived with the awkward onset of the expected war. Once a man on the run with his brother Jackson, Miles marveled at how far he'd traveled since then and more so since he'd come north before the war sprang to life, marveling just the same as the time he'd been fettered by disbelief when Jackson became suspected of murder, and the two brothers, truly not quite men at the time, had journeyed trails west, west to Texas.

"What are you gathering information on now, Maloney?" asked Fintan McCabe, a friend who'd once worked for Pinkerton. Finn knew Miles still wrote stories for a Texas newspaper, now defunct, so his friend's endeavors seemed fruitless to the soldier from Camp Chase.

"I'm writing about the conditions at that prison, where you're posted, and I imagine this one's not much different than all the others. I'd like to get into some of the Confederacy forts, but I have not worked out the details to go so deep in disguise," said Miles, "and live."

Miles chuckled, and Finn just shook his head.

"You have a wish to die, friend," said Finn, raising his glass of bourbon to his friend, as if making a toast. "I'm surprised the commanders at the prison approve of your revealing anything about our own prisons."

"I never said they gave approval. But you know of my

friend, Norton. He's rabid, like a bitten dog, about revealing secrets to the people. Besides, he has every aim to help those imprisoned, especially the Texans," said Miles. "I carry a deep concern for his safety since he may well appear to the officers as a threat, even a spy."

"Well, Maloney, you both walk a thin line. I imagine stepping on both sides of it. You may be my friend, but you shall get no information of maneuvers from me. As for the horrendous conditions here at Camp Chase, there's little we can do to hide the horrors. But remember, the men imprisoned here are the enemy, and I can assure you it will become more horrendous as the regiments bring more captured greybacks."

"No doubt."

The two sat in silence in the parlor of the house where Miles had let a room. The room was dim with only two oil lamps burning in a room draped in dark colors, but the bar was open as Miles called for two more bourbons.

"I do miss my days working for Allen Pinkerton," said Finn. "He spends more time in Washington now than in Michigan. Got the President's ear on matters. The old days of chasing trains and train robbers were more to my liking than processing prisoners and mustering in the field. I met General McClellan, briefly of course, down at Camp Dennison earlier this year. I fear I could get pulled into another regiment as the South keeps poking at the borders in Kentucky."

"I cannot fathom the moves McClellan has made in the East. Or, should I say, maneuvers he has not made," said Miles.

"I hear your beloved Terry's Rangers are moving into Kentucky. More Texans will soon show up at the prison," Finn said.

"I expected they'd head north to battle. Not ones to back down from a fight. Hey, what with the greybacks at the prison, you should be able to get a uniform off one of them, can't you? I certainly have need of one."

"Why did I not see that request coming? Damn you, Maloney, you're asking for trouble. You do know what they do to beagles, don't you? You're a lot more fond of ropes than I," said Finn, shaking his head.

Finn looked around the room. He was from Kentucky, near Louisville, a tall, slender man fond of being clean-shaven. Being based at the fort left him time and means to indulge in such hygiene as well as a bit of leisure in Columbus. Finn had always been distracted by the pretty women, but he wasn't meeting many of them at the prison—not as many as he'd charmed on stagecoaches and trains in the old days.

"See that woman over there at the desk," said Finn, nodding his head toward the clerk's desk. "The raven-haired beauty in the blue taffeta dress. Do ya think the man next to her is her father? Or her husband?" asked Finn.

"Damn, McCabe," said Miles, setting his glass hard on the table. "You ain't got time for earnest courting, and she does not appear to be the sort of lady to sport around. And, further, I'm certain that man, the one with a Colt in his holster, is her husband."

"Well, I imagine you are correct, as you usually are. You have the nose of a hound dog and the eye of an eagle." Finn stood. "I'm headed back to the fort. I'll see what I can do about a uniform. You are a foolish, foolish man, Miles Maloney. Bet Pinkerton wishes he still had you."

"Thank you, friend," said Miles, raising his glass and watching his friend, as he left, tip his hat to the dark-haired woman pacing near the wooden desk. Miles sat for a while, savoring what remained in his glass, watching the people in the room, sizing up their attire, their demeanor, as he wondered of the details of each life. Of their struggles. Their losses and dreams.

He was in no hurry to go upstairs to his room. He looked up to see the woman with the raven hair being escorted up the stairway by a man old enough to be her father, but likely her husband. She reminded him of Fidelia, her strong jaw, her fair skin framed by dark tresses. He'd thought before of writing Fidelia another letter and posting it from a state to the south, but he'd already lost her, which didn't mean he'd stopped loving her. The noise in the room began to fade, and he rose and climbed the stairs, took pen to paper, and for the first time since leaving Texas, he wrote to his pa and Jackson, not knowing if his brother had enlisted or been conscripted by the Confederates.

After another two weeks, Miles had recorded enough information, through inspection and conversations, to finish his article on conditions for prisoners at a Union prison. He'd managed, through the kitchen staff, to sit and talk with a small number of prisoners, including a Texan. He wrote down their names and where they were from, hoping the details would not be cut by an editor and might allow a few families to learn the fate of their sons. He'd thoroughly edit the article and post it by the end of the week.

He decided wintertime was a good opportunity to take the train east. To interview a few officials in Washington, maybe even schedule a meeting with Pinkerton for another article. Miles was not certain how Norton was distributing his news articles, now that the Intelligencer had shut down in Austin; nevertheless, Norton continued to pay Miles for his submitted pieces and underwrite his travel.

On Saturday, Miles caught up with Finn in the mess hall at Camp Chase, where Finn passed a package to him, and he pulled back a corner of the tissue to reveal the gray of a Confederate uniform. As a bonus, a much-needed perk, Finn handed Miles a second parcel.

"It's Confederate. The least ragged uniform I've

confiscated. Got it off a recent prisoner carried in, from a skirmish down in Kentucky. Needs laundering and both need pressing. I presumed it would come in handy for your mischief," said Finn, smiling.

"Yes. I'm certain I'll need this one soon enough," said James.

Miles untied the second package to find a blue uniform in decent condition with a lieutenant's insignia, a single gold bar stitched on the collar. But he had no hat. The Confederate hats signified cavalry versus artillery but having *lost* a hat could work to his advantage; however, he'd best have a horse if he showed up at a cavalry unit.

"Thank you, friend," said Miles.

"You be careful with those, my friend," said Finn.

The two men downed one more drink and played a few hands of Blackjack before parting. Miles stood.

"I'll stop by Columbus in early spring on my way back to Mount Vernon. At some point, I believe Norton will come down with me to Camp Chase. Thanks for the ticket, here," said Miles in a whisper, holding up the clothing, "into the Confederacy."

Miles had a voucher for the train, leaving early in the morning. Winter hung dismally as a new year was about to round the corner. Norton had told him to pass through Washington and go on into Baltimore, to hang out at the gatherings of the powerful bushwhackers at the Barnum Hotel. He wanted news of the Union's strategy, but Miles would need to be elusive in any articles he'd pen. The fine line he walked was clear in his mind, and he and Norton had discussed the use of pseudonyms on everything published. Miles would be thorough in withholding the army's orders and targets, vigilant in censoring information that would disadvantage the Union. However, he was certain that Norton would approve of any skullduggery.

CHAPTER 8

Kentucky

The door of winter was wide open upon Benjamin Terry's Texas Rangers when snows fell in Kentucky and measles spread through the regiment, culling the weak and the unlucky. James had been fortuitous so far, but nothing had prepared him for the frigid temperatures in the North. He thought often of the bonds the Kiowa and Comanche held with the earth—their buffalo blankets. And as he lay beneath his cotton cover, he understood the value of the heavy skins when the tribes would travel into the mountains. north to Palo Duro and on to Colorado. James wished he had such a blanket. Instead, the men woke weary each morning, having shivered half their night away.

Terry's Rangers, officially the 8th Texas Cavalry, held no small amount of enthusiasm. The men who'd volunteered for the regiment were educated men, professional men, farmers, and wannabe politicians—but these men were also cowboys and no stranger to a lariat or a gun. They knew their way around a horse and knew in their bones that the horse was their most valuable weapon in battle. So, when called to Woodsonville, they were ready.

Scouts had found a Union encampment beyond the Greene River, and the colonel sent a small group to engage them. The engagement grew to a battle where the Unionists greatly outnumbered the Rangers, and Colonel Terry sent Captain Ferrell one way while Terry and his men went another. The

Rangers held back nothing in battle and their battle cry was mighty, yet despite their gritty courage or, perhaps, because of it, the men were ambushed, and the beloved Benjamin Terry was one of the first to fall, felled by a shot to his jaw. The battle ensued with losses on both sides, but it was the Yankees who held back the aggressors. Back at camp, neither winter nor grief held respite, and within a week, elections were held for the regiment. Lubbock, second in command, became commander, but within days, died of the typhoid, so the regiment elected John Wharton to lead.

"We've lost our Captain Terry and I ain't happy about this defeat," said James to Pete as the two men saddled their horses one afternoon. Christmas would come in two days, but it felt like no Christmas these men had known before. "I pray it's not an omen."

"I can't believe we lost Terry," said Pete, his head hung in despair.

"Damn. And now Lubbock is dead before we've even moved on. It doesn't bode well for our regiment."

"What do you think of Wharton?" asked Pete.

"Wharton's a good man. The one who urged me to join the cavalry. He can be a bit hot-headed, but I trust him as our leader."

The two mounted their horses, neither animal having been injured at Woodsonville. James had been grazed by a bullet, near his shoulder, and it had been bandaged by the medic. Took but a bit of skin with the fabric of his sleeve.

"I took a revolver from a fallen soldier—not one of our men. It's an Adams revolver. Not sure it's better than my Whitney, but it's a second weapon should I need it. I grabbed the cartridge box from the fella's belt, but I'll probably have trouble getting more ammo," said James as he held up the revolver to show Pete and then dropped it into the holster.

"Seems wrong robbing a dead man," said Pete.

"Pete, they don't need it. You'd better keep yourself well-armed. And rest assured, they'd do the same to you if you fell."

Snow covered the ground into January with drifts hugging the tents, but the men remained near Bowling Green. Some of the Texans had never before seen a snowfall or the frost of barren trees, and they were in awe but ill-clothed. And in that same month, Colonel Wharton shared that he'd received word that a Confederate general was killed on January 19th, not far from the Cumberland River, and the battle was lost. Many of the men, including James, fell into glumness, but the following week their spirits were lifted when a shipment of goods came from Texas. A shipment of woolens—blankets, socks, shirts—arrived and dispersed, and a grateful Company D celebrated with venison and shared whiskey around the campfire that evening and slept like babies as new snow fell.

Word came of retreat soon thereafter. Winter held firm into early February, when General Johnston gave the order to move back to Tennessee after Fort Donelson surrendered to Grant. News of the heavy losses had spurred the departure.

"Retreat" was a word foreign to the men of Terry's Rangers, the men of Texas, and, in respect to their colonel and founder, the regiment had unanimously chosen to keep their title, Benjamin Terry's Texas Rangers. With the decision made to retreat, the General assigned Terry's Cavalry to secure the rear of the army's journey into Tennessee.

Morning light filled the sky, dimmed by heavy clouds, and the snow fell faster as James and Pete strapped down their blankets in silence and mounted their horses before falling in behind Captain Ferrell. Steven Ferrell hailed from Bastrop and had mustered Company D in only a week. James had heard from someone in the Company that Ferrell had health problems, but over time, James came to suspect the Captain's health was influenced by his desire for the drink. Ferrell had never garnered enough votes to fill Terry's place as commander. Wharton had won overwhelmingly.

In Nashville, General Johnston sent some of the Rangers toward Fort Donelson to pick up supplies salvaged from the lost fort, to pick up any straggler soldiers walking south, and the Cavalry rejoined the army in Murfreesboro, where Johnston left the Texan men camped to monitor the enemy's movements as the infantry moved farther south. The regiment did not stay long in Murfreesboro, but they would eventually return. Yet, as James sat at a campfire one night, his thoughts turned back to his wife and how he'd not written to her since that train north to Nashville. How could he have forgotten her in all these weeks—forgotten to write or even to mull over the softness and fragrance of her? He'd faced death in battle and never even thought of its impact on Fidelia. He swallowed his shame, dumped his stale coffee, and walked back to his tent, where he lit a candle and, with pen in hand, wrote to his wife in Austin. He would purchase a stamp from the sutler in the morning. On the following morning, in a chilled fog of early March, Wharton ordered the Rangers to dismantle camp as they would head south to General Johnston's army, to Corinth near the Tennessee River.

CHAPTER 9

Pond Springs

Letters came and went after Fidelia and Leona returned from Pond Springs. Letters to and from Fidelia's mother, letters from Grandpa, but still no letter from James. The newspaper had written about delays and blockades interfering with mail and encouraged families to refrain from worrying.

She sat at her desk, rereading James' last post—news of the places he'd been—when Fidelia heard the rustle of Leona's skirt as she walked into the room.

"Miss Fidelia. I've put supper on the table. You need to eat. I made a hearty soup of potatoes and onions to go with the bread you baked, and there's a bit of salt pork."

"I'm on my way, Leona," said Fidelia as she rose from her chair and smoothed the cotton pinafore over the early roundness of her condition. The baby's presence had grown discernable, palpable, with even a few twinges assuring her that the child was stirring.

"Maybe it would be best for us to travel to the farm before the baby's arrival," said Fidelia to Leona as the two women sat at the small table. Because James' parents had once done much entertaining, the kitchen and dining room were the largest rooms in the house, and the women's voices seemed to echo in the emptiness.

"Oh, Miss, I think the trip might be too much, and the doctor is here in Austin."

"True, but Grandma has much experience in birthing

babies. And there is a doctor in Round Rock," Fidelia said. "Besides, I am no delicate orchid, but I will think on it. Early March would be the time to go."

"But, what about the house? Maybe I should stay here while you are gone," and Leona looked at Fidelia before continuing. "But maybe helping with the infant would be too much for your grandma."

"I doubt that." Fidelia said and threw her hands up in the air. "It's too much to decide now. We'll think on it."

As winter neared and the wind blew outside, rattling the windows, Leona stoked the fire and added some logs.

"We need to do something for Christmas," said Fidelia. "It comes next week. I'm not sure where to get pine boughs, and I think we can forgo a tree. No, wait. Mister Cannon has a young grandchild. Go to the livery tomorrow and see if Gus can get us a small pine tree, and I will write a note inviting Herman and his family to join us. I can find the box of decorations James stashed away last year. You and I can scrounge a fine feast, and I'll find a trinket or toy for the boy."

Leona smiled.

"Yes, ma'am. I do think we should be festive, in spite of the war."

The two women busied themselves over the next days, readying the home for a holiday. When Fidelia opened the door on Christmas morning, she saw Herman Cannon and his grandson.

"Missus Hughes, I apologize, but my daughter-in-law decided to stay home. She does not like to socialize much, but Isaac is here." He smiled down at the boy when, at that very moment, a wagon pulled in front of the house.

"Mama!" exclaimed Fidelia.

The house was ripe in celebration with the opening of gifts and enough food for all, since Mariah, Fidelia's ma, had brought a mincemeat pie, roasted leg of pork, and a basket of freshly harvested beets to roast in the oven.

"We decided to spend the holiday with you, dear," said Ma. "However, you can see our old hog didn't survive." Mom smiled as she passed the pot of roasted pork to Leona.

"Oh, Mama and Pa ... you will stay the night, won't you? There is room upstairs."

"We can make it home tonight," said Pa.

"No, please stay," pleaded Fidelia. "It will be dark early, and it's cold. Leona will make a good breakfast in the morning. I'm so happy you're here."

Mariah looked at her husband, who grumbled and then acquiesced, and Fidelia hugged her parents. After Herman's family left, Pa brought firewood into the house. There was a small barn shared between the Hughes' home and their neighbor, and Fidelia's pa pulled the wagon between the houses and stalled the horses, spreading a bit of hay for them.

"How is James?" asked Ma. "Do you know where he is?"

"No, Ma. I've not received a letter yet."

"I don't know how y'all keep horses in the city in those tiny stables, with nowhere to graze," said Pa as he walked in the room.

"It's not like living in the country, Pa." Fidelia thought of the dreadful smells in the streets but said no more in mixed company. "At least it will keep your mares out of the cold."

"John, Fidelia has not yet received mail from James."

"Well, in that Confederate uniform, there ain't no good place to be," said John.

Mariah glared at her husband and put her fingers to her lips.

"I'm sure he'll be fine. He's in the cavalry and not afoot," said John.

Fidelia wanted to hear no more talk of the war.

"Can I pour you a cup of tea? Leona has the kettle hot."

"Yes, dear," said Mariah, and Pa shook his head.

"Some cider, Pa?"

He didn't answer, and Fidelia followed Leona to the kitchen. She returned with hot tea for her ma and set a cup of hot cider with a few drops of rum in front of her pa.

At breakfast, Mariah asked her daughter about her confinement.

"Are you staying here to have your baby?"

Fidelia's pa rose from the table.

"I'm going to water the horses before hitching the wagon," he declared and walked out of the house.

"Ma, I might go out to the farm, to be with Grandma. I have not yet decided."

"I hate your being alone here. I know you have Leona, but you'd be wise to trust your grandmother to help. She's helped birth many babies, and besides, I think she needs to be needed, as does your grandpa. I have no doubt they are lonely. Grandpa has said as much." She covered her daughter's hand and squeezed it before rising from her chair to go.

"I cannot wait to meet my grandchild."

CHAPTER 10

Train to Baltimore

The train ride east was slow, and snow began falling as they neared Wheeling. The dismal skies of winter did not ebb Mile's excitement for the task before him. Baltimore would be alit with activity, with conversation and cigar smoke and even a few tussles as opinions overcame a man's judgment.

Norton had told him where to find a room in the city, a boarding house that would meet the limits of his pockets yet in walking distance of Barnum's City Hotel. When the train pulled into the Baltimore station, the sky was dark, moonless, and Miles took a buggy downtown, to the heart of Baltimore.

"Calvert and Fayette," said Miles. "The Barnum."

The lights in the city sparkled down Fayette Street.

"Stop here," yelled Miles when he saw the boarding house Norton had recommended. He found himself in a shabby but clean room as he paid the woman for a full week. The room would suffice and was only a block from the hotel. He settled in for the night and, bright and early the next morning, he washed, dressed, and walked to Barnum's Hotel, a grand building of granite lit by sunrise, with its ornate balconies, drawing the famous and those of means. Though the air was chilled, an invisible excitement stirred in the city, but Miles felt it. He knew where it came from. The street was bustling with people on their way to work, and he found the hotel lobby to be equally lively with a sprinkling of accompanied stylish ladies and a few gentlemen checking out at the hotel's desk.

In the dining hall, he ordered the dropped eggs and dipped toast with coffee as he eyed the clientele in the room. He knew this was not the right time of day to meet up with the rabble-rousers, and he was certain that they would be fewer in number since the Union troops were peppered throughout the city after April's riots. Tonight, the gatherings would delve into loud conversations and whispers of schemes, and he would be there to listen.

At nine o'clock that evening, the lobby and restaurant were full of men animated in discussions, some loud, some whispered. A few sat at card games in the lobby, but Miles headed into the dining room, where he saw Joe Howard sitting with a large group of men. Howard worked for Pinkerton, and Miles had met him once.

"Hey, Howard. Good to see you," said Miles, hoping he'd be remembered. "We met back in the District, in February."

The man nodded, looking a bit uncertain, but Miles couldn't blow Howard's cover and said no more.

"Any friend of Howard is a friend of ours," said a gray-haired, mustached man. "Sit down. Here." The man pulled back the chair next to him.

"Miles Maloney," said Miles, and he offered his hand. "From Texas."

"Well, by God, you're one of us," he bellowed. "Theodore Pendleton. Call me Theo."

Across the table, Joe Howard smiled, and Miles knew then that the agent remembered him, likely upon hearing his name.

"Yes, sir," Miles said. "And my family is in the North Carolina mountains, so I'm sad to hear of the Union's aggression here in your city. A downright transgression in a state so prosperous from its plantations."

"Amen to that," they toasted as they raised their glasses. "What brings you to Baltimore?" asked Theo.

"Well, I've done some writing for a Texas newspaper, and now, I'm eager to get into the fight. Offering my services. Pamphlets. Posters. Whatever the South needs, and when the time comes, I aim to enlist in a Texan regiment, where my loyalties lie ... though my talents do rest with newspaper copy."

Clearly, some of that was a lie, and Miles had omitted the part about the newspaper being booted from Austin for its support of the Union.

"But for tonight, Theo, I've come to listen. Eager to be a part of this excitement in resisting the government's oppression," said Miles as he smiled at the gentleman. "Let me buy you a drink. What are you drinking?"

"Oh, Son. My tobacco sales have me rolling in profits. You don't need to buy my drink, but I'll order for both of us," he said and raised his hand to call the bartender.

"Bring me another quart of Scotch ale and a glass for my friend here."

Miles remained silent as he sat and absorbed the chatter around the table, hearing plans to support the new Confederacy in Richmond with food and leather goods for the soldiers. The men spoke of sending their sons to battle as Maryland wavered on its loyalty, and most of the men sitting around Miles were sending sons off to the South. One man of an age near forty, in fine clothes, bragged of his own commission in a Virginian regiment. The northern part of the state supported Lincoln, but Maryland to the south was farmland and plantations dependent on slavery. They could not abide Maryland siding with the President.

As the evening had passed and the group of men dwindled, Miles readied for departure, offering those remaining any help they needed. Offered to design posters for a printer, should they have a press sympathetic to the cause.

"Son, you're young enough to enlist. I can connect you with an officer who can get you a spot in Virginia's cavalry," said an older gentleman from Marlboro.

"Thank you, sir," said Miles, careful not to reveal his discomfort at the man's offer. "For now, I'm writing posters and pamphlets. Committed to scribing articles for my publisher. Whatever you need, just tell me. I must say that I'd give my horse for the chance to interview Henry May. I cannot believe the liberties Lincoln took to imprison the Congressman."

At the utterance of Henry May's name, the men stirred and grumbled at the atrocity. Though Miles supported Lincoln's effort to curb slavery, he had been stupefied by the bold steps of the Union to imprison citizens and officials for dissent without charges.

"Thank you, Mister Pendleton, for the drink," Miles added swiftly.

With the lies having fluently drifted off Miles' tongue, he sat a while longer with an ear open to conversations about the table, and as time passed, the noise began to wane, and staff stacked chairs in preparation for the cleaning crew, he rose to leave, bidding the men good night. The frigid night air in the street pricked his skin, reminding him of a run-in with a Texan cactus back in Lampasas, and he pulled the woolen scarf snug around his neck and over his mouth. As he loped down the street, the idea of interviewing Henry May materialized, and the chill drew his gaze up toward the stars that always shone brighter in winter, and then, he pushed away the notion of interviews for fear such commentary might fall into the wrong hands. A heavy silence in the sky presaged a coming snowfall, and he scurried back to the boarding house, where sleep carried him away from the bustling thoughts of his deceits.

Up until Christmas Eve, he would circulate through the lobby and dining room at the Barnum most evenings, forging feigned relationships, but decided, for the holiday, to gift himself some time alone and hired a horse at the livery. The snow had melted, but the air still held a chill, so he bundled himself in woolens and packed staples in his saddle bags. He'd decided to ride south along the Patapsco River, where he hoped to find some solitude. He'd met a young fella, Henry Fitzell, at the hotel one evening, and when Miles mentioned his desire to spend Christmas on the Bay, to camp in the wilderness as he had as a kid, Henry had invited Miles to come to Sparrow's Point. He said his pa owned the land, so that's where Miles headed, for the woods. He checked in at the Fitzell home, to acknowledge his presence on their land, nodded at his friend, and thanked Missus Fitzell for her welcome, but he graciously declined offers of a meal and warm room. He yearned for the outdoors and, most of all, to be alone in his thoughts.

The shake of a rabbit caught his eye as he rode down the river's edge, and on the eve of Christmas, he cooked the hapless creature over a campfire. He remembered the days not so far back when, with his brother Jackson, he'd traveled across the country, and they'd eaten such meals. Never had he believed he'd miss those days, but now he did. How he had bemoaned that journey, but now, this miserable war had robbed him of home. His thoughts turned to Fidelia, no longer his, now belonging to another man. Never had a woman been more suited to him. Never had he been happier than with her, and now she was James' wife. *And who's fault was that? His very own when he'd left it all behind. He should have asked for her hand before leaving, but his prospects had been all-consuming— the life his ma had dreamed for him—to see the world. It is what he'd wanted, but a life with Delia is what filled his heart. Why did he give up one for the other? And ... where was James? Gone to the war or still with her?* Nothing seemed right about the way things had fallen.

He buried himself in woolens and his bedroll, where he

reveled in the soft night sounds of the wild, and his thoughts veered back to the days he'd traveled across the land with Jackson. How, in all his frustration with Jackson, the memories of those days now came vivid and endearing, and it was those images of trial and venture that carried him to sleep.

He spent Christmas Day riding alongside the river toward the Chesapeake Bay. Snow began to fall, and the beauty astounded him. He could not fathom all the young men living, if one could call it living, and fighting in reckless battles, but they were. He almost felt cowardly for his failure to enlist, but he was doing what he knew—what had been expected. Norton's passion to publish, to shed light on disputes and trickery, was contagious and held Miles to task, and neither man had turned on their countrymen, only on the slavery edicts. It seemed the whole of the world was skewed.

Through January, Miles garnered enough information to write four opinion pieces, which he mailed to Norton in Ohio, careful to use his pseudonym, Jack Beidletter, as Norton had instructed him. In Baltimore, he met up with Joe Howard at a pub one evening. Joe had a slight French accent and knew a lot about the workings of the South, though Miles never discovered just how deep those connections went. For all Miles knew, the man's very name was likely an alias, which was not unusual in the Pinkerton Agency.

"The firecrackers at the hotel are more subtle and fewer in number than they were a year ago, before the riots," said Joe. "But these men are still passionate, as you've seen. Be careful. They'll keep an eye on you, and in all this turmoil, there are secrets aplenty. Listen intently and they'll be revealed, but one never knows true loyalties in these times."

With those words, Joe raised his ale, and, for a moment,

Miles wondered about his own leanings. He briefly mulled over which side he was truly on. He was appalled by the custom of bondage and slavery yet had grown up moonshining in the South. He'd come north from Texas, where he also had roots, an aunt in San Saba and the woman he loved and lost. And, with these thoughts, he knew, at once, the next article he would write would be how this miserable war had split states like Maryland, ripped apart families. Brothers, fathers, and sons—too many now fighting against each other. He thought of Jackson, quite likely a Confederate soldier somewhere.

Even his editor was torn. Old Norton loved Texas but was a free-stater at heart. It was that night in early February that Miles walked through the streets of Baltimore to his rented room and started penning one of the best essays he'd written since he'd left Texas—"Family Divided by War." He would edit and rewrite it, and in due course, he would add some personal accounts as he met men whose families were at odds—some only at the dinner table, some on the battlefields. There had even been a woman at the boarding house who'd spilled her agonies for her son, who'd run to fight for the South, and her husband, who was killed in Manassas fighting on the side of the Union, in Battery D, commanded by Captain Griffin. This woman was now widowed and unknowing if she'd ever see her son again. Miles researched and journaled for eight more weeks until the article was its best, and he sent the finished piece to Norton, in Ohio, at the end of March as the Union battled fiercely in North Carolina for Fort Macon. Fort Macon fell in April.

CHAPTER 11

Corinth, Mississippi

Spring of 1862 bloomed in Mississippi with its greening trees and the buzz of bees in the peach orchards, but the landscape would soon enough turn bleak and smell of gunpowder and dread. However, the Rangers were determined to show no fear, and their outer shell remained one of bravado.

While camped in Corinth, the Rangers reassigned to General Bragg, James added news to the letter for his wife and posted it with Chaplain Bunting, and on a Sunday morning, General Johnston made the decision to surprise Grant's army, knowing that General Buell's approach would soon turn the Confederate armies outnumbered. As plans filtered down, it was the Sabbath when they would attack the Union's camp by the river, and the army converged east of the city. In the dark, before the light of dawn, the Yankees were surprised. The camp was emptied by the abrupt surprise at dawn and left askew with the Northerners driven into the trees, unprepared, yet they resisted with a mighty force.

James rode through the tents in pursuit of soldiers, his focus that of the brigade's goal of gaining territory for the Confederacy. Gaining control and, at best, their foe's surrender. Yet, he'd never lost his revulsion of killing another man—men no different than him in their obligation to duties—but he was firm in returning fire when fired upon. With three of his comrades, they rounded up and bound prisoners, but as the give and take progressed through the day, word came of bad news. General Johnston from Texas had been killed.

"Said he got shot in the knee," said Paul Watkins to James and Wayne Hamilton, a comrade from Austin, as they rode back toward camp. "I saw him fall and, damn, then heard he'd bled to death right in front of his own men. The general's surgeon had been sent back to camp for others injured, some of 'em being prisoners. Damn."

General Beauregard had ended the day and called the men back. Word passed around that General Grant of the Union, who'd been away nursing an injury, had rushed back to his troops in the midst of the fighting. Too late to save face.

As dark fell and torrents of rain rustled the tent, James and Pete could not contain their frustration.

"We came close to winning this one," said James. "If Beauregard hadn't pulled us back, we could have chased the damn Yankees back to Kentucky. At least we hit the jackpot with their goods and wagons."

"Believe you're right, Hughes. We did have them on the run. Johnston had been wise—that surprise attack worked. Half of them were fighting in their long johns," said Pete.

"Watkins said he'd seen Johnston leading the charge when he was hit. Said he could have just as well been hit by our own fire," said James. "Such a shame."

Thunder echoed and a bolt of lightning hit close to camp. James shook his head.

"I don't know if I can forgive Beauregard. It feels like dishonoring General Johnston. His plan worked and we abandoned it too soon. Didn't stay the course," said James.

Pete started to pull off his boots.

"Hold off, Pete," said James. "I'm dead tired, but more than that, I'm hungrier than a mare nursin' a colt. We got goods today at the Yankee camp, let's go get some vittles."

"I'm right behind ya," and Pete pulled on his boots and grabbed his poncho and hat.

They found most of their comrades had beat them to the bounty but there was plenty, and excitement at the seized sutlers' wagons held the men awake well past midnight. Tired, satiated, and muddied by the storm, eventually the promise of sleep called the Rangers to their tents, where they stripped off their sopping clothes and slept like the dead till sunrise.

On Monday morning, the Confederate foot soldiers and cavalries returned to the battlefield to succeed only in holding the reinforced Union soldiers at bay as General Bragg awaited more troops. James and his comrades found themselves dismounted and creeping through woods on foot. Bodies of uniformed soldiers could be seen here and there as the men scouted the area where rains had fallen on dead and wounded men through the night, and the silence along the Tennessee River was as eerie as a bog full of ghosts gone mute.

"I'm not sure I signed up for a fight like this," yelled one of the men as they advanced through the trees without their horses.

By midday, swollen bodies of both gray and blue, some draped with peach blossoms, peppered the forested fields, and the fragrance of gunpowder burned James' nostrils. In his pursuit, he came upon three wild pigs feasting on a bulging corpse, a Union man—known only by the bits of blue cloth. James doubled over and retched in the copse of poplars. For a moment, he doubted his manhood, then retched once more before he rinsed his mouth and poured what remained in his canteen over his head in an attempt to wash away his fear of weakness. The smell of fire and brimstone had fleetingly overcome the smells of rotting flesh, and at that moment, visions of Hell swirled in James' head as he recalled the pastor's fiery sermons on Satan that had alarmed him when his ma had long ago sat him in church pews. He ran his hand over his face twice, as if brushing away phantoms, and mounted his horse to join his comrades in their pursuit of a group of Yankees running toward an old barn.

Nothing was gained on that day but the sinking of morale. By the time the battle ended, the loss of life was plain all around him, and the Union had surrendered no ground. Nothing gained but a great loss. But the Army of the Mississippi had shaken the enemy's confidence, and Beauregard decided to move the men back into Tennessee, toward Chattanooga. The Rangers crossed into Tennessee at Lamb's Ferry, taking prisoners with them. A detail would later carry the captured in wagons to a prison in North Carolina or Georgia, but Terry's Rangers were dismayed by retreat after retreat.

As the men rode eastward, James' thoughts turned to Texas. Seeing the fertile farms across the Tennessee hills, he wondered how the McCord family was faring at home. Fidelia had written that she'd visited her grandparents and her pa's farm and how she'd worried about her ma's isolation. He hoped his wife had brought his mother-in-law back into town with her, given her some respite. The presence of Mariah would be a blessing during Fidelia's confinement and the birth. And suddenly, a resilience filled him, knowing he needed to return to them. He would fight smarter. Maybe less recklessly, as impulse was the Rangers' custom, and more deliberate, shrewder. Then, more horrible thoughts sprang forth: *What if she was the one who was lost? Or the baby?* He decided he would kneel in prayer that very night when they next camped. Pray to God that He will not forget them, as James and the men around him had, in such frightful times, neglected their prayers to the Almighty—he would pray that Fidelia's bold spirit would carry her through. He'd pray another letter might find him, sharing nothing but good news, and that night in camp, he knelt.

Near Chattanooga, the Rangers released their prisoners to a detail, and their regiment was assigned to Colonel Forrest's brigade, a cavalry brigade. In July, the men approached Murfreesboro, having planned on raiding the Union camp. Forrest sent some of the Rangers in a different direction and then he and his men headed straight into Murfreesboro, only to have troops ambushed by the Yankees. It was in the city, as Colonel Forrest rode through town, that the citizens would run toward Forrest's befuddled cavalrymen, pleading for the rebels to seize back their city.

As James and his comrades approached Murfreesboro, they saw Confederate soldiers and horses, some down, scattered through the corn fields. James recognized them at once. It was Company G, and then James's eyes caught the sight of Colonel Wharton on the ground, where he sat injured beside his dead horse, and from his grimaced pose as his medic tended him, Wharton ordered a detail, including James, into town in search of Colonel Forrest.

As James rode on into town, the sight of his fallen comrades and his friend and commander of the Rangers sitting behind him in distress in a muddy corn field, consumed him with both misery and anger. He felt eager for the fight ahead. After they joined up with Colonel Forrest and informed him of casualties, the men were called to the tavern, where they found the Union's General Crittenden hiding in a room. Forrest was overjoyed at the find and held him prisoner, a hostage for barter.

"Hey, Watkins," James said as Company D prepared to attack the camp outside of the town. "Can you believe we captured a general? How many damn Crittendens are there?"

"Too many," said Watkins. "One's on our side, but I hear he's been taken out of command. Are they all related?"

"Think so," said James, wiping down his saber before shielding it and mounting his horse. "All cowards."

Colonel Forrest attacked the Union camp at dusk, having

assigned the Rangers to lead the charge, and by the following evening, having conned the enemy into believing he'd had twice the men his brigade had, he coerced a surrender from the Union. The bounty of the conquest was abundant, and Colonel Forrest proved himself a fine soldier and strategist, warranting his promotion to General that July; however, James would soon come to despise the man.

CHAPTER 12

Pond Springs

Fidelia's scream rang through the house, through the opened windows to the barn, where the animals turned their heads, and it hovered over the morning meadows. Grandpa couldn't bear the sounds of agony from the upstairs bedroom, so he swigged his coffee and left the house to milk the cow. The old cow his granddaughter had once milked every morning.

Fidelia's labor had ravaged her through the night. Water had been boiled, words of encouragement had been plentiful, and a few sips of whiskey had been dispensed, but the struggle endured through the hours of darkness and candlelight.

"Soon," said Grandma, who'd helped her daughters-in-law birth a few babies back in Indiana.

"We're almost there, dear. Almost." Her voice trembled, and Fidelia feared it was worry. Reka, the amber color of her face glowing and her eyes bearing comfort, held a fresh, damp linen to the young woman's forehead.

"I sent Abe to get the doctor," said Grandma, "but I don't think we'll need him. You are so close. One more push should do it, dear. Push. Hard."

"I'm so tired, Grandma. I can't."

"You can, Delia, and now is the time."

The sun peeped through the dark clouds after a morning rain in early April when Fidelia's next wail soared, and she felt the pressure release and heard Grandma's squeal.

"It's a boy. A boy."

Grandma busied herself with the child, and then, Reka wrapped him in a small blanket and placed him in Fidelia's arms. He was so tiny but had the glow of an angel, and Fidelia thought of James and prayed he would come home.

Fidelia slept until Grandma woke her, carrying a fussing infant. As her son soothed himself at her breast, Fidelia fidgeted before finding a sense of comfort, and she eased into memories of her trip from Austin to Pond Springs. It had been the first warm day in February when Herman Cannon had brought Fidelia out to Pond Springs for her confinement. It was a slow journey, as Herman was wary of Fidelia's condition.

"Oh, Herman, don't be so careful of the trail. I'm not a delicate flower," she said about the slow pace, eager to see her grandparents, to settle in for a life-altering stay. "I'm quite well padded," she said and laughed at seeing the old man's smile.

She'd left Leona behind to care for the house, but she'd told the girl she might call for her later if more help was needed. Herman made a trip out to Pond Springs in mid-March to bring two letters from James and some linens that Leona had stitched for the baby. As Grandma had admired Leona's stitchwork and ribboned finishes on the blankets and gowns, Fidelia had ripped open the letters from her husband.

"Oh, Grandma, James said that he received the woolen blankets we sent before Christmas and that citizens of Texas had sent bundles of blankets and socks and woolen shirts. He said they were in Kentucky, then Tennessee, and the cold was brutal. The men were so thankful for the blankets and socks. Oh, no, and Benjamin Terry was killed." Worry creased

Fidelia's face as she'd ripped open the second letter.

"This one is from February. Wharton is their new commander, and the regiment's into Tennessee and toward Mississippi." Fidelia could tell by the gaps in news, the unanswered questions, that her letters had not arrived timely, but that the letters arrived at all somewhat reassured her.

"Dear, the most we can do is keep them in our prayers," said Grandma, yet the letters had not eased Fidelia's mind at all. She did not want to birth a fatherless child.

By the end of April, Fidelia had settled into a rhythm of sleep and feedings with her newborn son, John Robert Hughes. She'd already jotted down and posted a short note to James. Knowing how slowly mail traveled in wartime, she wanted to send news of the baby on its way. She would write a longer letter later when she'd regained her rhythm of time. In May, Ma and Pa came to visit and meet their first grandchild, and Pa had been all puffed up that the baby carried his name. Robert had been James' grandfather back in Alabama.

Grandpa and Abe had been plowing and seeding the fields, and Pa helped when he'd come but had been anxious to get home for his own planting. He'd said he was fortunate to have the one farmhand since so many young men had gone off to fight.

"I've bought a few head of cattle for the far meadows," Pa told Grandpa at supper one evening.

"That's likely a good idea, Son," said Grandpa. "Probably be more money in that, what with so many young men gone, and the army needs the meat as much as they'll need potatoes and onions. Everything's short these days. I could use a good cup of coffee."

"Yes, if I get a good price on the cattle next year, I can hire more help."

"You look thin, Mariah," said Grandma. "Are you eating well?"

Mariah sat at the supper table, holding her grandson.

"I've been busy about the farm and just put in my garden, Ma." As she sat at the table, Mariah heard the voices of her husband and her father-in-law in the background, but all she thought of was all those years John had chastised her for giving him no sons. Now, here she sat holding a sleeping boy, the child of their only surviving daughter who was sleeping upstairs. She worried about the future for all of them but mostly for her daughter, who could as likely end up a widow as not.

She ran her fingers over the soft curls of the sleeping baby and sent a prayer up for him and his mother.

"We need to leave tomorrow," said John. "I got corn and sorghum to get in the ground. The farmhand's got the cotton in."

Mariah hated to leave, but Leona was arriving in a couple days, and her daughter and Leona planned on returning to the Austin house later in May. It didn't seem right to Mariah that the two women should be alone in the city. Her son-in-law should have made better arrangements before he left, she thought. Her daughter would be best off at the McCord farm. Mariah rose to take the infant upstairs, and once the baby was asleep in Fidelia's room, she retired to the room downstairs that had once been John's and her room, where she packed their things for the early morning departure. Just as she lay her head on the pillow, her husband came into the room and undressed for bed.

"That's a fine son you were holding this evening," he said. "We'll pray our son-in-law comes home to meet him," and John extinguished the light of the oil lamp. Mariah said nothing but sent up another curtal prayer for her daughter.

Herman and Leona arrived at the farm at dusk the following day, and Grandpa insisted Herman spend the night.

"I'll even pay ya a bit if you'd like to stay and help me and Abe finish the planting," said Grandpa at supper. "We gonna do another field of cotton."

"Sir, I'll take your offer. Work is hard to come by these days, but you can pay me with Missus McCord's cooking."

Grandma laughed as Leona sat at the table holding little Johnny and fussing over him.

"Miss Fidelia, I'm so glad I'm here. I can help with this adorable baby," said Leona as the baby's eyes never left the young woman's face.

"I don't know what I'll do with all this help, Leona. Ma just left this morning, and now you're here to help along with Reka and Grandma. Ma's help granted me time to catch up on my sleep yesterday. Did any letters arrive at the house?"

"There were no posts, but Missus Baily of the Ladies' Aid Society came to give you a parcel of sugar and a packet of coffee. I brought them with me," said Leona.

"Thank you, Leona. Let's watch and see how far Grandma can stretch those treasures." At that, the two women chuckled.

CHAPTER 13

Virginia

Miles had been in Baltimore and Washington long enough. He'd written ample articles that he'd sent to his editor, and Norton's recent letter said he wanted more detailed accounts from the field. He wanted material from the battlefields, from the privates, from the dead. Yes, that's exactly what he'd said—the dead—and Miles knew what he meant.

The last line of his boss's letter read: "Son, that essay you sent to me on the war's divided families was a masterpiece. I sent it to the papers in Texas and published it here as well. Good work." Miles immediately wondered if the McCords or even Fidelia would see his work, but it didn't matter, for they wouldn't know who wrote it since it was penned under an alias.

As spring began to bloom along the Chesapeake Bay, as the mountain laurels revealed some early buds, Miles packed his scant belongings and two journals, one blank, into a small satchel, all of which he wrapped in the bedroll he'd earlier negotiated for at the livery. He arranged with the missus at the boarding house to mail the large bag with his typewriter to Tony Norton in Mount Vernon, and he dressed plainly for the train ride into Washington, where he would purchase a horse. Horses were hard to come by, for even the cavalries were pressed to find enough, but Norton had given him the name of a farmer near Alexandria.

When he left there with a twelve-year-old chestnut mare,

he headed south and decided to remain in civilian clothing. He had learned that the Union had occupied Fredericksburg in Virginia, but there could also be Rebels lurking throughout the area, many having escaped the city. At some point near Richmond, he would need to change into the Confederate uniform, as he believed that might give him more freedom to move about. He wished for an enlisted insignia but could not wait for his source in Ohio to unearth one. Maybe he'd find some luck in his travels, though he knew well that such luck may come at someone else's expense. He checked his rifle and the Colt he'd bought back in Arkansas, making sure they were loaded before riding on. He was headed toward Richmond, but it took three days to arrive at Fredericksburg, where he realized he'd been not far behind the Union army as he rode the trail, camping in woods that has sprung to life with leaves and buds.

Union troops were everywhere in and around the town. He moseyed through the streets, at the general store he bought some vittles—jerky, beans, and coffee—for his saddlebag and eavesdropped where he could. He gathered from what he heard that the Confederates had scattered in all directions, to the south and to the west. He'd best stay in the civilian clothes rather than be shot by the enemy of whatever uniform he wore.

As he walked on the street, he realized the town was a fount of secrets and information, so he found a boarding house beyond the livery, one with a small room to let. A group of men played cards at the table next to Miles, and one of them, a uniformed Federal officer, eyed Miles in the boarding house dining room as he enjoyed a bowl of hot soup. Finally, the mustached man spoke up, but Miles had been clandestine long enough to be at the ready.

"Hey, Son, why aren't you enlisted? No young man in this war should be walking about in fancy clothes," said the haughty middle-aged officer as Miles wondered what might be fancy about his clothes. "You a Johnny Reb in disguise?"

"No, sir," Miles replied. "From Ohio and just working. I'm a courier, sir."

"For who?" the man scoffed.

"Congressman Leary," he said, his shoulders straight and looking the soldier in the eye. "Cornelius Leary."

"What the hell you delivering here?"

"Leary's arranged to contract some horses for the Union, as well as a couple for the livery. I've carried messages to three horse farms nearby and was told to await replies." Miles said no more, for a good courier wouldn't reveal information.

The officer glared at him and resumed his card game, and Miles squirmed at the realization of how easy lying had come to him. He quickly finished his meal and moved on, pondering how all his deception was simply survival.

He doubted he'd find any Confederate soldiers nearby, at least any willing to admit such, but the small farms outside town would likely not be sympathetic to the Yankees, yet Miles knew such discontent, once they trusted him, would loosen their tongues. The town was full of Yanks, only piquing resentment. Miles had a way of getting people to turn chatty, to trust him—a skill he'd honed over the years since he'd worked in Arkansas—at the newspaper in Little Rock.

In spite of the occupation, the farms near Fredericksburg appeared intact with small gardens and would be filled with stories. He'd plan his guise, either uniformed or civilian, continue to let his meager room, and he could keep in touch with Norton and Pinkerton, if need be, through the postmaster in Fredericksburg—maybe even through summer. He'd decided to keep a low profile with all the Yanks about. Fredericksburg would well allow him entry into Richmond or, maybe, even down to North Carolina. Yet, the war would dictate his future. Surely, the South would seek to regain the town and even further north, including access to the rivers. As always, he would need to remain quick-footed, like a whitetail on the mountain.

Before Miles walked to the town's edges, he wrote in his journal about the Union's occupation of the Virginia city and how it appeared that the Rebels had scattered. The morning sky was thick with clouds, threatening spring rains, and he swiftly came upon a small farmhouse south of Fredericksburg and asked for a bit of water and perchance shelter from the storm.

"Ain't sure where my son is," said the farmwife as Miles sat in her kitchen. The woman's hair was pinned back and graying at her temples, yet she was still an attractive woman. Miles sat at the dining table hewn of pine, and she set a cup of coffee in front of him, wiped her hands on the cotton rag she held, and sat across from him. The morning sun lit the kitchen as if it were a serene morning in the country, but it was not. It was wartime. A girl, about ten, walked in and stood beside her mother, and the woman pulled the girl's hair into sections and began braiding tautly as she spoke to me, as if she'd done this a thousand times. And she likely had.

"He's just a boy. My son. Only seventeen. But he left with his company, just nine men. Said they were headed to the river when the Yanks poured into town. I heard some of 'em burnt the bridge and lit fire to the boats."

"Do you think they'll be back?" asked Miles.

"One way or th'other," she said. "They ain't gonna let them Billy Yanks take our town."

Having finished the girl's braid, the woman, Maureen Banks was her name, rose and went to the pantry and fixed a plate of biscuit and jam for the girl.

"You want a biscuit, Mister Maloney? I got some blueberry

jam we'd put up."

"No, thank you, Missus Banks, but I appreciate your kindness. But you can tell me how life has been here, on your farm since the war started. And where's your husband?"

She was silent and did not look at Miles.

"Ma'am, I assure you I'm no spy. Just recording stories for my newspaper, and I'll use no true names."

She looked at him hard, and then her face softened.

"Jimmy, my husband, signed up with the regiment that went to Richmond. The artillery," she said. "He's sent me a bit of money from his pay a few months ago."

She sat back down at the table, and she told Miles how she got by with last summer's garden and the fruit and vegetables she'd canned and stored in the root cellar. "The old man at the farm over there"—she pointed toward the south—"I gave him a jar of my wild blackberry preserves, and he gave us bacon and ribs when he slaughtered his hog. And I still got my chickens and praying the Yanks don't take 'em from us. Just me and the girl here right now."

She looked him in the eye, then gazed out the window.

"Suppose I should watch my talk—you being a stranger and all. You could be a disguised bluecoat or a spy." She looked back at Miles. "You seem like an honest young man, learned and all," she said, uncertainty quavering in her voice.

Miles heard similar stories at three more farms outside Fredericksburg, and then, when days of heavy spring rains came in April, he holed up in his room, writing to the rhythmic beat on the windowpanes, a sound filled with the hope of spring flowers and a quick end to war.

CHAPTER 14

Tennessee

Company D, along with the Rangers and newly promoted General Forrest, spent much of August riding between McMinnville, Lebanon, and Nashville, engaging in skirmishes along the way. On their first visit to Lebanon, the townspeople treated the soldiers to magnificent feasts in a fine display of support and gratitude. James, among others, was grateful yet shamed at the thought of their families back in Texas likely eking out lives with sparse means. Nevertheless, the men stuffed themselves with roasted pig, fresh garden vegetables, pies, and cakes—plenteous with extra to stuff into their haversacks. After a year as soldiers, it never escaped the thoughts of these men that they were not promised tomorrow.

As the brigade moved through August, James had helped burn down a few bridges and make their way to Knoxville. The bridges always seemed a double-edged sword to James. The enemy was thwarted, but the townspeople had built such bridges for their needs.

It was near Louisville that General Bragg sent General Forrest on his way to form a new regiment and made John Wharton the commander of his brigade. James was glad to see Forrest go for now, at least. The man may have been fearless on the field, but he was merely a spiteful slave trader disguised in a uniform. James had once seen the man yank his whip from his saddle and slice a soldier's cheek for failure to perform a duty fast enough and, on another occasion near the Kentucky line, shoot a captured Yankee and the Negro standing beside him, both between the eyes, for the Yankee's impertinence. James had no use for the man and hoped never to serve under him again. Pete had told him he'd once watched as Forrest shot a farmer's dog that would not cease barking at the man.

As autumn began to chill the air and rumple the trees of Tennessee, turning leaves brilliant, heavy combat met the brigade in Perryville, where the Confederates came up against Buell's army. The fighting was fierce, as well as the losses. The battle revealed the desperation hanging in the air of this war, as James saw his friend Pete searching bodies for a pair of proper shoes, only to tug boots from a sleeping soldier thought to be dead, a private of Company H who rose to yell at him. Scared the bejesus out of his friend. Finally, Pete pulled and yanked the leather boots from a dead Yankee, and he was not the only soldier pilfering the dead. James' heart sank at their fate.

It was in Perryville where the brigade gained a hill but lost Mark Evans, and Ferrell was promoted to replace him, so Lieutenant Kyle became the new Company D commander. Having lost yet another commander of the Rangers, the constant musical dance of officers did not sit well with the men of the 8th Cavalry. From Perryville, General Bragg headed to Cumberland Gap, and the Rangers, once again, were guarding the rear of the Army of the Mississippi—General Buell was likely in pursuit. James was getting sick of seeing Murfreesboro, and in the dreary winter skies of 1862, the oft-ill Major Ferrell took leave of the brigade for health reasons. His exit was no surprise to those of Company D.

As winter settled near Nolensville and the Christmas season sat bleak, James lay in his cot, re-reading the letter he'd received from his wife in September. The pages had grown soft and frayed from all the times James had read her words since the chaplain had handed him the letter. Fidelia expressed her worry for his safety and said she'd received the letter

James had posted. *Where are you now?* She'd written her questions and mischievously made him await the second page of the missive for the news he'd long awaited. A son, John Robert Hughes, had been born in April, with Fidelia's grandmother in attendance and a doctor on his way since the delivery had been long. He stopped reading. His heart abruptly eased, just as each time he came to these words, *John Robert Hughes.* The names floated in the air after he said them aloud. Like a melody invoking visions of a curly-headed boy and his mama, the young Fidelia he'd met at his printing shop in Austin. He reached into his haversack and pulled out the tintype of his wife's image.

A healthy, squalling boy, in the words of his wife. She called him Johnny in the letter and wrote that she prayed for the end of this war and his safe return. He ached for another letter. He wanted, more than anything, to see his son and his wife. More than anything, and he thought of the soldiers who'd wandered home, gone absent, and risked hanging. He knew he had friends who'd thought about it, but the Rangers did not desert. Nonetheless, part of him understood those who did. He could not help but wonder if these meager battles with dubious wins and losses were worth his absence, worth the loss of his friends and comrades. He remembered how Sam Houston had stood against the secession, and at times, James doubted the war—but never did he doubt his loyalty to the men in his company or the regiment.

He extinguished the lamp's flame and pulled the blanket tight to his chin, seeking warmth, wondering if any unused blankets lay upon a now empty cot at camp. He dreamt of sweet Fidelia, dreams of how he'd return home and give Johnny a sister. A dream so at odds with his other dreams, the nightmares of whimpers from the injured and of mute bodies on battlefields or those wasting away in putrid creeks. He knew he would be blessed to see Texas again.

Winter still blew through the bones of soldiers in December, showing no mercy as, once again, the men fought in Murfreesboro as if it were the heart of Tennessee. The melancholy of another Christmas away from home, of gray skies and too much death, challenged the temper of the men. It was near there, in Nolensville, where James' friend Wayne Hamilton, from Austin, was felled and where John Wharton and James' friend Pete were both injured in the chaos, battling the Union's onslaught at Stone's River where, early on, they'd reached the summit of a rise to see the creek lined with canons and a lieutenant called out at them, "Run." The battle continued as the Rangers bivouacked nearby, but the Union had the advantage, and it was there that saw Wharton's promotion to Brigadier General. But James' composure was doubly trodden with the capture of P. J. Watkins, and Major Kyle ordered them back to camp when an eerie dusk fell.

The next day Pete returned to their tent with his leg stitched where a Minié ball, the hollow-based and rounded bullets so prevalent in this war, had struck his bone, and James watched Pete set his muddy boots beside his cot.

"Are those boots a good fit, Pete? You might need good boots, walking with that limp."

"A little big, but I wear two pairs of socks," said Pete. "The limp will be gone once it heals."

James wondered if the holes in the first pair were covered by the second and if hope was the medicine the medics had given him.

"They're a helluva lot better than my old ones, worn through. You shoulda picked out a new pair of boots at Donelson. Yours are startin' to look worn, friend. Mine were no use to that dead man."

James nodded.

"Do you ever wish you'd stayed home? With your family?" asked James.

"Don't matter. They're conscripting now."

"Yes. Yet, it seems these battles, leaving so many corpses to rot and children back home fatherless, are getting us nowhere. Bragg struggled to gain Kentucky. Can't fault him for his efforts. But I'm ready to go home."

"It's 'cause you have that new baby," said Pete. "My kid's probably running in the fields with the sheep by now. They can be noisy—babies and sheep." He laughed. "But I do wish I could see my boy, Jake. See my wife again. Missin' the soft touch of a woman."

"Yah. I can't wait to hold my Fidelia. Haven't gotten another letter since the baby came," said James, still sitting on his cot. "Imagine as many letters get lost as soldiers are now missing. And all of it's bearing heavy on my soul."

Pete mumbled agreement.

"I'm gonna write a letter to Watkin's wife," said James. "Praying he survives prison or, better, gets traded back. Heard nothing good about the prisons." He extinguished his lamp. "But I won't tell her that," he whispered in the dark.

"Sweet dreams, friend," said Pete. "They're few and far between." And the tent turned dark.

But in the darkness, James could not forget Pete's words, "the soft touch of a woman." All he could think of was the fervor he recalled at the touch of Fidelia's slight hand on his bare shoulder. The softness of her raven hair, let down and gracing the curve of her back.

The tingle of her caress along his hairline. The softness and draw of her lips on his. He had never tired of her kind heart and how her easy charm unwittingly seduced him—not since their wedding, not since that first stolen kiss by the window in Austin, that first frisson of his own seduction.

He turned on his cot to find sleep, but the sense of his wife's being still held him tight, as if the curve of her body were present with him on a cold winter night. Warming him. Him. She'd chosen him—yet he could not shrug off how it came to be. Sleep forsook him.

CHAPTER 15

Austin, Texas

Summer had been a precious time with her grandparents, and Fidelia had relished watching her son come to know her. In the mornings he would smile then giggle at the sight of her face. Johnny's feedings had grown more regular, as had Fidelia's sleep, and Henry arrived in September to bring the two women and Johnny home to Austin.

The house had long sat empty, and the musty smell of it greeted Fidelia and Leona.

"Henry, I might need some repairs or work done on the house. I will send word to you if need be."

"Yes, Missus Hughes, I can do it."

"Well, do give me a few days to check the house, and then I'll send a list to you. With that list, I will also add some compensation. And have you received posts from your son?" asked Fidelia.

"Ma'am, little Isaac was taken with a cough when I left, so I'll soon check on him. I've received only one post from my oldest son and naught recent from the other." Herman scuffed his boot and looked down at the ground. "I'll be over to do the work as soon as I receive your list, missus." He turned to leave, but Fidelia called after him.

"I'll have Leona bring some hot soup over as soon as we go to market," Fidelia said, and the man turned to wave at her.

"Thank you, ma'am."

By the following day, the two women had boiled a pot of vegetable soup, and Leona then took half of it to Herman Cannon's house.

"That baby's cough was something terrible. It sounds like the whooping cough. I've heard the croaky hacking before when I was in school," said Leona when she returned. "I'll bake some bread before we sit for supper."

Johnny slept in a basket near the table as the two women talked and laughed over bowls of hot soup and fresh bread. Fidelia wished she had some of that coffee Leona had taken to the farm, and Grandma had, with the help of some chicory, made the coffee last until September.

"Oh, sweet Mary, where'd you get coffee?" Grandpa had asked that first morning, back at Pond Springs, when Grandma served cups of hot coffee. "This don't taste like that scorched rye you boil and pass off as the real thing."

Leona and Fidelia had laughed at Grandpa's reaction.

"Well, William, I added a bit of chicory to the grounds your granddaughter brought to us, and you be thankful for it," and Grandma had walked back to the stove to mind the bacon and porridge.

The women laughed at the memory of the spring day. "I sure wish we had some of that coffee now," said Leona.

"Oh, Leona, I was just thinking the very same. We are, indeed, like sisters, aren't we?"

Johnny started fussing, and Fidelia bent to pick him up and nursed the babe as Leona washed the dishes in the basin.

"Johnny's sound asleep, and I'm praying that whooping cough doesn't come here," said Fidelia when Leona returned to the table. "Grandma gave me three bags of spun yarn for the soldiers. Tomorrow, between meals and tending to the baby, we'll start knitting socks, scarves, and sweaters for the soldiers. Winter's coming, and I remember how James had written to me of the harsh cold in the North. I do remember the cold, the snows of winter from my youth in Indiana, and when the wind blew, it was dismal. I know the Ladies' Aid Society is also gathering some more blankets and will get a shipment on the train next week."

"I'll do the scarves and some hats. I'm not good at doing the sweaters with all the fitting together and sizing," said Leona as she slipped two loaves of bread into the oven.

"Maybe I can finish a sweater before shipments leave. Leona, I have to say how much I appreciate you. Like the family you are to me. I know I'm a bit older than you, but all my sisters were younger, and, for me, being with you is as if I am once again an older sister."

Leona reached over and squeezed Fidelia's hand.

"I never had a sister, nor a brother. I was so charmed to have you and Mister James in my life when Mama died."

"Well, you won't want to live your life with us forever," said Fidelia, "though I could certainly use your help for years ahead of me, I'm certain. But you need to get out more. Find a beau. Live your own life ... not ours."

"Now you sound like my mother, trying to marry me off," retorted Leona.

Fidelia laughed. "Yes, I do. I remember when my pa sounded like that. I apologize. We both need to move on at our pace. All will surely change when the men come home."

Silence ensued.

On Friday, Leona delivered the bundle of hats, scarves, and a sweater to Susan Bailey. They were bound for a train ride toward the battlefields.

"We have enough yardage to bring you more in a couple

of weeks," said Leona.

"Well, thank you, Leona," said Missus Bailey. "Why don't you consider working a day each week with us. We could use the help in our outreach and deliveries, and I know Fidelia's hours are bound with the new baby."

Leona was surprised by Missus Bailey's comment. She'd never been accustomed to being included by the ladies of Austin, nor had her mother, but the city had changed since the war, since the men left.

"I will talk to Missus Fidelia about some time to work with you. What is the best day?"

"Any day is fine. There are always deeds needing to be done. Do let me know, and I'll pair you with one of the ladies for a start. And give my regards to Fidelia. Tell her I'll come by in a few weeks to meet the new baby."

"I will. Thank you, ma'am."

There was a new spring in her step as she walked down the street. A new boldness filled her.

It was a cool day in late October with the windows shut from the breeze when Fidelia heard Johnny crying upstairs, and she walked to her room. One day, she would move the baby to the empty room, one day when her husband came home.

"I'll see you later, Leona," yelled Fidelia as Leona walked down the stairs. "And make those women treat you right."

Leona smiled and closed the front door behind her. She was dressed in her best dress, caramel cotton with a white collar, and she'd pulled on her pale blue cloak to ward off fall's first chill. Her flaxen hair was coiled at her nape and pinned tightly. She'd wanted to look her best, to measure up to the fine ladies that worked at the aid society.

"Good morning, Leona," said Missus Bonner. "I'm so glad you're joining us."

"As am I," said Leona.

About thirty burlap parcels sat on the large table, tied with string. Each string held a small tag with a name.

"These are to go out to some of the women, on Pine and Hickory Streets. Many of them have young children at home. So, there is a half-pound of sugar, a pound of cornmeal, and just a bit of coffee or tea. It's so hard to get any. We'll load them in the wagon out front, and Jim Carter will drive the wagon for you, stopping at each address you have listed. Be gracious at the door, no matter their greeting. Knock twice. Any questions?"

"What if no one is home?"

"Just bring those back. There's no spoilage in them, so we can deliver them another day."

"Yes, ma'am."

It took much of the day to make the deliveries. Only four still sat in the back of the wagon, where no one had answered Leona's knock at their door or the rude man who had said he needed no charity. Besides the man, only one woman had been uncouth, but most had been most kind and thankful.

"That was a great day of work, Leona," said Missus Bonner. "We don't usually get that much done in a day. You return next week, won't you?"

"Oh, yes. I am glad to help. And to meet residents of the city I'd never before met. Two of the women even asked my name when they thanked me."

"Oh, you will get to know people throughout the city and through the ladies in our society. We're glad to have you."

Somehow, Leona was filled with a new confidence as she walked home. A sense that she was growing into a woman, and with that thought, she suddenly missed her mother, knowing her mother would be proud and delighted in her only child.

CHAPTER 16

Virginia, near Fredericksburg

As summer took hold with its sultry days near the bay, Miles donned his blue uniform in a copse of trees off the trail. He didn't want anyone in town to see the change, and he couldn't very well explain a military uniform while he remained at the boarding house, so he knew that his time in Fredericksburg needed to end before fall, if not sooner.

The day, a Wednesday, smelled of horse manure and the loam of fresh-turned fields, and Miles rode with confident ease out toward the army camp northwest of town and near the edge of a wooded area filtering the summer light. The camp buzzed like a hive of bees as men moved to and fro, and Miles hung to the edge, where he found a line of mostly women washing clothes in tubs, intent on their duties and not looking up at him. Miles dismounted and tied his mare to a rope running between posts and began walking. At the end of the laundering group stood a tall Negro man, and Miles approached the man as he pinned a blue shirt to a line.

"Name's Miles," he said to the Negro. "I'm a scout with Leary's regiment." He nodded to the man and hoped no one called him out for disturbing the Negro's duties. "I never saw a laundry crew like this before. Guess it's 'cause I'm washing my own clothes. Do you travel with the regiment?"

Miles saw, up close, that the man's beard had grayed and his eyes creased with weariness, probably years of such.

"Yes, sah," he said. "I's called Dabney. They's took me on

the line with the ladies after they's freed me at one of the plantations they took. We's get free meals and rarely a coin for the work, but some of the ladies here have husbands in the army."

"That's fitting," said Miles, careful not to give away where his loyalties might lie.

"Yes, sah," the man said, and Miles nodded back at the man and walked on toward where he saw the dining tables. He knew he wanted to get some of the stories from the women washing the dirty rags of war, but it would be chancy. He would learn later from a Pinkerton man that Dabney's wife was hanging laundry on the other side of the Rappahannock, where the enemy camped. She'd hang shirts in such a way as to relay to her husband what little info she was able to glean from what she overheard.

As if he belonged there, Miles walked up to the fellow handing out grub and collected a plate of what looked like stew, unsure of the meat they were using. Meat was hard to come by for the Union. He sat down near a soldier eating alone—a private.

"Theo Isaacs," said Miles, becoming accustomed to deceit. "From near Baltimore. And you?"

"Jesse Postlewaite," said the man looking to be more of a young'un. Maybe seventeen, possibly younger. "I'm from Chadd's Ford, just west out of Philadelphia."

"I'm scouting—for the Ohio regiment sitting west of here. Where've you been before here?" Miles asked.

"Just enlisted three months ago, so Fredericksburg was my first skirmish. Not much a skirmish. We just walked in like we owned the town. Heard we're packing up next week and heading south. McClellan is down there, you know—gathering the armies."

"Yes. I've heard," Miles responded, startled at how quickly he'd reaped information out of the recruit. "I hear there's a lot of Amish and Quakers west of Philadelphia. Not fighting people, so I guess you're not one of them."

The man chuckled. "No. No, I'm not. But if they was fighting, they'd be on our side. When we came down the trail, you shoulda seen the Confederates running and swimming the river. I hear they call us bluebellies, but I think I'd call them yellowbellies."

The two men laughed, and after Miles finished his meal, he wished the young man well and walked through to the end of the camp and eyed the officers' tents to see if there was anyone of note or any unusual activity, but it was quiet. When he passed the laundry crew, he nodded at a young woman with her hands buried in a cauldron of suds.

"Sure wish my regiment let our wives travel with us," he said, but the woman eyed him suspiciously, so he walked unhurriedly toward where he'd reined his horse.

Summer had infiltrated the countryside, and the barren sights of winter were gone. A movement to the right of the trail caught his eye, but when he looked straight on, he saw naught but a ripple of the leaves stirred by a breeze, yet he pulled the reins tighter and moved forward at a crawl. Then he heard it. A twig cracked. When Miles turned, he saw a man moving among the trees, really a boy, attempting to conceal himself. There was no weapon in sight, so Miles stopped and dismounted. The boy had disappeared behind a tree. The risks were evident, but, as always, curiosity got the best of him, and he called out to the boy.

"Hey, I can see you." Miles raised his hand to indicate he was friendly; however, the uniform he wore sent its own message.

The boy stopped, and as Miles approached, he reckoned the boy to be about seventeen, smooth-faced and wariness in his eyes. His shirt was yellow, and Miles suspected he was signed up with the Confederates.

"What are you doing out here?" asked Miles. "Thought all you Rebs ran across the river when the Blue showed up."

The boy's shoulders eased, and Miles offered his hand. The boy held back, still carrying a healthy bit of uncertainty.

"Look yonder. I left my rifle on my horse," Miles said, not revealing he had a pistol in his boot.

"Most of 'em are gone. My folks live up the road, and I stayed," the boy said.

"Are you feeding information to them, across the river?"

He stood silent, which was all the answer Miles needed.

"My name is Theo," Miles lied again, thinking he'd better keep these names he used straight. "I'm from North Carolina." I looked him square in the eye. "Guess you think I'm crazy, huh?"

"Why you fightin' for them?"

"Well, as I've been told, ya never know which side one's sitting on. Even you," Miles said, and he looked the boy squarely again, then looked deep into the trees. "Are ya camping in the trees here? Or living in the luxury of a room with walls and a pallet up the road?"

The young man shifted his weight to his left foot and turned to look through the trees.

"I could use some conversation with a fellow Southerner before returning to town. I got some whiskey in my flask and a bedroll. If ya tell me your name, I'll stay the night over there near the river with ya."

"Jimmy," the boy said, and Miles could tell the young man was confused. "I-I-I'm just out here hunting some for my pa."

"Sure. How old are ya, Jimmy?" Miles walked over to get his horse, took the reins in hand.

"Sixteen, sir."

Miles laughed on the inside at the young boy calling his enemy "sir" and followed Jimmy through the trees toward the Rappahannock River, where Miles hobbled his horse and spread out his bedroll.

"I'm not the enemy, young man. I'm just a Southerner looking for my next story, so ignore the uniform. Two sides of this war are two too many for me," said Miles.

The boy had food packed from the family farmhouse, and there was no need for any hunting for supper. The two men supped and talked through half the night, and Miles changed out of his uniform into his civilian clothes as the boy watched him warily. Miles knew that his words and changing his clothes had confused the young man, and the two finally crawled into their makeshift beds when the forest turned dark. They had lit no campfire for fear of being spotted. Miles had let the boy have all his whiskey in hopes it would loosen his tongue, and though he was uncertain that the boy knew much, that assumption turned out to be wrong.

Jimmy revealed that his commander had gone down to Richmond, and there were couriers running information to the Confederate capital as his unit's spies sent messages across the river. The regiment had left behind a few boys who could hide in their family farms, and these boys had a basic knowledge of coding messages with flags. Jimmy even showed his flags to Miles. The boy spoke of the gathering of troops near Richmond and their concern of General McClellan's growing army along the Chesapeake Bay. It became clear to Miles in this chance conversation that spying was rampant in the war, with undercover agents on both sides.

The young Virginian woke with a headache, and Miles found his bag of biscuits and made some coffee for the two of them. Once he'd packed up his horse, Miles thanked his sluggish host for the generosity and conversation.

"Boy, you're looking a bit like the enemy around here. If I were you, I'd get rid of that yellow shirt," said Miles before he rode toward Fredericksburg.

Miles was back in his room in Fredericksburg, and the following morning, the rain came both slow and then fast on a foggy day. He wrote in his journal most of the morning, documenting all he'd seen and heard the day before. He noted some details in a letter to Norton, feeling safe to post mail to

Ohio, but as he realized his own deceptions, he grew wary of even the postmaster. Then he wondered if he himself was not a journalist but a spy, for he could not know what Norton did with the information Miles sent. He wished, more than anything, that he was sitting in Norton's library back in Ohio. The more he saw, the more he feared this war would last forever.

CHAPTER 17

Tennessee

It was the freezing winter of 1863, and James was no closer to going home and befuddled as to the strategies of the war. All he wanted to do was to go home to Texas—to Austin and his family. Nevertheless, the following months were naught but a retreat from Murfreesboro, first to Fort Donelson. Never in his whole life had James felt frigid cold like the winter that had carried the Rangers to the Cumberland River. Waking beneath the weight of ice-covered tents and taking his horse through streams that left the horses' lower quarters covered in ice. Nightmares of those days visited him as he prayed for spring. All this struggle for naught, as General Wheeler had led them to Dover, a fruitless battle with unimaginable loss. The men had scarce ammunition and the battle was a slaughter. To James, it seemed the war was one slaughter after another, but he was alive. And so far, uninjured.

They'd stayed in Sparta, where spring had arrived, and the Rangers captured a mail train. Many of James' comrades amused themselves for a couple of days reading the letters mailed between Yankees and their loved ones, but James was not interested in such callow amusement. *What if it had been his own long-awaited letters?*

He saw no good outcome to these battles that lead nowhere or to the rash decisions made by the generals. One moment, James would be filled with gratitude, and the next, he'd be consumed with guilt for his good fortune. So many would not go home, not on this Earth. Not all were lost in battle; many had departed in the agony of disease and exposure in the brutal winter of 1863.

The regiment's slow retreat eventually brought the men to respite in Rome, south of Chattanooga on the dawning side of Horseleg Mountain.

He had received two letters from Fidelia just before the brigade left for the brutal cold of the Cumberland River. His evenings were spent rereading her words, these words being the first letter since the revelation of their son's birth:

—the 22nd of November in the year 1862

Dearest James ... I've received your letters and know well that you spare me the horrors of your journey, yet I pray for you each night. Sweet Johnny is growing pudgy and smiles at me now with your very eyes. Yes, they have the twinkle I remember in your gaze. I cannot wait for you to meet him.

My letter will be brief, as the demands of an infant are plenty. Leona is a dear help. My family is well, but I fear for Grandpa's lonesomeness and hope to visit Pond Springs again in spring.

I ache for your nearness and for the wretched war to end. You are forever loved,
Delia

Her second letter was longer, and she shared the hardships being endured in Texas. She baked bread for some of the widows in town and wrote that she was down to her last two sewing needles. She said coffee and salt were difficult to find, and she used her tea sparingly. Many people, those still in the city, walked about, for so many horses had been confiscated for the war efforts, and the government had taken his horse as well. She'd heard there'd been violence toward some German communities who rejected slavery and secession and some anti-secessionists had left Texas. She wrote about Matilda's marriage to a soldier who had now returned to battle with Hood's Regiment, and she wrote that her young aunt was with child and living in Bastrop. She said her pa hoped for a good crop come summer even though the war effort would take some of his profits, and she still prayed nightly for James' homecoming.

But there was something in the words of her second letter, mailed in early December, that left James wanting. An underlying tension simmered between the lines—an indifference he found fretful or maybe it was but weariness. *Had she heard from Miles? Had he returned to Austin?* Fidelia had never given him reason to doubt her, and he knew it was his own insecurities that stirred his anxiety. He should be ashamed. Yet, even he wondered what happened to the young man, now, James sat alone in his tent, not far from where Miles had grown up just over the mountains in North Carolina. *Was the young man there with his pa or fighting with the Confederacy?* No one knew—except maybe that old coot who was the newspaper editor. And now, even he seemed to have vanished somewhere into the North.

The eating was good in the town of Rome, a town yet undisturbed in the middle of mountains and war—the town's generous families beholden to the soldiers in their midst. Some of the soldiers didn't hesitate to call on the young ladies, some visited the saucy ladies on a regular basis, and one of the Rangers even married a Georgian girl.

Wharton had arranged social events for the men in Chatanooga, before it was taken, and in Rome, but James had no use for dancing or holding another woman in his arms. Yet the men greatly admired Wharton and had gathered enough money from throughout the brigade to gift their commander with a splendid bay courser and a new saddle. Pete and James enjoyed the ceremonial presentation and barbeque as the two talked about how long it would take for a Yank to shoot it out from under him.

"Where do ya think we're going next?" asked Pete as he folded his pants and shirt. "Sometimes I can't cotton to the decisions made by these generals. Like Wheeler, sending those troops into Fort Donelson short ammunition."

"I know," James responded. "I hear the Union's converging toward Georgia. Guess we're the last line of defense and suspect we'll revisit Chattanooga. Everyone wants Chattanooga. Not eager to climb that damn mountain again."

James sat down on his cot and took a sip from his canteen. The men had managed to get a bit of good rye in town, and he indulged a sip or two each night, hoping he could refill it to the brim before they rode on out.

"You know," said Pete, "Watkins is back."

"Really?"

"Yep. Got released on a prisoner trade. Did you write his wife, like you said?" asked Pete.

Ephraim Dodd, one of the pickets, popped his head in.

"Back at camp, fellas. Did I miss anything?"

"Nope, Dodd. 'Cept a home-cooked banquet tonight," said Pete.

"Hey, Pete. Got me some good tobacco today. Come by later if you want some," said Dodd, and the fellow moved on toward his own tent.

"Yes, I did, Pete. Write to Missus Watkins. Better let him know, but I'm sure he's written his wife of his release—or perhaps the colonel arranged for a telegraph to his missus," said James. "That Dodd's a peculiar fella. A bit of a church bell to boot. Nothing he won't share, which might just get him into trouble."

"Yes, he is," replied Pete. "I don't think I've seen him on the battlefield, so he'll get home in one piece. For certain. And when he ain't talkin' up the ladies, he's got his nose in a book."

"He seems well-read, but he is quite the ladies' man. And I've seen him walking a few on his arm. Hardly ever in camp. I heard he got reported as a deserter back in May—he'd been gone so long."

"Don't know I trust him," said Pete. "Ain't like the rest of us." Then Pete blew out his lamp's flame.

"Gonna get my horse reshod tomorrow. Before she goes lame," said James as the tent went dark.

General Bragg sent General Wheeler and the Rangers south to scout for a flank of Rosancrans' men and to guard the southernmost flank of the army. The true battle followed beyond the mountains as the forces converged. At the left of the fiercest combat, James did not see the worst of Chickamauga until the cavalry rode into the mountains. Corpses lay everywhere amongst the moans of wounded men untended. The fallen horses grunted and tried to get up. A couple of them did, but the many seemed to fade and tire from the struggle. Ammunition was precious, but James shot two geldings he found in agony.

James realized they were all doing duty for politicians and generals who were much too fond of war, and even their own leader, Jefferson Davis, was held back by the Confederate cause of states' rights, and General Lee's mulish willfulness would never allow surrender. James looked in the distance, across the creek, and saw a medic in a Yankee uniform moving from one fallen man to another, offering little more than comfort and a sip of water. With his head bowed, James followed his unit back to the campsite.

In late September, the regiment camped near Ringgold, waiting to move west once again. In the dampness after a heavy rain was when he saw them. In the trees behind the tents, Private Dodd and another Ranger, unknown to James, stood, talking to a Confederate soldier. Suddenly, it was as if a ghost rose in the mist sifting through tall poplars—a visitation in the fields. There stood the very likeness of Miles Maloney. Not a dead man, for he stood out in the crispness of a gray uniform, so distinct from the rag-tag dress of the Rangers. The conversation between the men appeared intense. James stood transfixed, staring, but no one noticed him as he watched.

Company D was not so distant from the North Carolina mountains where Maloney's family lived. The young man who'd once stolen his wife's heart clearly was fighting as a Confederate, but James could not fathom what the meeting would be about. *What brigade was he assigned to? Should he confront the scoundrel that broke Fidelia's heart? To what end?* It was all just foolhardy, and finally, James walked on toward the sutler's wagon. He would confront Dodd about it later and see what he might learn of the rendezvous. Yet, at dawn, James found that Dodd was gone scouting or to visit one of his lady friends, as was his custom.

CHAPTER 18

Austin, Texas

The letters that had come from James had not quelled Fidelia's worry. He seemed to be in the midst of one battle after another, and she'd heard enough from others to know he'd omitted the carnage and despair. She could only hope the shipments of wools and blankets had kept the men warm in the cold of winter.

The hearth in her Austin home burned bright and constant in the cold spells of a fickle Texan January, but Fidelia knew warmer days were coming soon. She and Leona had paid a short visit to her grandparents' farm over the holiday, Grandpa had shot a splendid wild turkey, and Grandma had preserved plentiful tomatoes and berries. Even the desserts were an indulgence, sweetened with a bit of honey. Life seemed easier on the farm than in the city where goods were scarce and winter skies seemed grayer.

"Herman Cannon just stopped by to share the news that the Confederates have regained the port in Galveston," said Leona as she rushed into the kitchen.

"Make a pot of tea, Leona, while the baby is yet sleeping. We'll sit and enjoy it with hopes for a bit of sugar next time," said Leona, smiling. "Let's pray we can hold on to the port so our goods can come and go again."

"Oh, yes, ma'am. But sadly, this Confederacy paper won't buy much," said Leona.

Fidelia looked at Leona with her eyes wide.

"Well, dear girl, I should probably have you draw up our budget. I don't believe I've been aware of just how much its value has whittled away, but George did warn me. The print shop may need to shut down, he's told me."

"Oh, no, missus. Will you be able to keep the house?" asked Leona, knowing well such a query was improper, but she feared for her own well-being. She'd seen firsthand how poverty was a side-effect of this war.

"Well, for now, Leona," answered Fidelia, "it's the Hughes' home, and I cannot imagine losing it. Upkeep can come after the war. I sometimes feel we'd be better up in Pond Springs, looking after my grandparents and with no worry for food and staples. I saw Grandpa had two more pigs, and that turkey we had at Christmas was the best meal I'd had in months."

She laughed, hoping to quell Leona's apparent fear.

Leona dropped dried elderberries into the hot water, leaving it to steep as she placed the teapot, two cups, and spoons on the tray.

"Besides," added Fidelia, "you will be with our family as long as you need be."

"Thank you, Miss Fidelia. I so enjoyed being at your family's farm and you teaching me to ride. You were so blessed to grow up there."

"Yes, I was, but there were hardships as well. So much loss for our family," and Fidelia's voice faded softer as the images of her sisters flashed before her, as if they might be present with her now. She looked up at Leona as she strained tea into the teapot and carried the tray to the table.

"Sit down, Leona, and let me tell you all about my sisters." Fidelia took the teapot and poured tea into the painted cups, handing one to Leona and taking a sip from her own.

Spring arrived with a welcome vengeance, with both rain and sunshine, and Fidelia filled her hours with planting a few vegetables and tending to shrubs and blooms in the yard as Johnny sat and played on a quilt, crawling toward his mother until one day he stood and took his first unsteady steps.

"Oh, Johnny. Look at you. Such a big boy." Fidelia beamed and called to Leona in the house. "Leona, come quick, look at our Johnny."

The baby was sitting on the ground when Leona walked out the door.

"Oh, Leona, you missed it. He walked toward me from the blanket."

"Oh, dear, ma'am. We'll be scooting to keep up with him now," said Leona, laughing as she wiped her hands on her apron.

"Mercy, I should have thought to bring old Chap back home with me. He would be great with the baby, but the dog does love the farm and running through the meadows, and I'm sure Pa needs him as well. We'll see."

It was April when the letter came. Leona laid it on the table.

"Ma'am, it's from your pa. In Cypress."

That caught Fidelia's attention. Her father never wrote her letters, and she looked at the envelope on the table, afraid to even touch it.

George had just told her yesterday that he was shutting down the shop. The presses were not running, and there were no customers to pay the expenses. She had told him to put the old press that once belonged to James' grandfather in the shed behind the house and to dispose of the rest as he thought best.

Now a menacing post sat on the table like a foreboding she

wanted no part of. *What could have happened?*

She sat down and looked at the handwriting on the letter, at the creases and soil marks from the days the envelope traveled. She picked it up.

Fidelia, I'm writing about your mother.
She has become frail, and the doctor came
yesterday. He said she would not likely heal
but only weaken. Something about her
blood, he said. Please come. Pa

Fidelia's head dropped into her hands.

"Ma'am. Is the news bad?"

Fidelia looked up at Leona. "Yes. It's my ma. She's ill. I must go."

"Oh, my Lord. I will help all I can. Including prayers, ma'am. Let the baby stay here with me. You go on and care for your mother."

"I'll leave in the morning, yet I'm torn about taking or leaving Johnny. My ma's illness could be catching, yet I'm still nursing," said Fidelia.

"Ma'am, I remember Herman Cannon saying he had a nanny goat. Until you get home, I can give Johnny warm milk from Mister Cannon's farm," said Leona.

"Let's do that. He's old enough, and you can mix some in his porridge. I pray I can get home before my milk dries up, but he's a year old and perhaps it's time to wean him. I can ride, and I'll borrow a horse from Herman Cannon, though he won't be keen on me going alone. I'll write a note for you to deliver to him as soon as you can go."

Leona went to the desk in the sitting room and returned with paper and pen for her mistress, and when she walked into the kitchen she found her friend, her caretaker, her mistress, sobbing.

"Oh, miss," and she put down the pen and paper and hugged Fidelia until her sobs waned. "This is all too much. All too much gloom to deal with at once."

Leona sat at the table next to Fidelia.

"Tell me what to write, and I'll pen the message to Herman, and then, I'll make you a cup of mint tea before I go across town to deliver it."

Fidelia left in the morning with a satchel, including her small Allen revolver, and a wrapped lunch Leona had prepared for the two travelers. Herman had arranged for his fifteen-year-old nephew to ride with Fidelia all the way to her pa's cabin, and Fidelia agreed to have her pa ride with her at least part-way on her journey home.

When they approached her parents' cabin, Fidelia saw no one. No sign of life; no one out in the fields or near the barn, but she saw the fields were planted.

"Please stay," she said to the young man riding with her. "I will get you a drink ... and if there are any vittles, I'll prepare you a meal. I think you should stay the night in the barn. There are cots for the help, and you can head home in the morning, but do as you deem best."

Fidelia opened the door to find it dark inside and her mother in bed, asleep. She did not wake her mother but instead scoured the kitchen for food. There were dirty dishes and, in the pantry, some hardtack and dried turkey. The kettle was empty, but there were some staples such as cornmeal and oats as well as preserved berries and tomatoes. She walked outside.

"Go take our horses out to the barn and feed and water them before you stall them," Fidelia said to the boy. "There should be oats in the bin near the barn door. I'll fix you a bit of food, but it won't be fancy."

"No need, missus. I'll rest my horse a bit and head on

home. I think I can make the main Lampasas trail into Austin by dusk. I'd be grateful for some cool well water if you please."

He turned and led the horses out toward the barn. Fidelia pulled well water for the basin and some for the young man. As she waited for him to return, she lit the oven and mixed some cornbread. Once it was in the oven, she washed the dishes.

"Give me your canteen," she said to the boy when he came through the door. "I'll fill it, and here's a cup of fresh water. While your horse rests, I'm making cornbread and will give you some jerky to take with you. Did you find the oats for the horses?"

"Yes, and thank you, ma'am. Kind of you."

"Not as kind as you coming all this way with me. And, when home, will you or your uncle Herman please go by and check on Leona every week while I'm gone? Ask her if she needs any help. I'll be so grateful."

"Yes, ma'am." He emptied his cup in one gulp, and then Fidelia refilled it before the two walked back outside, where she saw her father riding toward the barn on a gray gelding, her dog Chap wandering beside him, and she realized she still had not spoken to her mother.

"I'll have some food fixed for you as quick as I can. Go over and tell my pa who you are and that I'll soon have some food ready. I see he'll be at the barn before you get there."

The smell of sweet cornbread met Fidelia when she walked back into the cabin.

"Mama?" She sat on the edge of the bed and gently touched her ma's shoulder.

"Oh, Delia, you are here. I'm so sorry you had to come all this way. Is Johnny with you?"

"No, Ma. He's with Leona. What did the doctor say?"

Ma sat up in bed, ran her fingers through her mussed hair.

"He said I would have good days and bad days before I had no days at all."

Mariah smiled at her daughter, and in response, Fidelia struggled to hold in her tears. If her ma was going to be strong, so was she. She took her mother's hand and held it, but her thoughts were not still. She thought back on all the hard times and how hard her mama worked. How she subjugated herself to her husband's days and demands, except she could never give Fidelia's pa the son he so wanted. She remembered how her ma had once buried her sadness in laudanum until Grandma put a stop to it.

"Ma, can I get you something to drink? I will bring some cool water. I did not see any milk."

"Yes, dear, I can drink some water."

"I should have thought to bring some supplies. Some staples," said Fidelia as she walked toward the kitchen and poured the last of the well water she'd brought into the house. She could not fathom how her mother managed out here, so far from everything and everyone.

"It's good to smell something cookin' again," said Pa as he walked in the house. "The boy's out there brushing down his horse. Glad that fella rode out here with ya."

Fidelia said nothing. She was too near to letting her pa have an earful but thought better of it. As she cut the cornbread, she heard her ma stirring in the bedroom, and before she finished wrapping a meager meal in a cloth for the boy, her mother walked into the kitchen. She had put on a dress, but her hair was still tousled and loose.

"Mama, are you feeling any better?"

"Enough to join you both out here. Tomorrow we'll make a pot of soup. I'd put a garden in before I fell ill, and though it's untended, I can see it's bearing—some tomatoes and onions and squash. The squash is not likely ready yet."

"Sit down, Ma. Before the young fella who rode out with me gets on his way home, I'll make something to eat from what's here. I'll check for some ripe tomatoes. There's cornbread and I found a bit of coffee I'll brew. I'm staying a while to help you. Pa, I'll stay in the room with Ma."

"Good 'nuff. I'll sleep in the barn. There most of the time anyways," said Pa as he sat at the table. "Running a few cattle now on the land."

"Maybe it's best if Ma stays in Pond Springs," said Fidelia. Silence was his only response, and Pa walked out the door.

CHAPTER 19

Cleveland (Camp Chase)

Miles returned to Ohio in October and settled in. Anthony Norton had let a flea-bag room for him in a rooming house on Hague Street in Columbus, but this was wartime and Miles was not unaccustomed to meager abodes and not about to complain. Norton had found a room large enough for two so he could join Miles as they engaged in providing some relief and aid at the Camp Chase prison. Secondly, Miles had a history of staying nowhere long enough to expect fancy accommodations, and sometimes, he lay in bed at night seeking sleep and wondering just who he'd become.

He had spent much of the last year skulking through towns controlled by the Federal soldiers in Virginia and, in disguise, down into Richmond's confederate territory. He had met soldiers and families of soldiers, written their stories in his journal, and there had been stories he'd posted to his editor, Norton, to publish in papers—newspapers keeping their head above water in hostile times. Both men were walking flimsy lines, and Norton was still publishing some work in Texas. It was hard to take sides when the two men held Texas and the South in their hearts, yet they both decried slavery and the brutalities they'd seen.

Miles familiarized himself with the community where he now lodged, walking in the streets in the bustle of daytime and the muffled din of nighttime, conversing with shopkeepers when buying food. He cleaned his room, laundered the sullied bedding, and, since Norton had thoughtfully arranged delivery of Miles' typewriter, he unpacked and set it up at the desk. Norton had said he would come down to the city after the first melt of snow and trails were clear.

Columbus was quiet, lacking the bustle Miles had found in Baltimore almost two years before. It was now a town full of widows, like so many other American towns. Like farms all over the country where women were plowing fields and finding ways to feed their families. A couple of shopkeepers had told Miles about the Squirrel Hunters, the men Governor Todd had called up to carry their hunting shotguns to barricade Ohio's southern border when Cincinnati was threatened.

The leaves had begun to turn the colors that begged for winter, and Miles sat down at the desk and rolled a sheet of paper into his typewriter. He stared at the blank page. It did not speak to him, so he picked up his journal and his pen.

The world has gone mad. I've seen farms burned to the ground and horses slaughtered in the harsh struggle and strife on the battlefields in the South and am certain it happens in the Northern battles as well. Injuries to soldiers abominable, a few seen by my eyes, many detailed in stories told me. No matter whom I visit and speak with, their hearts open. Their stories pour out like milk into a bowl. It all comes down to family ... a mother worried about her son to the details of what he eats ... is he warm enough, and does he have weapons enough to defend himself? Women fear for their husbands, afraid they'd never come home. They'd heard enough stories of the dead and wounded. *They worry how they can feed their young children as well as farm animals. And I spoke to soldiers when I was able to get them alone. Most just want to go home and feel the battles to be futile and slapdash, while the Confederate leaders revealed a passion for their goals. The Yankees I spoke with were less passionate and plenty confident in the outcome of restoring the Union, but the soldiers on the battlefield just wanted the comfort of home. What spoke to me most was how these weary soldiers, most on foot, some cavalry, were all the same—regardless of the side they fought for. For what is the war?*

And there is plentiful distrust. Soldiers never spill their hearts to me when in the company of their comrades. Why they trust me, I do not know—but more often than not, people see me as a kindred spirit, even when I'm in a uniform.

So, who am I in all of this? A lost soul. I've seen so much in my travels. Would my mother be proud of who I've become, or would she see me as the lost soul that I feel I am? I'd promised her I would go beyond the hollow in the mountains, and I have done so. In a grand way. But now, I'm tethered to no one dear, to no place held as home, to nothing but my ideals and my stories.

Miles closed the journal and placed it back in his bag. A light began to fade outside the one window of his room, and he knew it would be, at least, a few days before Tony Norton arrived. He looked forward to getting into the prison at Camp Chase, to speak with some of the prisoners, especially those from Texas. He decided to approach the prison the following day since Norton had already made the arrangements for their entrance to provide aid. Miles had no doubt that what was needed most was nourishment—of all kinds.

He arrived at the gate to Camp Chase with his satchel and a small box of biscuits and a jar of jam he'd purchased on his way. He'd already spoken with the owner of the café where he sometimes stopped for hot soup—asked him if he would be willing to donate to Miles any produce and food uneaten, that which would otherwise be tossed or given to a farmer. The manager agreed but told him there would be little of that to give.

The guard who greeted Miles looked at him suspiciously.

"I work with Anthony Norton, who will soon be arriving to work with the prisoners, but I've decided to donate my services, any assistance, prior to Norton's arrival. We are newspapermen, but Norton is a long-time resident of Mount Vernon. Is there an officer present who can usher me into the duties I can provide to be of help?"

"What's in the box?" the man asked.

"Just some hardtack for the prisoners, if allowed, sir," Miles responded.

"I need to search your haversack," said the soldier.

Miles handed it over, and the bag was thoroughly searched and handed back.

Without a word, the fellow turned and walked away

toward a tent next to one of the shacks. Miles stood patient in the sun, hoping the sun would continue to shine and ward off winter, but winter would soon come with its frigid weather.

"Son," said a tall man wearing a hat and the voice of authority. "Captain Wallis here. And you are?"

"Miles Maloney, sir. Work for Tony Norton,"

"I'm aware of Mister Anthony Norton," said the captain. "We look forward to his presence here. When will he arrive?"

"He said before the first snow falls," said Miles, grinning. The officer laughed.

"That sounds like Mister Norton. He'll be here soon enough, and for now, I'll let you dispense some of that food once I inspect the box. Can't let you walk into the yard with it, or you will be mobbed. For now, I have a small group across the way being processed in. Follow me."

Miles followed the man down a narrow path between barracks, but he could hear the chatter and bustle of many beyond the buildings.

"What you can do today is to first share the foodstuff you have in your box. I'll have Private Daniels bring you some paper, ink, and a pen, so you can help them write letters home—tell their family where they've ended up and that the Confederates should concede and end this war."

The man turned and smiled at Miles. Miles smiled back and wondered if this soldier was scrutinizing his loyalties.

"I cannot disagree, sir. They all, on both sides, just want to go home," said Miles, meaning every word he spoke. "I can help them write letters, especially those who are illiterate, and I will post them if you wish."

"We'll post them," the captain responded abruptly, giving Miles his first clue as to how he'd need to guide the men in writing their letters.

Miles wanted to get stories from these captured soldiers, but he chose not to ask. He would just let the tales spill from the men as he knew they would, especially once they knew he'd come from Texas.

"That's good." The captain stopped. "Let me look inside your box." Captain Wallis examined the contents, and then he opened the door to where Miles saw eight ragged men sitting on the dirt floor. A couple looked up at him. No one smiled.

"Well, Rebs. It's your lucky day. This fellow here has brought some vittles and said he'd help you write some notes home. Tell your folks of your new accommodations."

Miles nodded to the prisoners. He could only imagine the thoughts whirling in their heads, and he knew right off that their greatest hurdle would be staying healthy. Disease would be their direst enemy, though Miles was certain that, at the moment, they thought it was the uniformed man beside him.

Miles spent the next few hours helping the men pen letters to their families.

"Got no who cares where I am," said one of them, a gruff man of about forty-five or so, long, scraggly hair.

"Where are you from?" Miles asked.

"Nowhere."

Miles stared at him, saying nothing.

"South Carolina. Near the sea," said the man, his words drawn forth by Miles' silence.

"North Carolina," said Miles, and the old soldier's eyes brightened a bit. "The mountains of North Carolina."

"You a turncoat?" asked one of the other men.

"At heart, I'm a newspaperman. Came here from Texas. Takin' no sides," said Miles.

The men muttered among themselves, and Miles opened the box of biscuits and jam. The bond had been made.

In November, just before the first snowfall, Tony Norton arrived in Columbus and took residence in the rented room shared with his subordinate and friend, Miles Maloney.

"I could not be happier to be here," said Norton to Miles as he unpacked his suitcase. "Being cooped up with young children and women was more than I could bear another day, and I enjoyed every minute of solitude on my ride down here. Stabled my mare at the livery."

"Yes, we can walk to the camp from here," said Miles.

"Maybe you can. We'll have to see about old me."

Norton, with the aid of his cane, and Miles made it to Camp Chase each morning. Sometimes Miles picked up vittles at the cafes and turned them over to the mess hall with naught but hope that some of it would make its way to the prisoners. It wasn't much, but any at all helped. Norton, benefiting from his acquaintances, and Miles had managed to collect a wagon full of donated blankets, some frayed but better than nothing. The two men spent their days talking to the prisoners, talking about Texas to the Texans, and negotiating a release where they could. Miles often sat with prisoners, especially on those weeks when Norton returned to Mount Vernon, and penned letters to mothers and wives all over the South, but the Yankees read most of them before sealed, and Miles never knew which ones would be mailed. Yet, every now and then a rare occasion came when he'd sit and read words from home to a cheered soldier that revealed the letter had been received by a loved one. On a day in early February, the prison rooms almost as bitterly cold as the outdoors, he recalled a prisoner from Texas sharing a letter from his wife. He read aloud the name of a James Hughes in the 8th Texas Cavalry who'd written to the man's wife of his capture, and the prisoner's gratitude for such a kindness stuck with Miles through the day, as did the news that his beloved Fidelia's husband was still alive.

Miles spent the evenings and weekends of winter writing stories gleaned from his everyday encounters. Newspaper articles about prison conditions and the scars of war and then more personal stories about matters of the heart. He found these days more rewarding than those he'd spent on the road infiltrating small towns and military units.

"Son, you've been a blessing to have here, in Ohio," said Norton to Miles one cold, February evening in the meager room they shared. Miles sat at the desk, and Norton's cane drummed the wooden floor as he paced. "You've worked so voraciously for the newspaper that, truly, you should have your own newspaper. Once this damn war is over, we should work on doing just that, boy."

Miles turned his chair.

"Tony, I will always write these stories, but once this is all behind us, I think I just want a bit of land down in Texas. Farming and raise some cattle." Miles wanted to add "raise a family," but he couldn't think of doing that without his Fidelia. "I guess what I'm saying is, that in addition to owning a bit of land and farming, I want to be a storyteller. In the written word, unlike my pa who never wrote down a word of his tales."

"You're selling yourself short, boy, but a man's gotta be true to his heart. That's a hard life—farming. Ranching's a bit less back-breaking, especially in Texas." Tony stopped pacing and sat on his bed. He stared at his friend.

"Son, life is only a minute long and full of demons. Look at me. I'm only forty-something, and I look to be about sixty. Most days, feel like I'm eighty, and I've never done a bit of hard labor like farming or fighting." He untied his shoes, and Miles watched him.

"You do what's in your heart but always think hard on an opportunity, Son. Texas could use a man like you. Hard-working and hard-thinking." And with those words, Norton caressed his beard and lay down on his bed.

Miles looked down at his journal and wrote, "Live like Tony Norton. As sweet Ma would say to us, *do not walk as a fool ... but holdeth your peace for your time will come.*" He closed the book, washed his face at the washbowl, and went to bed, hoping spring would bloom soon.

CHAPTER 20

Cypress Creek

Ma had rallied over the time Fidelia stayed at the cabin. She no longer spent her days in the darkness, in bed. Fidelia made her wash in the morning, put on a fresh dress, and sit at the table or outdoors in the coolness of mornings. Fidelia tended the kitchen, made meals for Pa, did the laundry, and when able, cultivated the garden, culling some okra to brew a meager makeshift coffee. Ma never complained. Pa was another matter, but he did work the farm from dawn to dusk. The farmhand, Boyd, was easygoing and forever expressing his gratitude for the homecooked meals. The man, his black hair grayed at the temple, appeared to be almost fifty and walked with a slight limp, which threw probable light on why he'd not gone off to fight with all the men. Seemed her pa was lucky to have him.

"Pa, I think Ma needs to be at the farm with Grandma. I need to go home. I have a needy baby missing his mother and too early on a goat's milk. Grandma would take care of Ma," said Fidelia at supper one evening in May.

"Who'll do my washing? Cook the meals?"

Fidelia couldn't even bring her eyes up to meet her pa's. She sat in silence and continued eating.

"Boyd, can I get you anything more," asked Fidelia after a time.

"No, ma'am. You're a mighty fine cook, and I'm as full as a working man can be." He smiled at her.

Ma had gone to lay down after she'd eaten but before Fidelia had mentioned she needed to go to Grandpa's farm. After Boyd left for the barn, Fidelia looked at her pa.

"I'm leaving in three days, Pa. I'm going home, and I plan to write to Grandpa about Ma's condition and her need for care."

Without waiting for a response, she rose from the table with her plate and walked to the basin. She knew she'd irked Pa when she heard his chair scrape the floor, but she knew her grandparents would not allow their daughter-in-law to suffer alone.

On a cooler than normal morning, Fidelia walked toward the barn with her satchel. Pa had left to check on his cattle, but he knew she was leaving. He'd said little to her since the supper conversation about Ma.

When Fidelia rose that morning, she helped her ma rise and dress, and Fidelia made a breakfast she knew Ma would barely touch. She wished she had tea or coffee to leave for Ma, but at least the laundry was done.

"Ma, I'm asking Grandpa to come get you. I must get home to Johnny, but Grandma will take care of you. I want you to sit out in the evening air. Pa will be fine without you. He'll grumble, but there'll be no one to hear him but Boyd and the chickens. I love you and will see you again as soon as I can. I'll bring Johnny."

Mariah held her daughter's hand, not wanting to let go. Fidelia kissed her mother on the top of her head and walked toward the door.

"I love you, Mama."

In the barn, she saddled her horse. She wanted to get home and decided to make the ride alone. As she'd tossed through a sleepless night, she decided she would go straight to the farm and talk to Grandpa. Posting a letter would take too long, and she could spend the night and ride into Austin tomorrow.

The skies were cloudy with but a drizzle of rain halfway through her journey, and she sighed relief when she, at last, saw the farm. Grandpa stood with a horse in front of the barn and appeared to be about to stable her. He looked up in her direction and waved, likely unsure it was his granddaughter, and Fidelia waved back. He would see her soon enough.

Grandpa took the reins of her horse as Fidelia dismounted and then hugged her grandfather.

"This is a surprise," he said.

"For me as well," said Fidelia. "I'm not staying, except for the night, but I've come to speak with you and Grandma about my ma. She's ill."

Grandpa's brow furrowed as he tied the horses to the rail.

"Abe had said she was poorly when he last went out to help John. But I didn't know she was seriously ill. Why did John not tell us?"

"I've been caring for her but must get home to the baby. Pa doesn't want her to leave, but, Grandpa, she needs help she is not getting at home. Can we talk at supper?"

"Sure, we can. We need to go get her, don't we?"

Fidelia nodded and smiled. She'd expected nothing less from her grandparents. She had considered bringing her mother to Austin, with both Leona and her to help, but she had no doubt that having Mariah here would put a spring in Grandma's step as well.

At supper that evening, it was decided that Abe and Grandpa would travel to Pa's cabin and bring Mariah to the farm. Grandma would care for her, and Grandpa planned to tell his son that his daughter-in-law deserved better.

"She's been the suffering wife all these damn years," Grandpa had said at supper. "My son might be a good provider, but he's never been a fit husband to that girl."

When he'd said that, Fidelia wanted to smile at his calling her mother "a girl," but the sad truth of his words filled her instead. She knew well that her ma had deserved more happiness than she'd had.

Grandma had decided she would send word to the doctor to come to the farm and check Mariah. Fidelia hoped that a proper diagnosis would offer comfort as well as hope. After breakfast, she penned a three-line note to James of her mother's illness and her journey back home. The sun had not been up long when she delivered the post into the hands of Mister Rutledge, the postmaster in Pond Springs, and rode south toward Austin.

Grandpa had sent Abe to ride with Fidelia to the city's edge, and she had been grateful for the company and some peace of mind. Little Johnny reached for Fidelia when she arrived home to find all was well.

"Oh, Leona, all looks well, as if I'd only left minutes ago. Thank you. I'm so weary and burdened by Ma's state, I just want to sit and hold the baby. To sip some minted tea."

Fidelia spun around once with Johnny in her arms.

"I will fix the tea. Do sit down and rest," said Leona, and she turned toward the kitchen.

Fidelia sank into a chair, where her whole body relaxed, and Johnny ran off toward the kitchen. How Fidelia wished James was here. She'd never missed him as much as she did at this moment. Providence had taken all control from her hands, even her heart. She could not even bring home James, and she cried her fears out to God, startling Johnny, who pleaded to be picked up. It was as if God himself had spoken to her, reminding her to be grateful for what she had.

CHAPTER 21

Tennessee

Near Knoxville, the November air was frigid, chilling the soldiers to the bone along the river's edge, and all was against the Rangers. *When will it stop?* James thought of all the deserters and how easy it would be to go. To be home again, with Fidelia. To sleep in a warm, soft bed. To hold his new son. It would be so easy to ride into the trees, and he'd heard of others who had done it. Some had vanished; some were in the brig. It was not in his character to abandon his duty.

Near Knoxville, the Texas men found themselves galled and unaccustomed to axing and felling tall trees merely to send them down the Tennessee River, in hopes of breaking the Union's boom that crossed the river for corralling supplies. Terry's Rangers were more accustomed to fighting with the Colts from their holsters and had more than a few curse words at being sent across the icy river. It was a fool's plan. The mission did little to weaken the enemy's incursion, but James had helped carry the weight of tall trees to the river's eastern shore. If the generals would only engage a strategy to gain ground, there could be a point to the damned war. A point to all the soldiers now buried beneath Tennessean and Georgian farm dirt, so far from Texan soil.

Now shivering, the men rode from the trouncing at Farmington back toward Chattanooga. Pete had lost his horse after a Yankee foot soldier had sabered it. He was still distraught over putting down the horse and now rode on a weary mare once belonging to a cavalryman from Company B. That soldier had been injured and sent off with no need for his mare, and James looked over at Pete, who rode beside him.

"When will it end, Pete?" James asked, not expecting an answer. "I think we are two damned men, by chance still riding in this war, still in one piece. One damned frozen piece."

"That's exactly what I think every mornin' when I open my eyes again. How damn fortunate I am to just hear the birds."

"Yeah. Let's hope our luck doesn't run out." The two men rode a bit in silence. James pulled his collar and scarf tight around his neck, and Pete pulled a blanket over his coat.

"Did you ever get some tobacco from Ephraim Dodd?" asked James.

"Nope. He'd left camp I was told when I stopped by, but I got some 'baccy from the sutler."

"Wonder where he is now. Dodd. Supposed to be scouting, I imagine," said James.

"Yeah, but he sold his mule last I saw him and still needs a horse since his went lame. Only God knows where he's at, but I's suspect he's wheeling and dealing wherever he's gone," said Pete. "Or maybe some young lady knows ... a pretty young thing lendin' him a soft bed and home-cookin'. Last time I talked to him, all he was talkin' about was angels' wings and a Miss Maggie. That skinny boy loves the ladies."

James laughed and saw Watkins ride up to join them.

"Hey, Hughes, thank you for the missive you mailed my wife," said Watkins. "She wrote me that your kind words gifted her the hope she needed. You're a good man, James."

"Glad to hear it. Was nothing. I must say—I feared for your life, Watkins. I've heard the tales of horror and death in the prisons, so I'm glad for your release."

"The place—Camp Chase, they called it—was grim, but the prison trades with the Yankees are what saves us," said Watkins. "They can't afford to feed us. Not sure they even cared to, but I met a couple Ohio fellas who'd come back from

Texas. Brought some comfort and vittles."

"Well, sometimes appears the Confederacy can't feed us either. All that hardtack back at Chattanooga was hard to swallow, but at least they got those wagons in. Thank God for the farm wives along the way who cook for us."

"Amen," said Pete.

"Hey, Hughes," said Watkins. "Before the war, my wife mentioned some gossip to me. She said your young wife was once betrothed to a Carolina fella. Said he'd worked at the paper. How'd you beguile her away from him?"

James looked over at Watkins, startled by the blunt question. His eyes turned dark for a moment, and he rode forward in strained silence.

"Sorry, friend," said Watkins as the silence lingered. "I may have I overstepped—prying as to personal matters in my curiosity."

Another pause came as the men rode three-abreast amidst the men of Company D.

"No, Watkins. It's fair knowledge," said James, his voice almost a whisper. "She was courted by a young man from the Appalachians. He worked for Norton at the Intelligencer. I won her back when the fella disappeared. Before the war, it seems Norton sent the boy up North—so he said—and no one heard from him again."

"Dang, James. I didn't know that," said Pete. "What happened to him?"

"We never heard. But I wasn't gonna just sit back and wait, so I pursued Miss McCord. Offered comfort through her melancholy. Just kept showing up until I knew the right moment came to ask for her hand."

"I'm sorry, Hughes," said Watkins. "I shouldn't pry. I'd say all's well if the prize is won."

"We have a son. A boy I've not yet seen," said James. The words, spoken aloud, filled his chest. Making his family materialize so real in his mind—a vision.

"Glad to hear it," said Watkins.

"Funny thing, though. At a camp near Georgia, I was certain I saw a Confederate soldier who looked just like him. Not one of us, not a Ranger, but he was talking to Dodd."

"Well, Dodd talks to everybody and anybody, though he prefers those wearing skirts," said Watkins.

At that moment, shots rang out in front of the men causing them to scatter, and James headed to his right to take cover in the trees. Turned out to be a Yankee scouting party, and Company D chased them to the west. Surely, another battle awaited the Rangers around the next bend, and the men prayed their guns wouldn't fail them in the persistent cold.

The cold did not relent, nor did the skirmishes as they traveled between Atlanta and Knoxville. James was getting tired of seeing the same landscape where the farmhouses now seemed to hold naught but sad stories and little food. Crops had not been planted nor harvested, and more often than not, it was the womenfolk holding families together. Some women had planted small vegetable gardens for sustenance and, with keeping their chickens fed and caged, managed to sustain themselves and a few soldiers who might pass through, but when Yankees came through, they'd go through a farmhouse and leave nothing behind, not even one hen. James had seen some Confederate soldiers just as harsh, and it had turned his stomach. A day seldom passed when he did not wonder just why he had joined this spectacle only to come to the conclusion that expectation had been his guide.

CHAPTER 22

Austin

The last letter Fidelia had received from her husband was filled with despair. He had not talked of it, but she felt it oozing between the lines of his words. Of his friend's release from a Union prison. The letter had been written in October, but Fidelia knew that winter would be blanketing the men in Tennessee soon, and if not now, then in late November. As before, the women of Austin had sent blankets, sweaters, and socks, but their destination was undefined, merely to the Confederacy.

Fidelia had visited the farm in September, mostly to visit with her mother. It came clear that Ma had rebounded a bit under the care of her mother-in-law, but she was still frail. The physician Grandpa had called had given no more hope than the charlatan who'd visited her back at the Cypress Creek cabin, but he had given Grandma some remedies for comfort. He told Grandma to stew butterbur from near the creek for dropsy, and a sip of boiled hawthorn now and then when she was weak.

Johnny was growing into a feisty young boy and had begun uttering a few words, including "mama." Fidelia decided to return to Grandpa's farm for the holiday. Ma would be overjoyed to see her grandson again. Joy is what Fidelia wanted to gift her mother, and she hoped her pa would be thoughtful enough to join them. Grandma had said that John came to visit his wife for a couple of days in August.

Tomorrow, Leona would be working with the Ladies' Aid Society group, making deliveries, so Fidelia decided to work on an afghan for Grandma and Grandpa, a Christmas gift. She'd purchased extra skeins of yarn from the Ladies' Aid Society, some leftovers in brown, beige, and white, and the blanket was now half-finished. Tomorrow she would spend the day with Johnny. She owed James a letter. She'd received two from him since she'd last written in October.

"Have a good day, Leona," said Fidelia as the girl grabbed her cloak. "Bundle up. It's getting colder."

Fidelia noticed that Leona stood a bit taller, that the girl had mended and pressed her blue wool shirtwaist and pulled back and pinned her flaxen waves, revealing the lines of her face. It was clear that Leona's work with the Ladies' Aid Society had been good for her as she grew into a cordial young woman. Her newfound esteem was seen in her smile and a new glow.

Leona enjoyed the morning sun on the cool winter day as the young man helped her load the boxes into the wagon. The young man holding the reins was new, and with a list of names and addresses, she climbed up onto the seat next to him.

"G'day, ma'am," said the slight fellow with tousled auburn hair. He was younger than the man who'd been driving the wagon. Deliveries were made once a month, and Leona had been told there would be two outings for the holiday in December. Leona would have to talk to Fidelia about her schedule for the holidays.

"My name is Leona Wells," she told him, followed by the first address on her list.

The young man turned and smiled at her, and at that moment, something unfamiliar and warm welled up inside of her. His smile was like a summer day.

"You can call me Dane. Dane Cannon. You're looking might pretty today, Miss Wells."

When her name rolled off his tongue like that, Leona again felt that warmth inside, and she fidgeted in her seat and sat silent. At the first stop, Dane jumped down and ran around to help Leona down off her seat before he reached into the back of the wagon and handed a package to her. She looked up into his eyes, her own wide with surprise at his help. She nodded and turned to walk to the first home on her list.

The process repeated at the next stop, and with that, Leona spoke up.

"I can dismount from the wagon myself, Mr. Cannon."

"Sorry, ma'am. I was trying to help. I'll get the packages out of the back for you if that's alright."

Leona noticed he appeared a bit bewildered, and though she felt competent, she had enjoyed his gentlemanly help. She was not accustomed to such courtesy, especially from a man.

"Well, it's not necessary, but if you'd like," she responded.

There were twenty-seven more deliveries to be made, and after five more stops, Dane started telling Leona about how he'd gone to Victoria to sign up with Shea's Artillery Battalion. He revealed the hardships after being shot in the leg, then coming down with yellow fever. How he feared he would die but finally rallied and was discharged because of his weakened state after the illness and his leg being slow to heal.

"I only got home two months ago but coming home proved a blessing since my pa and sister-in-law can use the help. And another income," he said.

"Are you related to Herman Cannon?" asked Leona.

Dane looked over at her with raised eyebrows.

"He's my father. Do you know him?"

"Yes. He's been helping Missus Hughes, my employer," said Leona. "And my friend. They took me in like family when Ma died. Your pa carried us in his wagon to Pond Springs when we visited the McCord farm."

"Ah. The McCord farm. Pa used to work for Jeremy McCord. Good people," said Dane.

Leona noticed the young man's limp before he dropped her off at the Hughes' house.

"I'll take that one undelivered package back to Missus Bonner on the way to the livery," he told her. He smiled. "I look forward to seeing you again in December."

Leona hung her cloak on the hook near the front door, feeling tired but realizing the day had passed so quickly. The smells of roasted pork wafted from the kitchen, and the warmth of the fireplace revealed how the outside air had chilled since she'd left that morning. As she passed the mirror, she noticed a flush in her cheeks and wondered if it was the chill in the air or the company she'd kept.

"Oh, Leona. You're home," exclaimed Fidelia when she looked up from the pot she just stirred. "Can you get Johnny, please? He's been down for a nap and should be up by now."

"Yes, ma'am."

The three of them enjoyed a savory meal since Fidelia had been favored enough to get some pork from the liveryman who had a farm outside of town. Even Johnny nursed to fullness after Leona had played patty-cake with him.

"I'll clean the kitchen after I bed the baby, Fidelia, so that you can write your letter."

"Thank you, dear. I do need to get one posted. My James has been so good about writing me in such dire conditions."

Fidelia could hear the baby's giggles from the other room as she laid sheets of paper on the desktop and pulled her ink and pen from the drawer.

Dearest James,

We ate a fine supper this evening thanks to Henry at the livery bringing me some pork. I am certain your meals are more meager, and I am eager for the day you return home to a soft bed and a home-cooked meal. To my arms. To meet your son.

I have decided to visit the farm for the holidays. I must say that I am distressed at how feeble Grandma and Grandpa have become, but they are managing. Ma is still with them. I must see her and, perhaps, stay to help. Grandma has written that Ma has some days she sleeps all day, but I am full of gratitude that Grandpa and Abe went out to the cabin to get her in the summer. She was reluctant to leave Pa, but he could not take care of her, and I must disclose, he expected her to perform all her daily chores in her weakened condition. Please pray for her, James.

I pray you are warm, wherever you are, and that you are well. The newspaper stories of the war are alarming, and how each side sings their own praises, I feel the conflict seems never-ending. May this miserable war be over soon.

I will write to you from the farm, in December. I cannot wait for you to meet Johnny who is quite well and running about with me and Leona always chasing him. I do not want to wait another day to be held within your arms, but I will fretfully await that day. I look forward to your next letter.

Sent with all my love, Delia

It was the second week of December when Leona wrapped herself in her wool coat and scarf and met Missus Bonner in town for the holiday deliveries. The wagon was full of packages, and the list handed to her was long, but she saw that Dane Cannon stood beside the cart and had smiled at her as she passed him.

It was a cold day, which only spurred the two to get the deliveries finished by mid-afternoon. The two shared childhood remembrances and laughed with each other all afternoon.

"I'm glad we have more deliveries tomorrow," Dane said as he braked the wagon in front of the Ladies' Aid Society.

"Why? It's so cold."

"Because I will get to laugh with you again," he said and smiled at her. The warm feeling once again rose inside, and she knew what it was. She liked him. She liked him a lot. Liked his strong hands helping her down from the wagon. His gentleness with the horses. His easy laugh and smile.

Dane saw the blush in her face and took her hand into his.

"It's cold out here. Check in with Missus Bonner and I'll wait here to take you home." He let go of Leona's hand.

There was little conversation in the awkward ride to her house.

"I'll see you tomorrow," said Dane as Leona stepped down.

The sun rose bright on the following day when Missus Bonner produced a shorter list plus the three undelivered packages from the day before. Leona wore her ruffled green dress with her plaid cloak, and Dane's wide smile greeted her at the wagon.

"Told ya I'd be happy to see ya today," he said as he took her hand and helped her to the wagon seat.

"Well, I must say, I'm happy to see you too. We're leaving

next week for the McCords'."

The wagon lurched forward, and Dane put his hand on Leona's shoulder to steady her.

"I'm sad to hear you're leaving for the holidays. Was hoping to see you again."

"I think your pa is taking us."

Dane looked over at Leona as he pulled the horses to a stop at the first house.

"I think I'll take y'all and let Papa take a day off, if'n that's okay with Pa and Missus Hughes."

"It would likely be fine," said Leona as they stopped, and he handed her a package from the back of the wagon.

The deliveries were finished by noon, and when Leona entered the front door of the Hughes' house, she saw Fidelia knitting and little Johnny asleep on a blanket near her chair.

"Miss Fidelia, I think I might be in love. What does that feel like?"

CHAPTER 23

Cleveland (Camp Chase)

Snows had fallen in early December, and there had been the loss of a Texan prisoner at Camp Chase when he'd frozen to death near the fence. No one knew why he'd been outside, but death at the prisons was not an uncommon thing except that it was usually brought on by disease more often than weather. In spite of the weather, Miles had decided to continue on into Tennessee and get more stories.

Norton encouraged him to wait until spring, but Miles wanted to see the conditions of living and how so many battles had distressed the once-bucolic hillsides and the families living there. He wanted to see first-hand the soldiers who had to be as weary as a cat nursing twelve kittens. He'd take a few blankets with him, but he always traveled light, so he'd only have a few to give away. The blankets he and Norton had gathered and donated at the Columbus prison were much appreciated by the recipients.

"If the soldiers can endure the brutal conditions day after day, I can do the same to get my stories," said Miles to Norton in their rented room near Camp Chase. "Yet I have license to leave at any time I choose."

Norton decided he would keep the room but return home to Mount Vernon for the holidays, then come back as weather permitted, expecting Miles to return in the spring. Miles began preparing, stocking up on some journals, laundering his borrowed uniforms, oiling his guns, and wiping down his saddle, canteen, and a few eating utensils. He'd get some beans, some coffee, and a new rain slicker before he left.

He left Columbus the same day Norton left for Mount Vernon. It was a cold day, two days before Christmas, and there was no precipitation nor promise of any, though Miles was certain it would come. There would be woods to cross through in Kentucky as he headed for Nashville. By noon, when he stopped to rest and water his horse, he felt like he was back on the trails with his brother. It truly had not been that long ago when he'd traversed the country back in 1857. He wondered why it had felt like decades—forever. *How could so much have changed?*

He bit into a biscuit and took a sip from his canteen as he leaned back against a tree near a rill. Parts of the trail felt forsaken and solitary, and Miles knew he needed to be cautious in wartime. He still wore civilian clothes.

Even in mid-day, the overgrowth of the forest made it seem the edge of dusk, so his mind went to dreaming. All the way back to his months in Little Rock, living in a cabin not so different than his childhood in Appalachia. He'd been happy working in the city and living in the woods. He'd met so many interesting people and saw the first railroads come west. Then, with the sight of one wanted poster, the law still looking for his brother for the murder of a farm boy, Miles and Jackson had gone on the run once again. On to Texas.

Texas seemed to be his undoing. He'd found everything he'd ever wanted and lost it all. Then, his thoughts traveled all the way back to his mother and their conversation on her deathbed. She'd wanted him to see the world. She'd encouraged him to be all he could be. And here he sat in the forest by rippling water in search of someone else's story. *Where was his story?* Jackson had gone home to his life and now had two sons of his own, last Miles had heard. He'd heard nothing from his pa or brother since the war started, but that was to be expected. Even Norton did not know where Miles was on any given day.

He mounted his horse and moved on to the south.

Winter found him north of Nashville—came in behind him like a bobcat pouncing on prey. He plowed on through stinging snow into the city and let a room for the night. The Union now occupied Nashville.

The snow ended overnight, and in the morning, Miles decided to stay another day. Even though many of the city dwellers had left for safer abodes, this city had to be full of stories. He pulled out his journal before he left the boarding house.

> *December 28, 1863. I've arrived in the center of Tennessee and have not yet found the South, but I'm certain I'll encounter disguised Rebels at every turn of the city, more at the edge.*

And off he went. The Union was everywhere, in uniform, and it appeared civilians were staying behind closed doors. Few were on the streets, and the walkways were shrouded in snowdrifts. Miles, in civilian clothing, found a hotel with an open dining room.

"Morning, sir," said an attractive woman, older than Miles with brown curls pinned high, her striking cheekbones accented with a flush to her cheeks. "Breakfast?"

"Yes. Passing through and hungry," said Miles. She smiled.

"Just some eggs, fried, and sausage, if you can," said Miles. "Where is everyone? Only saw soldiers."

"Well, it is quite cold, but"—she lowered her voice to a whisper—"most of our city folk left for Chattanooga or somewhere south. Those who've stayed—we've been made to sign an oath to the Union."

"I just need a biscuit and jam and a hot coffee if it's to be had."

Miles was surprised the woman revealed this information to him, and it reinforced his sense that there was no hiding his origins in the moonshine mountains.

"I heard the general moved on to Knoxville," said Miles.

"Believe that is true, but there are skirmishes everywhere in between," she said, and with those words, she was off to the kitchen.

A couple of civilians sat in the room, and there was a table of Union soldiers. Officers. Miles avoided eye contact with them, not wanting another interrogation. He downed the coffee, and after he paid the woman and left a generous tip, he bundled up with his scarf and gloves and walked the streets toward the edge of town. He wanted to talk to a resident and knew it would more likely be a woman. It was the women left at home, at the mercy of war and shortages.

He came upon a small farm at the threshold of Nashville, somewhat dilapidated with a few chickens in the yard revealing that someone lived there. He walked down the road a bit, hoping someone would come out. It seemed too bold to knock at the door, yet it wasn't the kind of day one would be outside, except to feed chickens or check for eggs.

Just as hoped, he walked back to find an old woman wrapped in a shawl leaving the coop with a basket of eggs.

"Good day, ma'am. Can you, pray tell, tell me the name of this road?"

The woman squinted at him and then approached.

"What did ye say, young man?"

"Asked the name of this road. I'm not from here and might be lost."

"Chicken Road."

Miles looked at the woman, unsure if she was jesting.

"Sounds mighty right to me. I see the town's full of soldiers now."

"Damn Yankees. I's surprised I still got all my chickens. They took my neighbor's hens and pig. Guess we don't need to eat, do we? You ain't one of their spies, are ya?"

He laughed.

"No, ma'am. I write stories, and I'm looking for some new ones."

She looked hard into his face, her eyes like steel. She looked frail, but Miles gathered she was not that at all.

"Come on in out of the cold, boy. I'll makes ya some hot tea. It's from my herbs, so don't be expectin' something fancy.

Miles didn't tarry but followed right behind the woman whose name was still a mystery. He hoped the old woman had a fire in her hearth as robust as the one in her eyes.

Sitting at a table that looked as old as the farm, Miles looked around the room while the woman busied herself with a kettle.

"My name's Miles," he said, "and just between us, I'm from North Carolina."

She kept working, and he wondered if she hadn't heard him. The room was large, with a table and chairs, a bench, a makeshift kitchen with a hearth, and a fine fire warming him. It was clean, and a small black and white cat rubbed against the woman's ankles.

"I'm Mildred. Mildred Sweeney," she said as she set two cups of steaming tea on the table. "Feel I've been here forever, but my parents came here from Virginia. Glad to hear you ain't one of them Yankees. Here's some honey in this jar. Ain't got no sugar and no dairy cow."

"Good to meet ya, Mildred, and where's your family?"

"None here. All that's left is my son and grandson, both gone off to fight. Daughter died in youth. I heard some talk that my grandson Billy got killed in Gettysburg. My husband's been dead since I killed him."

Miles didn't know what to say upon hearing her confession, but the old woman started chuckling.

"Love saying it to jolt people," she said. "Somethin' I cooked some eighteen years ago didn't agree with Joshua and he died in some agony. Bless him. This cat here showed up some months ago and keeps me company. And the chickens."

"Do you mind if I write some of this down, Miss Mildred?" Miles had his journal and cedar pencil at hand.

"No, sir. Not much to write down," she said. "We had a nice little farm here once. Crops of corn and potatoes. Onions. Saddest day of my life was when my girl died. Right here. In that room. She wanted to see the ocean, more of the world than this scrap of a place. I wanted it for her since she wanted it so bad. She and her pa are buried across the road."

The woman's words reminded Miles of the night he'd sat with his ma as she died. Her wish was for him to see the world. Pa was just keeping on till Molly married. The words pulled up old grief.

"Our life here is not like the fancy people in town with their crinoline dresses and dancing and teas. Do you know some still go dancing in the midst of our sorrows as if their world has not changed? All I can do is hope my son comes home one day. Otherwise, I'll just live lonely here till I die, suppose."

"Well, I don't think anyone's gonna stop you, Miss Mildred. At least as long as you got some chickens and your well don't go dry."

"Nope. Ya right about that, and if those damn Yankees take my hens, I got plenty of squirrels for stew and plump grouse out in the woods."

Miles sipped another cup of tea and a biscuit before he left Mildred's farm, and as he walked back to the boarding house, he knew then where the pull of her story would take him. East. He'd leave early in the morning, traveling east toward North

Carolina, dodging skirmishes and campsites and gathering what stories he came upon on the way.

Chapter 24

Tennessee

In the coldest winter James had ever seen, he wrapped himself in two worn wool blankets in the tent he shared with Pete, Watkins, and a fellow from Milam County. He wore gloves, two shirts, and long johns and still shivered.

The Union held Nashville and now, Knoxville. Skirmishes around the city happened on a regular basis, but the Confederates could not take the city. Colonel Harrison had led the regiment from the Holston River down to Rome, Georgia before the big storm arrived. The location was a good stepping point to both Chattanooga and to Knoxville, and the mountains were a good place to shelter.

Before sleep finally took him deep, he had dreamt of spring. He no longer dreamt of going home; now he only hoped for a few rays of sun and the cover of pines to shield them from the enemy. The men were so weary, and hope seemed but an indulgence.

In the morning, campfires drew the men to breakfast, and word spread from one to another that their scout, Ephraim Dodd, had been captured by Union soldiers near Knoxville. The story was that the enemy thought him to be a spy, and some of the men laughed at such an idea.

"He's nothing but a ladies' man," said one of the men.

"Well, think about it," said another. "What better way to get the goods from the enemy. Wooing the women."

The chatter lasted all day. *Was he, or wasn't he? And who*

was he spying for? Someone said that the Yankees might hang him. Everyone had an opinion of Dodd, and some even called him "odd Dodd." The men were told to stand down and wait for better weather before tracking to the west.

James hadn't had a letter for a couple of months, but neither did the rest of the men. They'd been on the move, and the brutal weather had kept deliveries at bay, not to mention the innumerable forays by both sides of the war to destroy bridges and railroad tracks. Now the regiments, most under the command of General Wheeler, seemed stuck by indecision and a brutal winter. Talk was that a Union attack on Atlanta was in the making, but, for the moment, winter was a relentless demon keeping the men cornered and sheltered. Vittles were scarce, like the supply lines, but the men were armed and the forests full of fowl and rabbits.

James volunteered, along with Watkins, to chop firewood. "Keep moving" was the adage amongst the regiment. It was the best way to not feel the cold, but the soles of James' boots had worn paper-thin, and he was thankful for his wool socks.

"Do ya think this will ever end?" said Watkins as he felled a small poplar. "I'm ready to go home. Some days my horse just wants to head west."

"I know. Crossed my mind too," said James. "I sometimes wonder what happened to those who just rode off. Deserted the army. Do ya think they made it home?"

"I imagine some of them did. And I wish I'd gone with them. We just keep losing ground, losing horses, losing comrades, and at every turn, we're risking our own lives for what appears to be naught but defeat and defeat. I just want to go home to a fire in the hearth and the gentleness of my Laura."

Watkins joined James to stack the cut wood into the cart.

"Well, if we lose Atlanta, I think it's done. I can't believe our army cannot hold on to Atlanta, but both sides will surely send all their brawn to that fight."

The cart full, Watkins hitched it to the two horses, and the men eased their way back to camp. As they unloaded and stacked the wood near the mess tent, there seemed a buzz about the camp, and Pete came running up to them.

"They killed him. Word just came," said Pete. "The Yanks hung Dodd. Someone said they had to do it twice to kill him."

We stood thunderstruck at Pete's words.

"Twice?" I asked.

"Yep. They hung him for spying. Last week, it's said." Pete caught his breath for a moment. "Someone said the rope broke on the first drop."

"Damn," said Watkins.

CHAPTER 25

Pond Springs

Fidelia rose early after the Christmas holiday and joined Grandpa in the milking ritual at the barn. They each sat on a stool milking the two dairy cows. Even little Johnny was still asleep, and as Fidelia always had, she enjoyed the early quiet of the day.

"Can you stay awhile longer, Fidelia?" asked Grandpa. "Your ma seems to wane a bit each day, and I think it's good for both of you to be together now. That baby of yours brings her so much joy. It's the only time I see a glint in her eye."

"I know, Grandpa. I've seen it, and I'm glad I'm here. I'll stay."

Fidelia knew she must. She knew her ma was failing faster than Fidelia was ready to accept, but she needed to be near her mother now and it was undeniable that the presence of Johnny seemed the best elixir for Ma. Even Pa had come for a couple of days but left for the cabin early yesterday as there were signs of storms coming.

"When the weather is clear," Fidelia said, "I might send Leona back to the Austin house to keep tabs on everything. Besides, she has become an integral help to the Ladies' Aid Society and met a young man she's fond of. The young man who carried us up here in the wagon. Remember? You met him."

"Ah. Yes," Grandpa mumbled. "Still romance in the midst of war. What better time than when the world is upside down."

Fidelia smiled. He sounded like the Grandpa she remembered, sharing his wisdom. She poured the milk in her bucket into Grandpa's and carried it to the porch. Grandpa rose and walked into Jeremy's old workshop. She wondered if he was visiting with Uncle Jeremy in the room where her uncle had once spent so much of his time and then, pondered if Gray Feather, the Osage who she'd befriended, had told Grandpa how spirits of the dead lingered. As a young girl, Fidelia's talks with Gray Feather had always enlightened and moved her in a way she did not fully understand as a child but appreciated now. He had moved through the forests with the French trappers as if he were a spirit and shared his wisdom with young Fidelia, guiding her path through harrowing grief. Now, she wondered if her grandpa had also received such wisdom—if Jeremy and Grandpa were now just talking in the workshop in the wavering light of the oil lamp. The very thought held her breath taut in her chest, and then, she thought of her mother and exhaled.

Fidelia was still at Pond Springs when Mariah died. There was snow in Central Texas on the brutally cold morning when Grandma went to wake her daughter-in-law and found her still. The touch of her skin was as cold as the meadows. She was not surprised and a bit grateful that her daughter-in-law had gone quietly in her sleep.

Abe first was sent to notify John of his wife's death, and when he returned, he built the coffin where Mariah had to rest a few days, maybe weeks, before the ground warmed enough for a grave to be dug in Round Rock.

"Seems the McCords are filling up this damned cemetery," said Grandpa two weeks later as he dug a hole with the help of Abe and the youngest Harris boy from the Stagecoach Inn. Before they were done, John arrived from Cypress Creek and relieved his father from the chore.

"It's my wife. My duty," John said and attacked the ground with his shovel as if his wrath could change the course of life. The women arrived later, with the wagon holding Mariah's coffin.

At the very sight of the wooden box in the wagon, back at the house, vivid memories had flooded Fidelia's mind. Two scenes. Two deaths. The first she thought of was Jeremy, who'd died coming to her rescue. Jeremy, the youngest McCord son, had been a jokester, at times sullen, but in his short life, he came to achieve success and build great friendships with those he'd helped and those who'd bought his crafted furniture. Then came the impressionable scene of Fidelia's aunt Audrey lying in a coffin, the very sleeping beauty she was in death, stolen of her vivacity and fearlessness. That loss had crushed young Fidelia. She remembered the day the man who'd loved her aunt came to find, instead, that he'd lost her and stood so sorrowful at her grave as Fidelia, only a girl of eight at the time, and her grandpa watched. Now, it was her mother's journey out to the small graveyard.

Her mother had found little happiness in life, mostly struggle and submission to her husband's indifference. Ma's joys were her girls, yet she'd lost them one by one, except for Fidelia. As much as she loved her ma, Fidelia wanted to live in the spirit of her aunt Audrey. She wanted to exact joy, to dance in life's puddles like Audrey had.

When the wagon arrived at the cemetery, Abe helped the women down. John walked toward his daughter and embraced her. She was his only child, but Fidelia felt confused by her father's affection after so many years when he'd shared so little affection with Ma. She was not accustomed to affection from her father and never quite understood what was in his heart. He said nothing, and after releasing his daughter he picked up his grandson, so like the son he'd always wished for.

The ceremony was short with an afternoon meal at the house. A couple women from the church came by to offer their condolences for they had known Mariah when the family all attended Sunday services.

That evening, Fidelia quietly asked Abe if he could take her small family back to Austin the following week, and he agreed. Her father stayed the night before leaving, visiting with Grandpa out in the workshop and retiring to the cot there for the night.

At breakfast, Pa revealed he planned to take a trip back to Indiana, to the old farm and to visit his brothers up north.

"I'm leaving after planting's done," he said. "I've got Boyd to keep up the work and animal care, and we've agreed Abe can go out a couple of times to check on things. See if Buster needs any help."

"You're going in the midst of this war?" asked Grandma.

"Yep. No time like now. I'm taking the train north ... not east, Ma. Probably to Chicago and then over to Indiana."

"Levi and the family are there," said Grandma, "but I think Junior is gone to fight with the Union."

"I'll be back in summer, before harvest for sure."

Fidelia sat silently through the conversation, only listening. Somehow, her father's journey seemed irreverent so sudden at the loss of his wife, of her mother. But her father had been distant from everyone since they'd all come to Texas.

The brutal cold of January kept Leona and Fidelia in Pond Springs until the beginning of February when Abe carried the Hughes family back to Austin. The weeks with her grandparents had given Fidelia time to help Grandma with laundry and churning butter. Leona and Reka made candles and soap, enough to last through summer, for soon, Grandma, with Reka's help, would be busy putting in her vegetable garden. Bundled in wools against the cold, Leona had learned how to set a broody hen, gather morning eggs, and feed the chickens, and she would let the cows and horses out to pasture when the sun broke through the clouds. The relentless cold of January caused Grandpa to bring the hatched chicks into the house, where he placed them near the hearth in a handmade box, and their constant chatter had Grandma praying for spring to come.

"Can we take one of the kittens back to Austin," asked Leona one evening at the farm. "Johnny would love its playfulness."

"I'm certain the kittens will be happier in the country," said Fidelia, "but I'll think about it. It would be a good mouser, I suppose, if it managed to dodge the wagons on the street."

Fidelia missed her dog, Chap, but knew he too was happier on a farm, now her father's farm. She knew Pa had found Chap to be a companion out in the middle of nowhere and on his rides through the hills to check on cattle, though she remembered how her dear mother had craved companionship and affection from her husband.

Once back home, Johnny and the women settled straightforwardly into their routine with a small cat underfoot.

"It will live in the carriage house," Fidelia had said, but now it bounced from room to room in search of attention and loose threads.

With the print shop shut down, finances were tight, and Fidelia struggled to manage the home. She craved a cup of coffee, of good coffee that was hard to find, but now it became a struggle to stock the cupboards with beans and fruit and dried meats. Grandma had sent some preserves, relishes, dried turkey, and salt pork. Shortages were rampant in towns, but the rural areas with farms, mostly managed by women in wartime, held their own with their gardens, field crops, and farm animals.

There was a knock at the front door. Fidelia picked up Johnny as he tumbled near her feet, and Leona opened the door to find Dane Cannon with a smile big enough to bring on spring.

"I'm so glad you are back," he said to Leona and smiled in Fidelia's direction. "I've missed you at the Ladies' Aid regular deliveries, and I've brought you a gift. A late Christmas gift."

"Dane, I have not even unpacked. But I'm comforted to be home. How did you know we'd returned?" said Leona.

"On the street, I saw Abe heading north with his wagon," said Dane, and he turned to Fidelia.

"Missus Hughes, I know you are not Leona's parent, but you are as near a mother as she has, so I want to ask your permission to court her"—he turned to look at Leona—"if she wishes."

"Well, young man, I do believe she wishes." Fidelia said and laughed, and Johnny laughed at his mother.

The gift he handed to Leona was wrapped in stenciled brown paper.

"Sit down," said Leona as she sat in the blue chair nearby. Dane sat on the edge of a caned chair, and Fidelia walked up the stairs with the baby.

"Naptime," she called back and disappeared.

"It's a book," said Dane before Leona had even unwrapped it.

"Oh, Dane."

"You always spoke of the books here in Missus Hughes' house, so I thought you would love these poems."

"I do. I do. I have not read Walt Whitman's poems, but I

have heard his name," said Leona. "Thank you." She turned through the pages, and then they both stood, and Leona rose on her toes to give him a quick kiss on the cheek.

"What's this?" he said, looking down at a kitten batting the laces of his shoes. He stooped to pick up the kitten.

"We haven't given him a name yet."

Dane looked at the cat. "Call him Sam. If he turns out to be a girl, which I think not, she'd be Samantha."

Leona laughed. "Why don't you come to supper one day next week. I'll have to ask Fidelia, but I'm certain she'll be agreeable. I'll see you on Thursday for the deliveries and tell you then."

"Yes. I will dream of you until Thursday," said Dane, and as he left, Leona watched him strut down the path to the street.

CHAPTER 26

Murphy, North Carolina

"Pa," yelled Miles as he rode up the hillside and saw his father outside the old whiskey shack. He was stooped over in the garden, and at hearing the horse approach he stood and looked toward Miles.

"Pa. It's me. Miles."

With those words, Pa waved and ambled awkwardly toward the path to the house.

"Son! By God, I thought you's was dead, it's been so long," yelled Pa.

Miles dismounted and hugged his father with all his might.

"No, Pa. I ain't dead. I've been working for the newspapers. Dodging the enemy just like Jackson taught me."

Jeremiah Maloney slapped his son on the shoulder. "I can't believe you're here standing before me."

"Where's Jackson?"

"The damned government took him to fight. Took Jacob too. 'Member? That's Molly's husband. The women are living together at Jacob's farm. Nora's got the two boys, and your sister, Molly, has a daughter, just a baby."

"I was hoping to see him. Jackson. But, Pa, I'm glad to be here." Miles hugged his pa again and then tied the reins to the post. "I'll stay a few days. Then gotta be on my way. I'm still writing stories for Norton, but I've been interviewing so many families, mostly women, broken by war, and all the sad stories reminded me how long it's been since I've seen home."

"Well, it ain't what it used ta be," said Pa. "With your ma gone, Jackson gone, and no Molly to cook for me."

Miles realized just how little had changed at the farm. How Miles' sister had been more a servant than a daughter.

"I'll ride over to see Molly tomorrow. Are ya still stewing whiskey?"

"Yep, but the local market for buying has dwindled. Let's stable your horse and go inside. Got me a new mule out in the barn and an old, crippled horse that Jacob gave me 'cause she's useless."

"Do you have some oats for my dun?" asked Miles as he let her drink at the trough.

"A bit and there's plenty hay," said Pa.

The next day, Miles found the farmhouse Jacob had purchased full of life and laughter, but he was not surprised. These two women were earthy and in their glory with a house full of children. Jacob's fields were fallow, but a small winter garden sprouted in the confines of a larger one that had likely been full in spring and was now being picked by free-ranging chickens. Except for the absence of men, the mountains seemed untouched by Union soldiers.

Molly sat her daughter, Lily, in Miles' lap as she busied herself in the kitchen. The infant appeared to be just less than a year old, and the baby pulled at her uncle's bearded growth and giggled. He lifted her high and she laughed as Jackson's two boys tussled nearby.

"I cannot believe you are here, brother," said Molly. "I thought you'd never come back, and Jackson said you'd found a girl in Texas."

He held Lily in his lap and took a sip of fresh coffee.

"I did, but seems she married another fellow after I left for

Ohio," he said, his voice turned soft and gray. "She could not wait for my return."

Molly kissed the top of her brother's head, and he realized how much his sister had changed since he last saw her. In that cabin with Pa, all those years ago, their mother ill, she was trapped and invisible—from dawn to dusk attending to the men as if she held no worth of her own. Now, in this life as a mother and wife, she'd bloomed full of life. Happy. Their small farmhouse was full of light, as were his sister's eyes, and at that moment, he realized with a staggering quickness how deeply unhappy he was.

Molly sat a bowl of grits in front of him with a biscuit and apple butter. He ate and spooned a bit of the butter into the baby's mouth as she grabbed for a taste. The weight of his niece on his legs sent a wave of regret through his core, and a leg muscle jerked his foot forward. He gripped Lily's waist, surprised by the smallness of her and realizing how little familiarity he had with babies. He and Fidelia had talked and dreamed of their own family, sons and daughters and a Texas farm. But what had he pursued? His own urge to wander a country and an urge to see new things, talk to people he'd never before met but who opened up to him as if they sat at the confessional. He recalled the dreams he'd spoken of with his ma on her death bed. She told him to be happy. *Where had he gone wrong?*

"Miles, where are you? You look like you've seen a ghost," said Molly. He left his reverie and turned toward her, at the light of gladness in her face, and realized she had found her way and he had not.

"Maybe I have, sister. Maybe I have seen my own," and he saw the crease of worry cross his sister's face. He handed Lily over to Molly and rose from his seat.

"I am so heartened, Molly, to see how happy you are here. You are blest," he said, and Nora smiled at him while Molly still appeared perplexed.

"I must be heading back to the cabin. I'll be leaving in a couple of days, but tell Jackson and Jacob of my regards when they return. I'll be heading back toward Ohio for now, and I suppose I can help Pa make some repairs at the cabin tomorrow. The porch is leaning."

Molly hugged Miles for a long time, as if she believed she'd never see him again. Then, Nora gave him a quick hug, and he left. He rode his horse up the mountain as winter dusk eased in from the east.

That evening, Miles sat at the table with sheets of paper, missing his typewriter that sat abandoned in Ohio with Tony Norton, and words flowed from his pen.

What Have We Sacrificed—and at What Price?

This bloody war is nothing but loss and sacrifice. How many widows have I spoken with who have lost all hope and mothers uncertain they'll ever see their sons again? All this pride and opinion for naught but the death of so many. I've yet to meet a family across these agonized states that has not been broken somehow. And in all of this, what happened to our humanity? I've seen the despair and squalid compounds of the war prisons. I've come upon fields with abandoned bodies of the fallen, their voices muted forever, and let me tell you, we are no longer the patriots that once sought our independence as a new country.

For what? I've talked to the Negroes who've walked to freedom and a couple still enslaved, only to find they are no different than us, but their pain is deeper and their desire to be free greater. Yet we fight over the right to enchain them, to use them—for profits. With the vacant chairs at supper tables, even the widows understand this battle's empty value of words spouted so brashly by commanders in the battlefields.

...

But before I go, let me tell you what I've sacrificed. For naught but an emptiness in my heart, like the hearts of all the others I've spoken to—like the hearts of the soldiers bravely fighting for their own lives as well as a cause or a duty. I've lost my home and my adopted state, and my friends and my values—and saddest of all, I've lost the only woman I've ever loved. I've given up the family I'll never have now. All of this sacrificed in the middle of this damned uncivil war. Everything that I've held in my heart and taken for granted, lost—the price of my ambition.

This new land of ours, made up of people with their own dreams, needs to stop sacrificing the very things that matter. It's too grand a price to pay. I will say here that I've read accounts of how the heavens draped the sky in divine northern lights of glorious colors as men died, men on both sides of the war, in Fredericksburg in 1862 as they battled at the Slaughter Pen farm, and I can only pray to the God that sanctified the souls on that night, that He will end this war tomorrow, so the light of who we are will seep back to light the day. I doggedly hold hope.

Miles read through his scrawled article once, edited a couple of words, and sealed it into an envelope he addressed to Norton in Ohio.

When Miles woke the next morning, a light snowfall

covered the ground, his father was still asleep, and he made a pot of coffee before heading out to the old woodshed. The room was quiet and dry, the opposite of what it had been when he and Jackson manned the still. A few jugs sat against the wall, some empty and some filled. Clearly, the moonshine business in Murphy, North Carolina, was not what it had been in the days before. He walked on to the barn and fed the mule and horses before he threw some feed to the chickens.

By the time his pa came outside, Miles had fixed the barn door and replaced some rotted siding on the barn.

"Pa, I'm gonna work on the porch this afternoon. See if I can level it out and replace two of the joists and some rotted boards if I can find enough lumber."

"There's some up in the cave," said Jeremiah.

"Damn, Pa. Up in the cave? Why would you have wood up in that cave? Take me a good piece of the day to get up the mountains and back."

"Well, I had plans. Thought I might move up there," said Jeremiah.

"You're crazy, Pa."

"Don't be hasty, boy. It's a lot warmer in winter than this old house."

Miles carried a piece he'd cut to support the porch and walked toward the house, his father following him.

"I made coffee. Let's fix something to eat before I head up the mountain. I saw you have a wreck of a wagon in the barn. Can your mule pull it?"

"Sure can. I'll go see if the hens laid any eggs." Jeremiah walked back toward the barn.

Miles stayed an extra day, and with his Pa, they ran some mash through the still. He wanted to make sure all worked properly before he left, and his father said he had a few customers still in the hills. Money was another issue, what with its decline of worth, but Jeremiah managed to meet his needs through barter, a common practice in wartime. Miles had made the trip up to Pa's cave in the mountainside to get the wood and found the cave well-stocked with whiskey jugs and a sleeping pallet. He stood and shook his head, thinking his pa was never meant to live in civilization, but Miles did notice how warm it was in the cave on a cold January day.

"Where ya going after this?" asked Pa as the two men sat on the mended porch the night before Mile's departure. Jeremiah lit his pipe.

"Not sure, Pa. I'm heading west. Norton, my editor and friend, and I still have business rendering aid to Confederates at Camp Chase and more stories to write. I wanted to head up through Richmond and explore Castle Thunder, where they keep the women prisoners. Imagine, imprisoning women in a war like this, but I believe I'll head to Tennessee toward Ohio. And, one day, at the end of this goddamned war, I sense I'll head back to Texas."

"Damn, Son. That's some terrible chancy places you're wanting to go. You better be careful and there's soldiers riding about in these woods, in both those dreary colors they wear, and some of 'em going rogue. Had some ruffians last month come here looking for moonshine. And, when you get back to Texas, give my thanks to Beulah for helping you boys. Wish you weren't headed so far, but you know where we're at. So glad you found your way back here."

"Pa, I did see how Molly and Nora were thriving over at Jacob's farm. I was overjoyed to see her so happy."

"Yeah, she's done good. Brings me a good home-cooked meal once a week. Sometimes twice," said Jeremiah. "I sure pray Jackson comes home. Got one letter from him. From down in L'isianna almost a year ago."

"What about Jacob? Has Molly heard from him?"

"Think so," said Jeremiah.

"I'll be leaving early tomorrow, but I promise to send you a note from Ohio and letters when and if I get back to Texas." Miles stood and headed out to the barn to check on his horse.

Dawn came with the falling of snow, and having packed his saddlebag and filled his canteen, Miles headed down the mountain and towards the east. When he arrived at the edge of town, he dismounted and, with bridle reins in hand, led his gelding. Miles stopped at the post office and mailed the envelope to Norton. He walked slowly, taking in each house he passed, the place where he'd attended church services with his ma, and he even saw Missus Jones wrapped in a wool cloak on her porch, setting down a bowl for a couple of cats. He waved, and she waved back, but he knew she didn't recognize him though she'd taught him years before in the schoolhouse. When he reached nothing but forest, Miles mounted the horse and rode down the very same trail he and Jackson had taken years before when they began their journey to Texas. The snow had stopped falling.

As the day ended, Miles found a copse of willows near a creek deeper in the trees so he could light a fire. He had traveled near Coker Creek in Tennessee, once the lands of the Cherokee, and he would keep the campfire small and short, for its light would seep through the night and reveal his presence. He watered his horse and cobbled him before gathering kindle and wood for a fire. He had coffee from Pa's house and set to brew a cup to warm himself before laying out his bed. A biscuit and dried pork abated his hunger as he planned the next day's journey.

Though the cold still quaked in his bones, Miles kicked dirt onto the waning glow of embers until the fire turned dark and he bound himself into blankets and the comfort of sleep. A deep sleep.

He woke to the jubilant trill of a warbler and the muffled sound of voices, and then, a thrust to his ribs. He sat up in the dimness of dawn to see three disheveled Confederates looking down at him. Based on their appearance, they seemed deserters. One of them, who appeared the oldest of the three, held his emptied sack and the Yankee uniform, and Miles looked about to see his personal things scattered at their feet.

He knew at that moment that he'd not gone deep enough into the forest. In the moments that followed, he felt only the loving warmth of his father's arms around him, his father who he'd left only the day before, and in the waning light, in the willows like an angel, a vision of Fidelia reached for him.

CHAPTER 27

Tennessee

Terry's Rangers, still under command of General Wheeler and Colonel Harrison, remained encamped south of Knoxville and scouted between Knoxville and Chattanooga. With a brutal winter, the regiments on both sides had hunkered down and major battles turned scarce through winter, though a skirmish erupted now and then when troops were on the move.

The ground had warmed enough to melt the snow, and Companies D and H of Terry's Rangers were moving on trails around Knoxville to monitor activity and subvert the enemy's encroachment south. There was a chilled wind blowing as the men rode two or three across along the narrow trail. Snow still dropped from the boughs of pines along the hills.

"Spring's around the corner," said Pete, riding alongside James.

"I hope you're right, Pete, but then the fight will be on again." James pulled his hat down tight about his head. He lowered his voice to near a whisper. "It'll take us longer to win this war than to lose it. That's certain."

"This wind is a demon," spoke James in a louder voice.

"We all wanna go home, friend. Maybe the wind will blow us yon," said Pete, his voice carrying a weariness that had become all too familiar.

By noon, the wind waned to a breeze and the sun shone brightly, warming the men. Far ahead in the line of men before them, Miles and Pete saw some men veering from the trail into the woods.

"What's happening?" asked Pete.

"Dunno. Don't think they'd be relieving themselves at once," said James, noticing that the horses moved slower.

"I'd say it's 'bout time to give the horses a rest. I thinks we're to head back to our encampment, so we should be turning around soon," said Pete.

"I haven't seen any enemy all day."

There was mumbling through the companies as they approached the spot of interest in the woods.

"There's been a hanging," yelled one of the men in front of them. "They say it's a Confederate."

A couple of soldiers in front of James broke off to go look. Pete followed them.

"C'mon," yelled Pete.

"Don't need to gaze upon such," said James. Pete kept waving his friend on, and James gave in and guided his horse toward the woods.

"Damn," said Pete. "Who hung him?"

"Looks like he got found to be a spy," said a soldier riding back toward the trail.

James looked up and caught his breath. He couldn't absorb the atrocity before him and dismounted. His throat tightened and his hands rose to his head in disbelief.

"What is it?" asked Pete.

"It's Miles Maloney. The fella I told you about who courted my wife," he said to Pete. "The one I thought I saw with Dodd."

"Is he a spy?"

James looked around. The gray uniform torn from Miles

lay on the ground, and Miles' body had been stripped, revealing the certain evidence for which he'd been deemed treasonous by troops or renegades who'd found him. A man stripped and shamed for impersonation.

A few more soldiers rode up to gawk, but in short time, the detachment had passed the sight. James looked around for Miles' horse and saw no sign of one; it was surely taken by those who'd done this deed. He walked about and found a few shreds of a blue uniform that had been burned and a ransacked satchel. Some sheet-iron crackers lay on the ground—unworthy of theft. Near a shrub, he found a book. It was a journal with handwritten pages, some torn out and shuffled along the ground by the breeze.

"Whatcha gonna do? We should get back with the regiment," said Pete.

James picked up loose pages scattered near him, and he bent down to pick up the journal and then opened it. He saw clips of phrases describing locations and conversations, and on a page near the end of the written notes, he saw the name "Fidelia" scrawled in the lad's handwriting, words of the loss of her, and he abruptly shut the book. He walked back to the clay-cold form of Miles hanging from a leafless sycamore. Looked into the young man's ashen face and almost retched. This man had been his nemesis, but nowhere in his heart did James believe the man deserved the wretchedness that had been dealt him.

He furtively slipped the loose pages into the journal and put it into his saddlebag before mounting his horse.

"We leaving?" asked Pete.

"Not yet," said James. Reaching for his Bowie knife, he swiftly sliced the rope holding Miles to the tree and dismounted. He wanted to bury the boy, but the ground was not sufficiently thawed and, more importantly, doing so could well bring the wrath of his commander if Miles was a spy. The two uniforms bode badly for the dead man and anyone who chose to help him.

James knelt down and cut the rope from the young man's purplish neck, and then he cut the rope binding Miles' hands behind him. Miles' frame was slender, and he was not much younger than himself, but James saw naught but a man too young to die.

"Pete, go on if you must, but I'd prefer you stay. Give me a few minutes. I'm struggling to grasp this sight, this revelation. No matter what the facts be, this was the man my wife once loved."

Pete dismounted, and the two men drug the body to the foot of the tree. James sat him up and leaned him against the tree, only hoping it would discourage scavengers but knowing it would not in the long run.

He took the blanket from the back of his horse and covered the body.

"What are ya doing? No time of year to be throwing out your only blanket."

"It's only right, Pete."

James foraged Miles' satchel to see if there was anything of value mistakenly left inside. A pair of socks was all that he found left in the bag, surprised the rogues who'd done this, who were clearly Rebels, had not found them.

"We best go," said James as he looked sternly at Pete. "Not a word to anyone of this."

Pete nodded and James paused.

"I know I should bury him. He ain't that far from where he came from, some town in the Appalachian Mountains. I just cannot seem to fathom this tragedy."

"Well, we can't bury him. The ground's too hard to dig and we ain't got no shovel."

Everything's a blur," and James looked at his friend. He walked to the tree where Miles sat, stilled forever, and knelt as if in prayer. He envisioned the scavengers who'd come in the thaw, who'd polish his bones and be holier for their work.

Finally, he stood and said, "*Requiescat in pace.*"

"I thank you, Pete, for lingering here with me. For being my good friend."

"What were those words you said? Like foreign words," asked Pete as the men mounted their horses.

James looked at Pete and then, understood.

"*Requiescat in pace.* Meaning 'rest in peace.' My grandmother was a Catholic and always said those words at a grave or when someone had died. Then she'd cross herself."

Pete nodded.

"It's the best I could do for him."

The two men rode at a trot to catch up with their comrades, soon bringing up the rear of the scouting party.

The clouds gathered in the sky as the detail rode back to their encampment to the south of where they'd found a sad chap hanging in the woods of Tennessee. After three hours with his rump tight against the cantle of his saddle, James was numb and oblivious to the sway of his horse. He could not unleash the image of Miles—the young man who'd once stolen the girl he loved and would now forever hang lifeless in that place behind one's eyes. James had remembered the young chap as quite full of life. How could he ever tell Fidelia what he saw—tell her what happened? If he told her, would it change forever how she felt? If he didn't tell her, Miles would be forever vanished. The choice seemed straightforward, but the fear of being haunted seemed too real. And a lie would be forever.

The hanged spy was the talk of the camp when the men returned, and as James sat at the mess with his plate of beans and biscuits, Paul Watkins walked over with his plate full and sat down next to him.

"Did you see the man hung in the woods today?" asked Watkins.

"Sadly," said James as he spooned beans into his mouth. "I couldn't believe it when I saw him. I'd seen him at Camp Chase when I was a prisoner there."

James almost choked on the beans as Watkins continued talking.

"I cannot believe that he was spying for the Union, but he and a fella called Norton came to the prison often, bringing us blankets, a bit of food, what little comfort they could give in a hell like that camp. One day that young chap gave me a pencil and paper to write my family. Said he'd post the letter for me."

"Do you think they were gleaning information?" asked James.

"Hard to tell now. They both seemed to love Texas, and I didn't see any cunning in him. Damned shame. At least Ephraim Dodd got a trial, sham that it may have been."

James said nothing. The world was spiraling. He sat with his empty fork in hand.

"Hughes. Come back," said Watkins, seeing his comrade's far-away state. "Where are you?"

Miles turned to look at his friend with eyes still blank, and he laid his utensil on his tin.

"Just wishing this war was over. Thinking of home," he replied to Watkins, knowing full well that he, at that very moment, dreaded looking into his wife's eyes and lying to her. Lies of omission were still lies.

"Just tired," said James as he rose to return to his tent where he found Pete sitting on his cot.

"Pete, when did we all become wild men?" said James, pulling off his boots. "All this savagery has hardened our hearts. Changed us. We drink to drunkenness just to numb memories of what we've seen. I've watched some men ride straight toward a cannon to end their misery, and some just walk away never to be seen again. Who are we, Pete? How can we go home to our loved ones, being the savages we've become?"

James pulled the blanket up to his chin and turned away from Pete, expecting no answer.

CHAPTER 28

Austin, Texas

Spring came with the same vengeance that winter had exacted on the Texas landscape. Flowers bloomed around the Hughes' house in Austin—cannas in whites and reds sprouted from the ground as fast as little Johnny had grown into a boy. Fidelia would watch her small son run about the yard, jabbering, and think of all the days his father had missed.

With the printing shop gone, it became harder and harder to bear the financial burden of the home in Austin. Leona's beau, Dane, brought a box of eggs every week or two from his father's coop, and Fidelia had even considered putting a coop near the shed, but she worried about the noise and movement of the city for domestic animals. It was why she left her dog, Chap, at the farm, and now she had the barn cat to worry about. If it had not been for the help from the Cannon family, her home would be in disrepair like some in the city. Herman and now Dane were godsends.

She'd received Grandma's letter that Pa had arrived home from Ohio, but she wrote little of his trip and said he may come to visit. It was planting season, so all the men were busy, and Fidelia found it odd that Pa would come to the city. *And why?*

In the letter, Grandma said that Matilda, Jeremy's widow, had remarried and moved to Bastrop. Fidelia had met Matilda's new husband only once, when he'd come by Grandpa's house at Christmas, and he'd seemed a kind man, but she found he couldn't measure up to her uncle Jeremy, who'd adored Matilda.

Johnny pulled at Fidelia's skirt as Leona walked by on her way to her delivery duties with the Ladies' Aid Society.

"What a lovely day, Leona," said Fidelia as she bent down to pick up her son. "Spring is in the air, so you be careful."

Leona laughed as she walked out the door, and Fidelia smiled and turned toward the kitchen. After she'd put Johnny down for a nap, she brewed some mint into a weak tea and sat with the newspaper, the *Star Gazette*, a nemesis to the employer of dear Miles. As she perused the pages, she found no words of James' regiment but saw that many prisoners had been taken near Knoxville, and a knot twisted in her stomach as her most recent letter had spoken of the skirmishes near Knoxville, even how one of his comrades named Dodd had been captured.

A loud knock at the door pulled her from her readings. When she opened the door, she found herself face-to-face with her father, looking serious. Behind him, she saw his horse tied to the rail.

"Pa. Such a surprise for you to have come so far to see me," said Fidelia as she leaned in to kiss her pa.

"I have a matter to discuss."

"You sound so serious, but I want to hear about your travels to Indiana. About my cousins. And did you see any troops on the way?" asked Fidelia. "Come, sit down. Johnny's asleep, and I'll make you a cup of tea."

"No need for tea, and I look forward to seeing the wee one if he wakes in time." Pa sat down in a chair. "I must get back to the land by nightfall. To get to the point, I am marrying again in the summer, to widow Ashton back in Fort Wayne. I'm leaving, but there's the issue of the farm, the crops, and my cattle. I want to leave it for you, with the help of my farmhand, until your husband returns. I know you know how to work the farm. The army will pay you for some of the crops, and living in the country would be good for Johnny."

Fidelia sat staring at her father, struggling to latch onto what he'd said. No words came to her, and then she thought of James and how he'd react to such.

"This is my home, Pa. Here, with James."

"Fidelia, I have hundreds of acres. James will not turn that down, and besides, he came from a farming family. His business is gone. This is an opportunity for your family," said Pa.

Tears began to gather and drop. *Where was James when she needed him?*

"What am I to do with James' home, Pa? This is his home. The house his parents built. You wanted me to have this life in the city with James, and now that I have, you want me to give it up?"

The two sat in silence for minutes.

"I want you to give it up for more," said Pa. "You can let this house, and you know you belong in the country. Seeing to the animals, the gardens, taking care of your Chap who loves it there. When James comes home, he can choose. Most important of all, you will be closer to your grandparents. All Papa speaks of is his loneliness, and I know he and Abe will help as much as they can. Besides, you don't know when or if James will be back."

Upon hearing those words, Fidelia stood up and walked into the kitchen. How dare her father say such words? From upstairs came the cries of her son, now awake. She gathered herself, took several breaths, and walked upstairs to get Johnny.

She didn't know if her pa would still be there when she returned to the sitting room, but he still sat where she'd left him.

"Johnny, here's Grandpa," she said as she put him down. The young child stood hesitant looking at his grandfather, unsure of who he was, but when John reached out to him, the child walked over and climbed up into John's lap.

"Are you sure you cannot stay for supper, Pa?"

"No, I must point my horse to the north shortly. I'm leaving in about six weeks, so you think on this. I really need you to take it on, and if you come a week or two early, either Boyd or I can show you the cattle side of the homestead. Though Boyd can handle it for you, you need to know it. Post a note to Cypress once you've made up your decision. I'm not of a mind to give up the homestead, nor the cabin. It's a fine cabin for your family."

He chatted with Johnny a bit, tried in vain to get the boy to say "Papaw," and then Fidelia's pa ruffled the boy's hair and stood to leave.

Leona arrived home before supper to find Fidelia sitting at the kitchen table and Johnny playing with the pots on the floor. She could tell her friend was troubled about something.

"I invited Dane over for supper tomorrow evening," Leona said. "Did something happen? You seem fretted."

Fidelia told Leona all that happened during her father's visit.

"I don't know what to do," said Fidelia.

"Well, after Johnny is abed, let's talk about it. What your pa's asked is a lot to take on, so we can figure out if we can do it. I do think Johnny would thrive there, though I've yet to see the place. Or would you leave me here? I'm certain talking it through will ease your doubts."

After supper, when the two women were alone, they mulled over the possibility of moving and pondered what problems might arise and what James might want. They found there was so much to consider what with the print shop being gone and the value of currency near nothing. What would James return to? The old typeface machine that had traveled all the way from Alabama was now sitting out in the shed, and that was all that remained of her husband's business.

Just like in the old days, the ranch would have her up at dawn milking the cows, but that would be an experience Johnny would never forget. The family would be self-sufficient, and, of course, Leona would go with Fidelia. She would need to find a way to care for the Hughes' house until James came home and decided what to do. She fell into bed that night weary of worry, but she had to admit to herself that she felt a bit excited about the prospect of being a farm girl once again, and she was not one bit happy about her father's upcoming nuptials, knowing what her ma had sacrificed for her family during her life cut short.

CHAPTER 29

Tennessee

James ran his fingers over the image on the ferrotype in his hand as he sat outside his tent near Chattanooga. The image of his beautiful wife stared back at him—her face still at the moment the photograph was made by William Bridgers on Pecan Street. He remembered that day in April 1861 and how happy they were. Bridgers made three images, one of each of them and one of them together, and now he carried Fidelia with him.

"Who's in that tintype you're holding?" asked Watkins as he walked toward the mess tent.

"My wife, friend."

"Can I see it?" said Watkins as he sat on a stump next to his friend.

"Yes." James held the tintype up for Watkins to see.

"Lovely. Now a mother, you say?" he asked.

"Yes. Our son, Johnny, is about two now. I cannot wait to see him," said James. "Do you have children?"

"Two. Two girls," replied Watkins. "Hoping I live long enough to see them again."

The two men sat silent, both weary of war and homesick.

"Time to mount up," said Lieutenant Decherd as he walked past them. "In thirty minutes, we're leaving on a scouting into Georgia, so get to the mess tent if you haven't ate."

The sights and breezes of spring in the mountains filled James with gratitude, of which he'd had little since winter. The haunting sight of Miles never slipped from his head. The vision would materialize in the most unexpected moments as if a sleuth looking to startle him, but the gaiety and warmth of the new season offered a distraction that disguised the war all around then. Carried him to a different time—even reminded him of his youth in Alabama. He was happy on his father's farm in those days, filled with hard work that carried one to a restful sleep at night. The blooms along the trail make him forget his nightmares, his fears of all that could be lost, and even the stress of deadlines in his beloved print shop. So many of the businesses were gone in Austin, including his own, according to letters he'd received from his wife. The loss had not been unexpected.

There was a pother at the front of the column of soldiers, and then, James heard the gunshots and horses fleeing into the woods toward the left. Decherd was only four horses in front of him, behind Company B, and he urged his men into the trees to the right.

"Come on," he yelled, and as the company gathered in the forest, he said they'd sit in silence a few moments, in scrutiny, and come in behind the enemy. Company D wound their way deeper and then forward to find a small detail of Yankees shooting from a gulch near the trail. Lieutenant Decherd led the charge, all unloading their weapons from behind the enemy and taking them by surprise. They scattered, and before the men killed three of the shooters and sent the rest of them running, James felt the burn in his shoulder and the wet warmth of his shirt. He reined his horse to the left and back with his left hand. When he slowed and looked down, he saw the blood dripping down his sleeve.

"Hit," he yelled out to his comrades, hoping someone would come to his aid. He dismounted, believing the wound was near his joint which prevented the use of a tourniquet, but he needed to stem the flow and pulled a cloth from his saddlebag, holding it tightly at his shoulder.

Watkins came to help. James yelped as Watkins pulled off James' shirt, ripped it into shreds, folded a strip to cover the wound, and tied it tight with a strip from the sleeve.

"Let's go," said Watkins. There were two more men wounded, and the commander decided to head back to the encampment, ending the mission.

By the second night after the skirmish, James lay fevered in the medic's tent, where they'd cleaned and bandaged the wound and then arranged for a medic to take him to surgeons at the field hospital.

James, unconscious and fevered, was wrapped in a blanket and placed in a wagon with two other soldiers heading south. The crippled cavalryman from the Rangers' Company H sat frail next to James, the cavalryman's left leg bound in bloody gauze, and a middle-aged man with a head wound, still oozing, lay next to a young medic and held tenaciously onto life. The wagon would take the men to Catoosa Springs in Georgia. The medic in charge watched as the wagon moved down the trail, believing only the cripple would arrive home alive.

The middle-aged man died on the way and was carried off when they reached the hospital. There, a surgeon operated and removed the Minié ball that had torn through the muscles of James' right shoulder, and for three days the wound oozed and swelled. In a moment of lucidity, James heard a young physician say he could do little but wait for healing as the infected wound had been treated with bromine, which turned the inflammation angry. Soon, James developed dysentery and lay delirious for days, fallen into dreams. The lines between wakefulness and sleep became blurred, and James saw Fidelia's smile welcoming him home, the sun behind her like a halo, a young child in her arms. He turned fitfully until pain woke him to see the young man from Company H nearby, his leg vanished as if never there and wrapped like a gauzed tree stump. Cries and moans filled the stale air around them. Then he felt the hard rim of a bedpan neath him.

A young soldier came and took the pan from beneath him, telling him he had dysentery. The same man soon returned and placed the pan where it had sat, uncomfortable, beneath James's rump.

"I'll change your dressing. It might burn since the doctor used bromine and it's sorely inflamed. I'll give ya a sip of whiskey."

James asked for a second sip of the whiskey and prayed it would return him to sleep, where he'd seen Fidelia welcoming him home. He squealed as the medic added iodine to his swollen shoulder and, shortly after, returned to a sleep he'd not bargained for. In his nightmare, he saw the ashen face of Miles staring at him, dead but not dead, as if pleading for help. Then the birds came to claim their prize beneath the tree where James had left the dead man, their squawking delight heckling James for not burying the man. For leaving him undignified as had the scoundrels who'd hung him. As a dark night fell in the forest of his dream, it carried James to a deep and dreamless sleep.

On a misty morning, James woke again to the sound of rain and the chatter and moans in the tent. He woke to the dismay of his circumstances, exacerbated by snippets of the nightmare he'd had, and he grabbed the arm of a medic passing by.

"I'm awake. I feel better."

The man looked at him with an expression of pity.

"I will have the doctor come."

James lay in his bed until dusk came, his eyes wide and still unable to turn his head or move his arm.

"Let me see the arm, Son," said a doctor James had not seen before.

The doctor first felt James' forehead, then he lifted James' right arm, eliciting a scream of pain.

"Can you feel the arm? Can you lift it?"

"I felt the agony," whispered James.

"That's the swelling in your shoulder, but agony is a good sign of healing. Try to lift your arm."

Nothing happened when James pushed through the pain to raise his arm.

"Your fever's waned but not gone. It's not promising that you will use the arm again," said the doctor. "But we'll wait for the swelling to abate. You won't be shaking that daddle for some time more. Meanwhile, you're still afflicted with dysentery, and I've no doubt you are aware of it. Try to take some broth and warm water. I'll check you tomorrow, but you will be here some weeks yet."

James sighed and craved to sit up. To stand. To be a man again.

"Good to see ya awake, James," said the fellow who'd lost his leg. "I'm Clark. R. Clark Hughes from Waco."

"Wish you were on the other side of me, Clark. I can't turn my head but a sliver. I'm James Hughes, from Austin. What's the "R" stand for?"

"Stands for Ragnald. My mother's grandfather of the same name was from Scotland, and Pa sometimes called me Ronald. But you best call me Clark."

"Guess we're kin, huh?"

"Maybe. My kin er from near the Delaware River," Clark said. "Now I lost my leg for the other side of this goddamned war."

"Pa's from Alabama. I think his grandpa sailed to Georgia

from Wales. So I'm told. Guess we're all kin if we go far 'nough back. And now we're both going home missing parts. Or, at least for me, the use of a limb."

"If we make it home."

Silence sat in the air between them when a woman approached James with a steaming cup of broth. She was soft-spoken with her brown hair in a bun, and as she raised the cup to his mouth, he saw the weariness in her eyes. No different than the war-weary men.

When June came, the Union was eyeing to topple Atlanta and breathing down the neck of General Forrest, thus, the hospital dismantled to relocate. James held his discharge notice in his hand. He wasn't alone as other men stood in disbelief beneath a cheery summer sky, about eighteen in number standing in skepticism that they were going home and then, in wonderment of how they would get there. Most of these men were disabled and being released for such reasons, and though James was a cavalryman, he stood horseless.

He could stand and bemoan his circumstances all day, or he could head west, and that's just what he did before he ran into Clark Hughes bumbling down the road on his crutch. Two men, each crippled in body and spirit, with a long way to go.

"Can I keep you company, comrade?" said James.

"Aye, if you choose to take twice as long to get home."

"I got my satchel and my gun, which ain't much good with a bum arm, but I don't have my saddle. Sure do wish I had it, but it's a heavy load with no horse," grumbled James. "Don't even know where our regiment is now, but if I had a horse, I'd lift you on it. Hell, I'd likely only try to lift you up."

The men had little in way of supplies or food, but Clark had a shotgun slung over his shoulder, and both were determined to wade through the throes and ruins of war to get home and see family. Now in civilian clothing, with the sun risen high, they'd walked three hours in the direction of Knoxville and were headed westward when horses approached from behind. James turned to see his friend Watkins leading two horses, one with his saddle on it.

"What marvel is this?" yelled James. "Have you deserted?" Watkins laughed.

"Damn, friends. It's good to see ya alive, but you fellows don't look good for the trip." Watkins dismounted. "Lieutenant Dechard thought you'd need these and wanted to make sure I got them to you. He couldn't bear you two walking home. We heard you were discharged, and I can promise they'd not have sent me with these two horses if there were more men remaining to ride them into Georgia."

Watkins had attached rolled blankets and the men's satchels to each saddle.

"Pete gathered your things, James. Made sure he put all your personal stuff in your haversack," said Watkins, and James immediately thought of Miles' journal and was grateful his friend had been discreet.

The men were harkened to have their saddles but saw the horses were likely the worst of the ones left back at camp. Still, gratitude filled them both.

"Pastor Bunting told me to remind you of Colonel Fremantle's words: 'No Texan walks a yard if he can help it,' and he blessed these two horses for you. I gotta get back to camp, and we're all praying for you, so please pray for us."

Watkins helped James up into his saddle, then did the same for Clark before he rode back to the east.

"Y'all be careful and stay out of sight. God send," Watkins yelled back at the two men, and his thoughts could not comprehend how the two could travel so far in such as state as he saw them.

Nevertheless, as James and Clark rode down the road, they each felt blessed in the Tennessean sun. To have horses. Just to be alive.

CHAPTER 30

Cypress Creek

The move to the country had been awkward, both the relocation and the goodbyes to Fidelia's father. She knew she loved her father, but his retreat from the family frustrated her. Now he was returning to Indiana, the land he'd regretted leaving all those years ago, and he'd always held his wife and his daughters within that misery. He would likely be happier in the North, and the only family he now abandoned were his parents and his only daughter, Fidelia.

She was grateful that Leona had agreed to come with her, for she'd dreaded the loneliness of this place, the memory of the scoundrels who'd burned down her pa's first cabin, but the guns were loaded, her dog Chap was here, and Boyd was present. Leona had brought the barn cat, and if any more showed up, she'd welcome them as mousers. She was indebted to Boyd, the farmhand, who was always kind and had been invaluable in taking care of matters, in addition to Abe coming every week or two.

Fidelia had decided that she would take care of milking the one cow each morning at sunrise and leave the care of Johnny and preparation of breakfast to Leona. Her childhood memory of that chore reminded her how it had eased her into a day, so when Boyd walked toward her, she smiled in his direction in the dim light of morning.

"Ma'am, I'm riding out today to check on the cattle. Leaving after breakfast if you'd like to join me." Chap sniffed at the man's boots. "I know you wanted to get acquainted with the cattle side of the farm and today is set to be a fine day for doing it."

"I'll be ready to go after my breakfast, after I let Leona know that she has Johnny all day." She wiped her hands on the skirt of her work dress and stood. "She will be safe here alone, won't she?" asked Fidelia with a tremble of concern in her voice.

"Yes, ma'am. We've had no problems here at the farm with marauders."

"Well, having met our neighbors gives me some comfort, knowing we're surrounded by good farm families. Maybe we can leave Chap here with her," said Fidelia

"Yes, ma'am."

Fidelia had pulled on the breeches her ma had made for her and mounted her old horse, Trapper, who'd she'd brought from Grandpa's farm. Boyd watched in amazement as she rode astride like a man, more confident on her horse than he'd expected.

"I'm a thinkin' your pa chose right on your running this ranch," Boyd remarked.

The two of them headed north across the shallows of the creek and toward the hills and valleys near the river.

"You know," said Boyd, breaking their silence as they neared the herd, "your pa was never content here. He worked hard and was miserable in it all, but I see somethin' different in you. Like you own this, which, of course, you do ... but I'm talking about somethin' deeper. You move through the work and ride across these fields like you're a part of it. No offense, ma'am, but you move like the Indians, like you're one with it."

She smiled at him as they slowed their movement forward.

"It's funny you say that, Boyd. It was an Osage who guided me as a girl, helped me through troubled times. We'd met him in Missouri, Gray Feather," said Fidelia.

"What's an Osage?"

Fidelia laughed as she dismounted Trapper.

"The Osage are a peaceful tribe of Indians from the forests and mountains of Missouri. They have a history of working with the French trappers, but now, the government has forced their movement west. Mostly to Kansas."

Boyd nodded.

"This group here has two new calves," said Boyd. "I'll brand them when I come back next week, unless you want to learn it."

"No. Later, if need be. I need to decide if the cattle will be worth the investment, in time and the money we don't have."

A total of seven new calves were counted on their ride, though one was nothing but the remains left behind by a pack of coyotes. They arrived at the house before dusk, and Leona had a pot of beans cooking.

A welcomed storm passed through the creek in early July, and Fidelia found the air a bit cooler and misty. It was Saturday, and that meant Dane Cannon would show up with the mail, though Fidelia knew the real reason he came. There was no letter from James, and Fidelia was worried that the last letter she'd received was written in March. She wondered if this war would ever be over.

Dane sat at the table talking to Leona as she mixed batter for a cake to put in the oven once the biscuits were done. Fidelia grabbed a basket and picked some ripened strawberries from the garden her ma once tended, then she grabbed a blanket and took Johnny's hand.

"Leona, we are going down to sit by the creek for a bit," said Fidelia as she and her son walked unhurriedly toward the trees, where she spread the blanket under a willow. She played patty-cake with Johnny and then they ate the strawberries. The toddler was soon fast asleep in the fresh air.

The recent conversation with the farmhand made Fidelia think of Gray Feather and her precious memories of their conversations—his gentle and wise guidance. She thought of the "white Indian" that Miles had described to her, how the boy whose name she'd forgotten, captured by Comanche and years later returned to his home, was close to the land and could not give up the Indian ways. Then she sank deep into her thoughts of San Saba and Miles.

The stillness of the meadow filled Fidelia and carried her thoughts to the past, to another life. It was in 1859 when Miles had courted her with a vengeance, a quiet vengeance, as if he were already a part of the McCord family. So often he'd be sitting at the dinner table in Pond Springs.

She remembered a night back in February of 1860—it had been late in the afternoon, the sun setting on a pleasant day in a Texas winter, and after a Saturday supper in Grandma's kitchen, she'd wrapped her shoulders in a shawl and walked outside with Miles. She had walked to the swing under the big oak—the swing her Uncle Jeremy had built for her. As she sat on the swing, her feet dangling, Miles leaned against the tree.

"Do you know how beautiful you look with the last of the day shining on you?" he said.

Fidelia had smiled and pushed herself on the swing, rising in the cool air.

"Our children will follow you everywhere, just as I will," he'd said. She winced for a moment at the memory of those words. She remembered how she slowed the swing and walked over to him, how he'd encircled her in his arms and kissed her as if he'd never kiss her again. She'd melted into his warmth, and then they'd walked, holding hands, through the meadow to the pond.

"I think you should marry me before we have all those children," Fidelia had said.

Miles laughed. "Have no doubts, my love," he'd said. "I want to buy some land where we can build a home. Or maybe there will still be grants for married men—something between your pa's cabin and Austin."

He stood in thought with his brow furrowed. "But Norton and I fear a battle is coming. Not to trouble you, but the country is torn in two directions."

Solemn, he looked into Fidelia's eyes.

"You're always what matters most to me. And your family," he said.

Fidelia put her arms around his neck, drawing his face nearer to hers, and Miles kissed her again. A kiss so resolved it almost felt like a *goodbye*.

Now, sitting in the Junegrass, Fidelia wondered if that's what it was. But his words had said otherwise—or not. She'd gone over this so many times after he'd disappeared. Six weeks after that day, Miles had left after a Sunday supper and never returned. Never sent a message. *Would he show up one day and expect her to still be waiting for him?* She remembered that day so long ago after they'd first met, when she'd sat with Miles in the very spot she sat now, when she saw he'd wanted to kiss her. But she'd moved on, married, and now had a son. *Why did she still feel so uncertain?*

The soft chirping of a wren fetched her chin up, and she saw the sun through the trees. She stood, gathered up Johnny and the blanket, and walked home.

CHAPTER 31

Knoxville, Tennessee

James and Clark had managed to skirt the enemy between Knoxville and around Nashville. They'd been cautious, but their first few days had been slow. They knew they were in no fit shape for such a journey but were grateful to not be walking; however, mounting their horses had turned into an escapade. That first morning out, it had taken half the day to find a way into their saddles. James had tried to help Clark up onto his horse, but with one good arm, it was a struggle, and Clark, unable to hold his balance, swore to the heavens each time his right foot slipped. When weariness and frustration got the best of them, they sat under an oak and commiserated and then talked for almost an hour about all the things they used to be able to do when they were unbroken. The two horses stood ready to go and stared at the men.

All at once, Clark said, "James, pull my horse under this tree, this low-hanging limb."

James did as he was told and stood in amazement as Clark grabbed the branch and inched his way upward until he was over the horse, and James nudged the horse into the right spot as Clark dropped himself into his old saddle.

"Damn, Clark. Brilliant," said James. "Now, you're up—what about me?"

It took James five tries to pull himself up onto his horse, using only his left hand and all the might he could muster. He knew, over time, he'd need to strengthen that left leg and try to regain use of his right arm, so as the men started down the trail, he put his reins in his right hand and, with the help of his legs, guided his horse through the day on trails. New realizations came to each man through the coming days on how their lives have changed and how critical it was that they find new strength in themselves. They became adept at laughing at themselves and at each other, a camaraderie grown firm.

It came clear to James, early on, that they would need to depend on the big-heartedness of those who lived in farmhouses along the way, usually women, and the men would have gone hungry without these kindnesses. With their frail appearances and civilian clothing, most farmwives and farmers took pity on the men, but James always remained cautious and reminded Clark to keep his gun loaded. The two men often rode the side roads where farms lay in meadows and away from the covert missions of the war.

One late July day, when dusk crept behind them, they pulled their horses onto a path, hoping it might lead to a farmhouse. They slowed at the sight of bones, large bones, the remains of what seemed three horses in a field, merely graceful skeletons picked clean. Like so many horses the two men had seen felled by bullets and cannons, these appeared lost in a likely skirmish of soldiers from an earlier year, and James thought of all the sacrifices of the past years. Unsung sacrifice, one battle after another.

The two men had only had a bit of dried beef in the past two days.

"I need to stop here," said James.

Clark pulled his horse to a stop. They'd been riding enough days together for him to know why they'd stopped. James' dysentery still troubled him, and Clark couldn't imagine how hard it was for his companion to ride his saddle all day.

When finished with his deed, James stood and barely had his pants up when he saw a plump rabbit in a mossy patch about ten yards straight in front of him. Using his left hand, he pulled his Whitney and took the shot. Got it.

"James!" yelled Clark, panicked at the sound of a gunshot until he saw his friend walk from the trees with the rabbit in hand.

"Supper."

"Look at you. We'll be true woodsmen by the time we get to Texas," said Clark.

"Let's ride further down the path, away from the trail, and find a good place for a campsite," said James.

"We'll ride till we find a creek or flowing rill, and we can fill our canteens and water the horses," said Clark, knowing well that his companion needed water more than the horses.

The ravenous men devoured the roasted rabbit, and James was filled with a new confidence for having shot his gun left-handed and hitting a target.

"Are you feeling better about our gettin' to Texas—alive?" asked James.

"Better every day, friend," Clark responded.

"Ya know, in the beginning, I wasn't sure we'd last a week. But look at us!"

"Well, James, I'd still like a new leg but must say my arms are stronger. Still thanking God and the colonel for our horses, but what I wouldn't give for a bit of whiskey and a hot bath."

"Amen," they said in unison, snuffed the campfire, and then slept like children lost in the forest.

Early August was hot, and the men neared Jackson, Tennessee. Clark's horse needed a shoe, maybe two. They found a farmhouse at the edge of town.

"Got a bit of food for two soldiers headed home?" asked Clark of the old man sitting leaning back in a wooden chair by the barn. "Maybe a pallet of hay in your barn, where we might sleep?"

"Who'd ya fight for?" asked the old man.

"We're headed home to Texas," said James.

"I'm certain my daughter has a bit of food in the kitchen. Go knock on the door. You fellas better go way south and cross the river. There's soldiers everywhere in Memphis."

"Thank ya, sir," said Clark.

The men enjoyed a meal of cornbread and beans with some roasted turkey in Missus Collins' kitchen. Her two teenage daughters helped serve the meal, and her young son took a plate out to his grandpa at the barn.

"You look sickly, sir," the woman said, looking straight at James. "Are you taken ill?"

"Ma'am, I'm improving day by day. Have trouble keeping my sustenance since my surgery," said James. "Thank you for your concern."

"Well, you men be careful near Memphis."

"Your pa told us there are soldiers thick as thieves 'round here," said Clark. "The Mississippi is like the spine of the nation, a coastline in the middle, and they're all fightin' to control it, aren't they?"

"He's my husband's pa, but it's good to have a man about, even an old one," she said. "Your General Forrest came through here in April. Caused quite the commotion. Left the bodies of prisoners through the streets here, especially the Negro ones. From what my friend's son saw from the livery, the man took great joy in shooting 'em where they stood."

She shook her head, and James wasn't sure what to say as there were none but Southerners at the table.

"Well, Missus Collins, I've met the man and can't say I like him much, but I'd better say no more," said James.

"That would be a wise decision 'round here," she responded and started gathering the men's plates.

"Coffee?"

"You have coffee?" asked Clark.

"I do but don't tell anyone." They all laughed as the two girls looked at the adults and the older one pulled a face.

"You're an angel, ma'am," said James. "And, if it's not much trouble, can I use a sheet of paper and a pen to scratch a note to my wife, if you could post it for me. She must be fretting not getting any letters."

"Susan," she called. "Bring this man a bit of paper and the ink and pen at Pa's desk." She turned to look at James. "Sure wish I knew where my husband was. Haven't got a letter for over five months."

The two men rose early in the morning when the sun was but peeking at the horizon. James milked the cow and set the bucket inside the kitchen door before the two men rode off to the south through narrow back roads. It was the least he could for her kindnesses. The old man had told them where to find the trail heading south to a ferry on the Mississippi.

CHAPTER 32

Cypress Creek

Abe did not show up at the farm to help with the harvesting, even though Grandpa had promised. Fidelia and Boyd managed to finish the harvest and sell the onion and potato crops at a negotiated price to the state. They were impressing the farmers' harvest for the army, but a negotiated price was better than none.

When Dane arrived on Saturday, Fidelia saddled Trapper and asked Boyd to ride over to Pond Springs with her. She had realized it best to be more careful in her travels in these unsettled times, not to mention there'd been recent Indian attacks not far to the west. She wanted to check on her grandparents and found it odd that Abe had not come for the harvest.

"What will we do with the cattle?" she asked Boyd as they rode toward the rising sun. "Can the government take them from us?"

"Ma'am, we don't have a large number, and I'd recommend we just keep them into another calving season. The embargo keeps us from running them north or east. Can't say what the government will do. Let's just wait."

"Well, let's hope the war ends soon," she said and the two rode on to Grandpa's farm.

She saw Reka hanging laundered clothes on a line as they rode up to the porch, and Fidelia found her grandma fidgeting about the kitchen.

"Oh, Delia. I'm so glad you are here. Grandpa is down in spirits—spending all day in Jeremy's old workshop in the barn. Part of our crops are going to waste."

"Boyd came with me, Grandma. Where's Abe," asked Fidelia.

Grandma's hands went to her head in distress.

"I can't bear to tell ya," she said. "The government's come and taken him—to work crop plantations near Houston."

"What?"

"They're impressing the slaves, just like they did the crops. We couldn't tell them Abe was free," Grandma whispered, "or they might a taken your grandpa, arrested him, and we'd never see Abe again."

In disbelief and dismay, Fidelia put her arms around Grandma and held her a moment. She knew well how this would crush her grandpa.

"I'll talk to Grandpa. Will they let Abe return after harvest? Please say they will."

"I am hopeful. In this maddened world, it is hard to know," said Grandma.

On her way to the barn, Fidelia stopped and told Boyd what had happened. "Go inside and ask my grandma for some hot tea and something to eat. She needs to keep busy."

She found her grandpa hunched over the workbench, cleaning Jeremy's old tools with a wire brush.

"Grandpa."

He turned quickly to see her.

"Fidelia, he's gone."

"Oh, Grandpa, I'm sure he'll be back. No matter what happens, he'd find his way back to Reka and his children."

"Well, I hear they've taken some to serve the army, but they said Abe was going to a farm just north of Houston. Said crops needed to be harvested for the Confederacy but look at mine. Some startin' to rot."

"Grandpa, we'll stay through tomorrow. Boyd can help. Reka and I can help as well, while Grandma watches the children. Which crops should we save?"

"Not sure it matters. The government might take that as well," he responded.

Fidelia had never seen her grandpa so dismayed, not since her Uncle Jeremy had been killed.

"Grandpa, I negotiated a price with the state. We'll try to save what we can," and she hugged him as she had her grandma.

She borrowed one of Grandma's old work dresses, and she worked with Reka and Boyd all day to harvest the onions. On Sunday, the three brought in a good bit of the cotton crop, and as the sky turned the pinks and oranges of the evening, Reka and Fidelia stripped to their chemises and bathed in the pond. The two women found a bit of scarce joy in the coolness of the water that evening, and the grime was gone when the water dripped off them at dusk. Once the women returned to the house, Boyd decided he would indulge in a dip in the pond.

"I'm sure Leona is worried about us, but I'm certain Dane stayed with her, at least through today," said Fidelia at the supper table. "We'll leave in the morning, but, Grandpa, I'll contact the agent I sold my crop to and send him over here. You'll have to yield on prices, but I found some is better than none."

"You are a blessing, Delia," said Grandma.

As Boyd and Fidelia rode back to Cypress Creek, they came upon Dane, who'd been sent to see to everyone's wellbeing, and Fidelia was distressed that Leona and Johnny had been left alone.

"I know, Dane. Leona has been fretting, hasn't she?" asked Fidelia.

"Yes, and I must return to town but was not willing to do so until I saw to everyone being safe. Since you are on your way home, I will get on to my job and see you next week, Missus Hughes. I hope there will be a letter from your mister."

"Godspeed, boy," said Boyd as Dane rode away.

The mention of a letter set Fidelia to worry once again. Why has she not heard from James? There was more harvesting to come and then winter would be upon them, chilled days much milder than what she remembered as a young girl in Indiana. She recalled the day, when she was maybe six, when they'd buried her sister Hester as snow fell deep around them, and in an early Indiana spring, they'd left for Texas.

It was two days more, after she'd come home, when her world fell apart. She spent the morning in the barn brushing her horse as Johnny climbed and rolled from a hay bale. When she finished, she walked over to the workbench, and she saw the wooden toolbox Jeremy had kept in the McCord barn, surprised that her pa had carried it to his farm. In it, she saw some papers and found a stack of envelopes, yellowed over time.

On top was an opened envelope with a letter to Pa from Grandpa, another letter from Uncle Levi in Indiana, and then, she saw the letter, postmarked in Maryland and then Dallas, in Miles' handwriting. It was addressed to her and had been opened. She looked at the date of the post—it was March 12, 1860.

Her knees gave way and she sunk to the ground, hearing her son's giggling in his play behind her. She pulled the letter from the envelope. *Dearest Delia*, it began, and fear filled her as she knew she must read the words.

"Boyd," she called toward the stalls. "Would you please take Johnny into the house?"

"Yes, ma'am."

She felt the throbbing in her chest, and with the letter in her hand, she walked out of the barn and behind the house to a large sycamore, where she sat. She had to be alone.

> *Dearest Delia. I want to write you pages and pages of what's in my heart, but this must be a hasty message full of love. Norton is sending me north and I'll become an enemy of the state in these times. War is coming, and I will be meeting unsavory people. I cannot put you and your family at risk in times like these, and we're certain our newspaper will be driven from the State.*
>
> *You are everything to me, but I must be silent in the months to come. I beg you, wait for my return. You are my future and everything I want to return to. I cannot wait for this conflict to end and to wed you, to grow a family in the countryside we both love so much. You are what I will see every day I am gone, so please, have heart for you are held*

firm within mine.

I feel the worst of war will be to the east,
and I pray for your safety and wellbeing as
well as that of your family—all of whom I love.
Yours forever and forever, Miles

She felt nauseated, light-headed. *How could this be?* Her father had read this and held it from her as he'd always wanted her to marry James. *How much misery could my own father have inflicted on his family?* She knew she'd faltered in her pledge, the vow of love to another, when she'd accepted James' proposal, when she married him ... and now, this.

She saw the ink smudge on the paper and realized tears were falling. She set the letter aside as she realized how alone she felt in the wild of Texas, not knowing if either her husband or Miles were alive. But she wasn't alone. She had Johnny. She had her grandparents and the gift of friends. *She wanted so desperately to strike out at her father, but of what use was that?* He was gone, and it would change nothing. The price had been paid, and now everything was naught but waiting. Waiting.

Yet, that night, when her head hit the pillow, her thoughts consumed her, and she tossed in darkness the whole night.

CHAPTER 33

Louisiana

Clark and James camped in the cover of trees near the banks of the Sabine River, sometimes hearing the churning of a boat passing. Their journey through Arkansas had been uneventful except for an evening as the sun fell west on a backwoods trail when they'd run into three men appearing to be deserters, one of them still in a Confederate uniform, though torn and dimmed by dirt. James had told the men that they were discharged, merely traveling home, when the younger one saw Clark's sawed-off leg and the frailty of the two men and drew his pistol.

"You. Get off that horse. I thinks I wanna see you dance a jig, old man," as the scoundrel looked at Clark and waved his gun about.

Within a second, Clark had drawn and sent two of the men falling back with three blasts of his Colt. The third fella turned on his horse and swiftly rode off. The young one who'd taunted Clark was not quite gone but was bleeding out, and what with the noise of the gunshots, James and Clark thought best to ride off into the woods. They kept going till darkness surrounded them. They had no plans to meet up with any more renegades or regiments. They had, over their long journey, become adept at survival by remaining naught but shadows, and it was not lost on them that they needed to be even more careful.

Two nights before they sat beside the Sabine, deep in the Louisiana woods, the two men had neared a shack when they saw only an old woman in the yard, a Negro woman, stooped and with gray hair braided down her back. Her house was near a creek, so James and Clark approached her on foot, Clark on his crutch and the men leading their horses.

"We're friendly, ma'am. Just heading home and asking for a bit to eat if you have some," said James.

She stared hard at the men.

"We mean no harm."

"Looking to me like someone got to y'all first," she said.

"Yes, ma'am. Wounded in battle and discharged. We got nothing to give you in exchange but some kind words," said Clark.

"If need be, we could maybe rustle up a wild turkey or a rabbit for you in these woods here," said James.

"Don't need no gift and don't have much. Nowhere for ya to sleep in this shack, but I'll fix ya some eggs. Got some dried turkey," she said, looking straight at James, "and some tea for you."

"We're grateful, ma'am."

"Well, you'll be the first. Last men who came through here took three o'my chickens and kept going. Thank the Lord I had a few more hens roaming in the woods. And don't be calling me ma'am. I'm just called Mamaw 'round here. Too old to have a pretty name."

"I'm James and this, here, is Clark."

"Well, mister," she said, still looking at James, "I can see you got the runny flux from some infection, and I'll brew ya some bark and sweet milk with fired brandy." She walked into the house. Clark and James looked at each other, speechless.

"Sounds like bark juice to me," said Clark after the woman

had gone inside.

James laughed and said, "I could use some bark juice," and then the men led their horses to the creek, hobbled them, and left them to graze.

"We can camp in the trees over there, other side of the creek," said Clark.

Mamaw never invited the men into her house, but she brought out a steaming cup of a milky brew for James. He wondered where she got her milk, but later Clark and James heard the soft bleating of goats.

"This won't taste so good, but it'll help your innards. Drink it up. I'll bring some boiled eggs and wild plums out to ya. You can sit on that log there."

The old woman sat and ate with them and gave them some dried turkey to take with them along with a pouch of the bark she'd used in the healing drink.

"Ya gonna have to find your own sweet milk and brandy," she said, "but you should feel better tomorrow, Mister James."

"We thank you, Mamaw. You are a kind woman, and we were fortunate to chance upon you. We'll be gone in the morning," said Clark.

"Bless you," said James as the men led their horses down to the trees and across the creek. In the early dawn, Clark slipped his wooden crutch into the scabbard that he'd made from a bit of leather he traded for back in Tennessee, and the two men mounted their horses and rode off.

There was still a morning mist when the men reached Logan's Ferry and crossed into Texas.

"Home," said Clark. "I feel it in my feet and in my bones, even the sad one that's gone."

"Well, there's still some rough ground to cross, friend, but

I think we're through the worst," said James. "Let's stay together all the way to Marlin, then I'll move on south. You can make it on from there, can't ya?"

"I'm sure I can. I'll be seeing the light of home, where my folks might wait for me. I hope they're not too disappointed in what's left. A flukey chance you have a wife to go home to."

James stared at Clark and then laughed.

"I suppose it is, friend. She shoulda got my letter by now. The one I hope that Tennessee farmwife posted for me."

"Or maybe you'll surprise her. My folks still have my tanning tools, so I'm gonna open shop again. I know this war's gonna have to end soon, and there'll be a need for new saddles and such," said Clark. "You'll know where to find me."

"And well might, friend. My shop's gone. Damn this war. Got no idea what I'm going back to, but suspect I'll stop at my in-law's farm as I will ride past it. My Delia might be there for all I know," said James as he bit into a persimmon pulled from a tree on the Texas side of the river. "If she mailed any letters since May, they'd never find me."

Two days later, the two men rode into Nacogdoches and found it appeared the likeness of a ghost town, and the sight of it disheartened them. About five or six more days of riding and they'd split up. James was so close to home he could smell the cedar scrub and prairie grass. But as the days wore on toward the trail into Austin, James thought of little but the sight of Miles in that tree back in Tennessee. The closer he got to home, the larger his dilemma hung in his head, and he'd yet to figure on how he'd handle it. All he wanted was to hold his Delia and their young child and to feel the warmth of home, and he had no desire to thwart it with the sights he had seen or stir feelings in her heart of someone other than himself.

The two men were about a day and a half from going their own ways when James could hold it no longer. In all the miles he and Clark had traveled, all their limitations, including fear of infection and renegades, surely facing death's reach, James had never shared the quandary that haunted him more nights than not.

"Clark, you and I have come a long way together. It's more than just the miles. It's the journey we've been on. But a terrible thing happened before I was injured, and I've never shared it with anyone but my friend Pete."

"What's that? Lord a'mighty. How could our situation have been much worse, other than us being dead in a gulley?" asked Clark.

"Well, let me tell you what I've gotta decide in the next few days," said James.

And with those words, James told his friend the whole tale of who Miles was and what he'd seen on that fateful expedition back in February.

"Criminy, James, I don't think I'd tell her. But it ain't me that'll be haunted by it, and what if she finds out? You won't be able to dig out of that hole."

James stared at Clark, knowing he was right.

"I didn't bury the boy. I hated leaving him there, but the ground was froze, and if anyone in our regiment knew I'd even done such, it would make me suspect. But even I felt bad propping him against that tree, let alone my Delia knowing. To be truthful, I'm afraid she still loved him."

"Well, he might have been a spy. Right? That's no hero," said Clark.

"I don't think he was a spy," said James, "but don't know for sure. The boy was a storyteller, wrote articles about people. I kept part of his journal I found. Haven't even opened it yet."

"Damn, James. I woulda read it and burned it long before now."

All the way to Marlin, Texas, James' stomach twisted and grumbled, more from worry than the scarcity of food, and it was a rainy day in October when the two men went their separate ways.

CHAPTER 34

Cypress Creek

The day Dane came with the mail, with the letter from Tennessee, Fidelia could not sit still. She could not believe he was coming home.

"I'm not sure he'll know where I am," she said to Leona. "I'm certain he did not get my letter if he's been traveling. What will he think if the house is empty?"

She turned to Dane.

"Maybe we should go back to Austin."

"Ma'am, no need. I can put a note at the house, or I could stay there in the evenings if you'd like."

"Oh, dear. I don't know what to do. I don't know when he'll get here, and there's still harvesting to be done. I need to clean the house."

"Sit down, Fidelia," said Leona. "I can take care of the house and Johnny. Don't worry, and when Mister Hughes gets here, Dane can take me back to the city, so you two can be alone, at least for a bit."

Dane finished his biscuit and jam, and then he turned to Fidelia.

"Missus Hughes, I know I should have talked to you before today, but when you were gone looking for Abe at your grandparents' farm, I asked Leona to wed. I, though belated, am asking your blessing before it is agreed on. I mean to put no burden on you in these times, and we can wait for you to be settled."

"Oh, dear. So much blessed news, but I am not surprised. I knew this day was coming. Yes, yes. You have my blessing and, I am certain, that of James."

"Thank you, ma'am." Leona smiled at Fidelia, and Dane left the women alone and joined Boyd at the barn.

"I am so happy for you, dear," said Fidelia. "Dane is a kind young man. And, yes, Leona, you're right about James' homecoming. It's been three years since he left. It's much like a new courtship, isn't it? I do feel giddy."

As soon as the words of courtship left her mouth, she thought of the letter she'd found, about the courtship she'd abandoned. And what if he came back looking for her. But she knew she had to let that go. She'd made a vow to James and now he was coming home. Maybe he'd be injured since he was discharged, and in addition to that, he'd have to deal with the loss of his printing shop—maybe even the house. This godforsaken war was a never-ending nightmare. She sat and remembered poor Reka over at Grandpa's farm, not knowing if her Abe would ever come home.

Not knowing where James would go when he reached Austin, Fidelia sent word of his return to Grandpa, asking Boyd to ride over to Pond Springs when he was out checking on the cattle. Leona helped her ready the house, and Boyd, at last, completed the harvesting of the field of cotton without help.

"I'll help you till the fields before the cold of winter, Boyd," she'd told him, unsure if either Abe or James would be back.

"It's a lot of work for a woman, but I've seen ya do it, so any help would be appreciated," said Boyd.

"I know my pa usually let you go for the winter, but I'd appreciate it if you were still here. I don't want to be out here alone and don't right know whether or not I will be. Even Leona will be leaving shortly, to wed. Don't you have any family, Boyd?" she asked, feeling ashamed she had not asked before.

"Just a sister back in Maryland," he said. "My Ginny and the infant died in childbirth about seventeen years ago."

"I'm sorry to hear that. You surely can stay here, but I don't think I can give you more than room and board till we harvest next summer."

"Ma'am, that's about all I need. I look forward to meeting your husband."

"Well, he doesn't know yet that Pa left me this farm, so we'll have to see what happens. I'm pretty certain James never got that letter when I told him, but maybe he did."

Chapter 35

Williamson County

The sun was moving toward the western horizon, splaying pinks through the clouds on a pleasant day as James' horse, as weary as James himself, ambled along the trail and past the Stagecoach Inn in Round Rock. He would arrive at the McCord farm before nightfall and wanted to go on to Austin. But he would stop at the farm since he'd not had a letter from his wife for a good part of the year, the last one in February when she'd told him the shop had closed.

He had opened the journal, once belonging to Miles, when he'd camped near Salado Creek. The sun had not set when he made camp, and he knew he would be home on the morrow. He read through pages of conversations Miles had had with widows and farms and even a couple of soldiers, though he gathered up some loose pages and others were missing—the pages that the killers had torn out. James found notes of the days he'd worked at the prison in Columbus, Ohio, including tidbits of Texas prisoners he'd talked with—even an annotation about Watkins, who'd been held there.

But interspersed with Miles Maloney's notes were words of loss. Mighty grief and the loss of Fidelia when he'd learned she'd married, when, according to the entries, Anthony Norton had told him Fidelia had been wed to a printer, and there, in Maloney's handwriting was his own name. *Why had the chap left her behind? Not told her where he'd gone?*

Now, he saw the familiar farmhouse before him in the dim

light of evening. Candlelight revealed the windows, and he tied his horse and knocked at the door.

"Oh, good God, praise," said Missus McCord as she greeted him. "Fidelia sent word you were coming. Said you might stop here if you came home from the north."

"Welcome, Son," said William McCord as he shook James's hand and felt it held no strength.

Grandma said, "Boy, you wasted away to nothing. Sit. Sit, and I'll get you a bowl of stew. Some biscuits."

"Glad you stopped, Son," said Grandpa. "You know, or may not know, she's not in town anymore. My son—you've met John—moved to Indiana and left the farm to her. She's out at Cypress Creek but has someone watching your house in Austin."

James was too weary to even show the surprise he held at hearing the news.

"She's so excited you're coming. We'll ride out early tomorrow if that's good with you. I know you'd probably like to see her tonight."

"Morning is good, sir. I think what I desire more than anything in this world right now is a soft bed."

"We got plenty of those, James. And I'll fix you a big breakfast. We got plenty of eggs and milk and biscuits. No coffee."

"You injured, Son?" asked Grandpa.

In spite of his weariness, James told the story of what had happened to him, that he yet had spells of dysentery, and about the bark tea an old woman in Louisiana had given him.

"It seemed to work, and she gave me a piece of the bark. It's in my saddlebag."

"Go get it, William," Grandma said to her husband.

James panicked.

"No, I'll get it. Give me a minute and I'll bring in my satchel." James rose and walked out the door.

Grandma made a brew of bark and milk and brandy, as

James described to her, and once downed, he went off to bed. James fell into a deep and dreamless sleep in the warmth of feathered down in the quiet of Fidelia's old bedroom.

Early in the morning, James rode west toward the cabin. Grandpa had wanted to ride with him, but Grandma forbade it.

A chill filled the air as James traveled, and he could not grasp his wife managing the farm and foregoing their home in Austin. His father-in-law had said there were now cattle at the farm, and he'd shared how the government had imposed restrictions on the Negroes in the city and how it had impressed, seized, both crops and slaves. James struggled with the idea of such restraints so contrary to the wild ways of the Texas he'd left only a few years earlier.

The tea Missus McCord had given him the night before had eased his discomfort and allowed him a sleep like none he could remember. *Still not a whole man, how would he face his wife? How would she see him?*

And then, looking up, he saw the large barn before him and a young woman and a young child walking toward it. After the woman looked in his direction, she grabbed up the child and ran to the cabin, and another woman walked out the door looking in his direction. He urged his horse to quicken its pace and saw the woman was his Fidelia, dark strands of her hair dancing in the breeze as she strode toward him.

The sight of her pressed all worries from his mind. He was home.

As he held Fidelia in his arms, he saw Leona and the child walk out the door.

"Johnny?"

Fidelia turned to look back.

"Yes. It's your son. He'll be shy since he hasn't met you. On the night he was born, I prayed to God you would come home. And you have."

James kissed his wife on the cheek and walked over to his son, stooping to meet the child at eye level.

"Good to meet you, young man," said James, and he struggled to extend his right arm as if to shake hands, and the boy hid behind Leona's skirt. James stood up.

"Leona, you have grown into a young woman since I've seen you," he said. "Are you women running this farm on your own?"

"With the help of Boyd, the farmhand, we are doing that," said Fidelia. "James, you have lost so much weight. Were you injured? Is that why you've come home?"

"Yes. Shot in the shoulder. Laid up for a good spell and discharged, but the man I traveled home with, Clark, from up near the Brazos, he lost a leg, so we were a sorry sight sneaking across the land. Like a couple of snakes in the grass, trying to avoid renegades and battlefields."

"I'll fix a good dinner for all of us. Dane, Leona's betrothed, has been keeping an eye on the house for me. Dane is Henry Cannon's son. He'll come tomorrow, on Saturday, to bring the mail, and he keeps us abreast of the news. Really, I'm certain he comes to see Leona. I didn't know what to do with the house, James, and I was surprised about pa leaving this farm to me. We can talk about it more when you're quite rested."

"I'm certain this Texas air will help. Even a Texan winter will be a blessing to me. Never knew just how cold it could get till I saw Kentucky and those Tennessee mountains."

"I'll take your horse out to the barn, Mister Hughes," said Leona. "I'm certain you are both tired to the bone." Johnny followed her as she took the reins and led the horse to the barn.

"I'm not sure what to do with that horse; in truth, it does belong to the army," said James as he watched his son follow Leona and his horse.

Fidelia stood tall on her toes and kissed James on the cheek, took his hand, and led him inside. Once in the kitchen, James turned to face his wife, put his left hand behind her neck, and kissed her with all the fire his weary body held as she leaned against the wall and the weight of the world held them together.

"Home is with you, Delia, wherever we are," whispered James. "I'm almost in disbelief that I'm here. You don't know how many days I doubted that this could come to be. That I would be here. That I would see you again."

Fidelia felt all the pain in and between his words. He sounded different yet never closer to her. But she was cautious in the autumn of 1864, when so much had changed and the smell of war still hovered in the air.

Chapter 36

Cypress Creek

Saturday arrived covered in gray clouds and the threat of rains, and Dane arrived at the Cypress Creek farm to find Leona in the kitchen feeding Johnny.

"You look beautiful this morning," he said and sat at the table across Leona.

"I am still in a morning dress and my hair not pinned, and I think you're a smitten man," she responded as she encouraged Johnny to eat his porridge. "We are being quiet. Fidelia and Mister Hughes are not up yet.

"Mister Hughes is home?"

"Yes, he came yesterday. Looks poorly," said Leona.

"I'm sorry to hear that. Now, regarding this love-sick man, when are you and I going to visit the preacher? I have a job at the Institute for the Deaf, and we can find a place of our own. Maybe even consider a grant of land if there's any to be had."

"I want to give the Hughes some time together. Maybe we can schedule a small ceremony at your pa's home after Christmas."

"If I must wait till Christmas," said Dane, "I will just have to be patient. You are a girl worth waiting for." He winked at his betrothed.

Leona gave him a kiss on the cheek as she walked to the basin with dishes.

"Would you like some eggs and grits?"

"Yes, ma'am. I would. There was no mail for Missus

Hughes." Dane picked up Johnny and walked outside, grabbed the reins of his horse, and led her to the trough. Johnny watched the horse drink and splashed his hand in the water, and Dane looked up to see Boyd by the barn. He waved.

"Eggs are ready," called Leona. "Come on in and meet Mister James."

The two men hit it off right away. Both had seen the battlefields, though in different places and from different angles, yet their reluctance to speak of the misery did not escape Fidelia's notice. James was not the man who'd left in 1861, and she well knew she was not the woman he'd left behind.

During the night, Fidelia told James about her mother and how she'd found her in the cabin that day she'd come—her slow passing under the care of Grandma and then, her father's quick exit. As the two came together that night, the gaunt frame of her husband and his jutting bones had shaken her, yet the unexpected gentleness of his touch introduced her to the James Hughes who had returned from war.

They had slept past sunrise but had reveled in the union of their bodies in a soft moonlight arcing through the windowpane, yet Fidelia had heard the moans of her husband's dreams and could only imagine what he lived through in his sleep.

The baby, now two years old, smiled at James across the table and giggled when his father winked at him. Fidelia sat next to James and put her hand over his right hand, and he managed to turn his hand over and clasped hers.

"You know, two months ago, I couldn't have done that," he said, looking into the smile in his wife's eyes.

"Have you met Boyd?" asked Dane.

"No. He's been out checking the fields and cattle when I came yesterday, but I've heard how he's been such a help to Fidelia." James turned to Fidelia. "Though I have no doubt you could have done it all on your own."

James stood and walked around the table, reached out to his young son, and picked him up. The child scrutinized his face.

Dane stood up and said, "Let's go meet Boyd."

"So, Dane," said James as they walked to the barn. "I hear you've asked to marry our Leona. She is like a daughter, or more like a niece, to us, so we'd expect you to take good care of her. Do you have work?"

"Yes, sir, Mister Hughes. The Institute of the Deaf hired me.'

"To do what?" he asked.

"As an interpreter, maybe later, an instructor. My sister-in-law is deaf and lives with us, so Pa and I have learned to speak by hand. Your Leona is a treasure. I met her working with the Ladies' Aid Society when I drove the wagon for their deliveries. I still do it when they need me."

"Leona volunteered with the Ladies' Aid Society?" asked James.

"Yes, sir. She's very gracious, especially concerned about all the widows."

Almost to the barn, James walked in silence, then spoke. "We've left too many dead on the fields of sorrow. Needlessly."

Two days after Dane had returned to Austin, James mounted his horse and headed out to inspect the fields and the cattle with Boyd. He liked Boyd, an easygoing man who knew the land and his way around a ranch. Fidelia had told him that Boyd was a widower. Running cattle was something James had never considered doing, yet the idea of it intrigued him, and if he was to choose life at the farm, he had no desire to farm that much land. James found that most of the crop fields had been turned over and was impressed by the work Boyd had done.

"I must say, having been working this farm a couple years now, what with John and then working for his daughter," said Boyd as he beside James. "Your Missus Fidelia is one devoted and shrewd farm woman. She knows how to handle a horse and even is equal to me in plowing a field. She had a hard time when her ma was ailing. Her pa wasn't much of a family man. She told me you had a print shop in the city, but this is a mighty fine ranch here, sir."

"I'm saddened to hear that about John. He did often seem withdrawn from his family. Delia told me last night about her ma taking ill and how Missus McCord, her grandmother, cared for Delia's ma. I'm taking it from your words that you think we should stay at the ranch."

"Well, I'm hoping," Boyd responded. "I like it here, and the city's gonna grow when the war ends. This is a mighty fine piece of land for a family."

James pondered the man's words as they rode on and Boyd noted of the whereabouts of the cattle and new calves. James had been so eager to get home and be with Fidelia, see their son, that he'd not thought much of the future. There would be more children. And the cattle, that might be sluggish trade now, but at war's end, maybe sooner, there will be a demand. He'd have to talk to his wife. There was the house in Austin to consider. He owned it outright.

"I think I need to make a trip into Austin. Tomorrow, I'll ride into the city, check the house, and meet with George who used to manage the books at my shop. I can't imagine there's any business to drum up now, but one day the city will be buzzing again."

"Just let me know what you need me to do. It's a bit slow

until planting season, but I'm gonna mend some fencing on the corral tomorrow."

"Will do, Boyd. I appreciate you being here."

As James rode from Cypress Creek into Austin, his thoughts turned back to the awful day in February. He sometimes dreamed of it; sometimes, it woke him with a start. But he had not found the courage to tell Fidelia, and he knew the longer he waited the harder it would be. He knew the right things to do, but he feared the outcome.

Winter was coming and would empty the trees of their leaves and the sky of promise.

CHAPTER 37

Cypress Creek

To Fidelia, the cabin at the creek felt empty without Leona. She and Dane had wed at the Justice of the Peace in Austin, a simple ceremony with the Cannon and Hughes families present. James and Fidelia had decided to let the Austin house to the newlyweds, and it was agreed they'd pay rent when they were able.

The skies were gray in late November and, with the baby in bed, James and Fidelia sat in front of the fireplace wrapped in a blanket.

Fidelia had been quiet, and James kissed her—a kiss most passionate as he'd gained back some vigor after his long journey, but she met his desire with a sadness in her eyes he'd not seen before.

"What's wrong?"

"James, I have to tell you something I've discovered. It's hard for me to say it."

James' heart sank and a knot twisted in his stomach. He should have told her about Miles right away.

"One day, in the barn, I found some letters in the toolbox. Letters to my pa from his brother and from Grandpa, and in the middle was a letter to me. It was opened, but I'd never received it. It was from Miles."

The muscles of James' back tightened, and he felt the ache in his injured shoulder as if a phantom.

"He said he was chasing stories in the North and asked me

to wait for him. Now, I don't know where he is or if he'll come back. I'm committed to our marriage, James, but I should have known. It was so careless of me, to make such an oath to you and not know of this, and there are days I hate my father for doing this."

James didn't know what to say, yet he knew what he must reveal.

"But I love you with everything in me, Delia."

"I know. And I love you."

He wanted to kiss her, but he had to spit it out. She was speaking the truth, so he must follow.

"Delia, I know." He continued, "I know where he is."

She pushed away from him and looked into his eyes.

"He's dead. And what I saw, what we came upon, is too horrible for me to tell you. But he died in Tennessee."

"You saw him?"

"My regiment found him, but he was gone. Dead. But I recognized right away who it was."

Tears were falling from her eyes in silence. She looked muddled, seemed unable to speak.

"I didn't want to tell you, Delia, for it was a horrible thing to see, a shock to me since I knew who he was. But some renegades killed him, and I am sorry to be the one to tell you."

He took her in his arms and held her, wrapped the blanket tighter around them, held her as she cried into his shoulder that hurt no more, and eventually she fell asleep. Then, laying down they slept, together, until Johnny woke them in the morning by the cold ashes of the hearth.

Fidelia rose and picked up Johnny.

"When was it you knew Miles was dead? That he was in Tennessee?" asked Fidelia.

James paused, reluctant to answer that question.

"In February," he answered, his voice humble.

She turned and walked to the basin in the kitchen, where she cleaned the child and washed the dried tears from her face.

She fixed breakfast but said nothing of last night while she fed their son and then went about her chores. James felt a chill between them, as if he may have lost her forever by revealing only a bit of what was so horrible. Revealing what would have been better unseen and unsaid. If only he had not been swayed by the curiosity of others and rode straight ahead on that day, he would have never known.

At supper, Boyd sat quiet at the table, detecting the strain between the couple.

"We have two new calves birthed this week," he said, breaking the silence. He looked at James. "Pass the potatoes, please."

As James handed the bowl to Boyd, he smiled at him. An awkward smile, and then Johnny jumped into his father's lap.

When James walked into the bedroom, Fidelia was brushing her hair. He wanted to take the brush and do it for her but feared her rejection.

"Fidelia, I'm broken-hearted to have brought you such dire news, but I didn't kill him. I wanted to bury him. The ground was frozen." He didn't mention the risk that Pete and he might have taken in doing so.

After a long silence, after he was under the covers, she spoke.

"It's all too much to deal with. Both the letter and what you've shared but should have told me sooner. It's more than I can bear. More than I can comprehend."

On Saturday morning, Dane arrived at the ranch with

some mail. He came alone, without Leona, and handed the letters to Fidelia.

There was a letter for James from Waco, and the Austin newspaper from Wednesday.

"And here's a bit of coffee that I picked up at Hollander's on Pecan Street," Boyd said and handed Fidelia the package.

"Come in, Dane; I'll brew a pot and we can indulge," said Fidelia.

James took the letter from Waco and walked away from the house as he opened it. Clark wrote that he'd bought a livery in Waco, was working with the horses, and still had time to do some tanning, but his news was sad. He had Pete Mullen's name listed as being killed in July near Murfreesboro in a skirmish.

I know you two were friends, James, and I wanted to let you know, his friend Clark wrote. Again, all the death, so needless, thought James, and he pushed the letter into his pocket. "Seems letters carry nothing but sad news anymore," he muttered as he walked into the kitchen.

"I'm taking a ride today. I'll be home in a couple of days," said James, and he walked upstairs.

He rode west with his gear stashed so he could camp on the trail. The ride felt familiar, like the long journey he and Clark had just been on, and he wondered why he wasn't resting his body at home. But he had a chore to do, and the chill in the air was warmer than the chill at home—a home not his own, having lost the life he'd left behind for the muster in Houston in 1861.

After everyone had been fed and Johnny was napping, Fidelia sat in the sitting room near her desk. Grandpa had asked Abe to bring her old writing desk over after she'd moved in. She put her feet up and opened the *Weekly Gazette*. She read of all the movements in the East, the names of generals she did not know, and then there was an article written by Jack Beidletter. The title drew her attention, "What Have We Sacrificed and for What?" She read the words, and they felt familiar. It sounded like Miles, but Miles was not the author, and besides, he was dead, according to James. *Could James have been wrong?*

She read the article again and was moved by it. She felt as if the whole world had shattered.

James arrived in San Saba near dusk. He thought the boy's aunt was named Beulah but was unsure if her last name was Maloney. A young man walking alongside the trail looked at him, then away.

"I'm looking for a woman named Beulah. Don't know her last name," said James.

The man shook his head and said nothing.

"She had a nephew named Miles, Miles Maloney,"

The man looked at him, and James saw the man's hair was long and tied in the back.

"Up the road. The house near the creek, with a windmill."

James held little back when he explained to Beulah what he'd found in the Tennessee woods. He did not talk of the gruesome sight he saw, but he told her the boy was hung, likely by Confederate renegades or deserters, who thought him a spy. And he told her who he was, the man that Fidelia had married. He could see she recognized Fidelia's name as he sat at her table with the hot chicory drink she'd poured for each of them, the drink reminding him of the bark juice he'd drank not so long ago in Louisiana, and he wondered if Miss Beulah had poured spirits into it.

"Ma'am, I don't think your nephew was a spy. I think he was just a storyteller looking for stories, but I don't know. I didn't know how to tell his family, back in North Carolina, except for through you."

"I'll write to his pa," said Beulah, "though I hate to bear such news to him. The boy had his life in front of him, and the war took it, but he's certainly not the only one to pay such a price. I appreciate your comin' all this way to tell me. You're a good man, and I welcome you to spend the night."

"Ma'am, you're kind, but I want to get home. I'll ride past dusk toward Lampasas and camp for the night."

"You fill your canteen at the well and take some cornbread, and you can take with you that horse of his, Marco," she said as she wrapped the bread.

"Ma'am, I can't take your horse."

"I don't need to be feeding another animal I can't make use of. Besides, I'm thinking my nephew Miles might want your wife to have him. He did love that girl I never got to meet, and I hope that does not sway you from taking the horse." Beulah looked up and gave James a firm look. "Or you can use Marco on your farm. Take him," she said as she busied herself wrapping the cornbread.

James was confounded as to what to do. He wasn't sure he wanted to take Miles' horse home to his wife. One more memory of loss, of the man she'd love and maybe still does. He considered going outside and just riding away, but she followed behind him to the porch.

"I'll show you which one. You don't want that feisty mare or my old mule out here." She stopped before the stall of a fine chestnut gelding. She bridled the horse and handed the reins to James. He thanked her and wished her well as he mounted his old army horse and rode away, leading Marco and thinking he might saddle the fine gelding tomorrow and ride him home.

CHAPTER 38

Cypress Creek

With Christmas coming, Fidelia planned for the family holiday in Pond Springs with her grandma and grandpa. She readied for the trip, knitting and stitching gifts. She wished with all her heart that her ma was still with her, for she needed someone to confide in. Her heart was torn between the man she'd loved and the one she'd married, and now, James had been the one to rip her hope into pieces. She couldn't abide what had happened and knew her life would have been different if her pa had given her the letter. *Or would it?*

In spite of her dilemma, James had gone off somewhere, left all of a sudden, and still wasn't home after three days.

As Johnny played with his blocks, Fidelia walked over to her desk, opened the drawer, and pulled out her old journal. She had not written in it for years now, but the ache inside poured onto blank pages before Johnny demanded dinner.

Gone

You, carefree and easy

stole my breath when you wandered

into Texas as if you'd sprouted

in a hot cotton field,

had always been here

and we were like children

swinging, back and forth,

back and forth drawn together

like piglets to the teat—

we were like clay

pulled and kneaded into a thing

that had never been before.

Now, I've heard you died.

How did I not know?

How did the sun rise anew?

The air I breathe is stale

and empty of our laughter

that once lingered here—

Still, you are forever, forever, forever.

She set the book aside, feeling like she'd released some of her agony, had let it go, before placing the journal back in the desk drawer, out of sight. She took Johnny's hand and walked out to the barn, where she had not been for days, to check on Boyd.

"Ma'am, James is not yet back. Should we be worried?" he asked.

"I don't know, but I feel certain he'll be back soon. I think we'll leave for a few days near Christmas, over to my grandpa's. If you want to take a few days away, before or after we're gone, please do."

"Got nowhere to go, Missus Fidelia."

"You are welcome to join us for the holiday. Grandma

always loves one more mouth to feed." Fidelia laughed, hoping he would accept the invitation.

James arrived home that afternoon and quietly stabled the horses before walking into the house. There'd hardly been a sentence spoken between him and his wife since that night in front of the fireplace, and he didn't know how to mend the rift. It almost seemed as if Miles was a greater threat to his marriage now than when the man was alive, and he pushed such thoughts away as his young son started squealing with joy at the sight of James.

Fidelia put a meal on the table and, leaving Johnny with James, she went upstairs to nap. James gobbled down the dumplings and wiped the child's face and hands before he placed the dishes in the basin and took Johnny out to the barn. The child ran to the dog and chased Chap in and out of the building in between giggles brought on by licks to his face.

"Boyd, how'd you manage not to get conscripted?" asked James.

"First, I'm sure they thought me too old, and, second, I got me a limp," said Boyd.

"Well, they're so desperate for men now, those things wouldn't matter."

"Sir, I have a tendency to lay low and keep my name off lists," said Boyd and he grinned. "Your missus invited me to go to her grandpa's home for the holiday. Though it's rare of me to mix with strangers, I just may go, if that is good with you."

"You don't need my blessing, but I'm glad to hear it. You probably noticed there's a new horse in that back stall. Can you say nothing about it to Delia? I haven't yet figured out how to explain it to her and not sure how she'll feel about it."

"Will do, James. He looks a might sounder than the horse you've been riding."

"He is a fine horse, and I appreciate it, friend. I may ride over to the McCord farm tomorrow to see if the old man needs any help. You're welcome to go with me."

"Appreciate the invite, but I'm checking on the cattle tomorrow. Haven't rode out for almost eight days. Since it's winter, I'd be glad to go over on the holiday. The old man's in his eighties, isn't he?"

"Yes, he is, but he keeps the farm up. I'm certain it's hard without Abe, but I think it's the company of others he misses the most, so they'd be most glad if you join us at Christmas."

Boyd nodded and led the two cows toward the door to the pasture.

When James looked around to see Johnny sitting beside the dog, he remembered the swing that his friend Jeremy had hung for Fidelia in the McCord barn. That was a great idea. He could hang it low for Johnny and raise it up as he grew.

By suppertime, he had sanded the edges of the swing, knotted the rope, and hung it over the rafter. The process of planing and sanding the wood had been good therapy for his still-weakened shoulder. As James had worked, Johnny slept on a hay bale, and when the boy woke, James enjoyed the delight in his boy's eyes when James showed the boy how the swing worked. Boyd was impressed with James' work as the two men watched the child try to swing as his pa had shown him, and then a call came from the house. A call for supper, and James realized they needed a dinner bell.

Fidelia said little at the supper table and only nodded when he said he'd ride over to her grandparents' farm. He was hoping she might ask to go with him, but she did not.

CHAPTER 39

Pond Springs

The weather turned cold overnight, and James put on his woolens for the ride over to Pond Springs. He thought of the miserable treks through the Northern ice and winds and how he'd learned to adapt in the scourge of winter. The nine miles was not a long ride, and he took it as slow as the chill would allow, taking in the light of winter, the shape of the leafless trees and cedar scrub—the chipping of sparrows and warblers chattering as they flit about seeking shelter in oak and juniper. For the first time, since he was a child in Alabama and the long trip to Texas, James took in the sense of the open space and the rush of water as he crossed the creek. For all the brutal days he spent in the wilds over the last three years, this felt different. Almost hallowed.

"Praise the Lord," said Grandma when James walked into the kitchen. "I'm glad you're here and look at you. Delia must be feeding you."

"She is, Missus McCord."

"Well, sit down. I've got some of that make-believe coffee if you'd like some." She walked toward the hearth. "Grandpa, James is here."

"I'll try some of that coffee. Dane brought us some coffee beans from the city. I'll bring them at Christmas. Hey, William," said James, looking over toward his father-in-law. "Sure was a sweet ride over to your farm without worry of any Yankees in the bushes.

Reka came inside, with her young daughter following and a bucket of milk. "G'day, Miss Reka," said James. "Have you heard from Abe?"

"He's home, sir. Like a holiday gift," she said as she sat the bucket in the kitchen.

"Thank you, Reka," Grandma said as she rubbed Reka's daughter's head, and the young girl giggled. "James, you've been my Delia's husband long enough to be calling me Grandma. Stop calling me Missus McCord. You're family, Son. The only son I got in Texas now."

"Hey, James," said Grandpa. "Giving Abe a rest after his impressment. Ain't much work as winter threatens, but I'm glad he came home with no scars. He got home a bit weary from the wear this week, walking all the way from Houston. Damned government."

"Well, I came to see if you needed any help. I'm getting accustomed to being in the country," said James, taking a sip of the coffee Grandma had set in front of him "You'd think it would be easy after living in forests and tents for three years, but that wasn't the same at all. Delia will be delighted to hear that Abe has returned, and Missus McCord, this coffee is better than some I had in the war."

"Ain't much of anything, Son. And it's Grandma. Remember to call me Grandma."

"Yes, ma'am. Grandma. I will have to get accustomed to the moniker."

"I cannot believe how much better you seem than when you dragged yourself into this house back a few weeks ago," said Grandma.

"A little better each day. Someone dropped a two-cent coin in my hand at a general store outside of Memphis, and on it, I found the Union had printed *In God We Trust*. What an odd thing to put such words on their money in this war," said James, who turned toward Grandpa. "Mister McCord, I built little Johnny a barn swing like the one Jeremy built. Hung it yesterday."

"Where is the boy?"

"I didn't bring him, sir. We'll bring him at Christmas. Just two more weeks."

"Well, we have much to celebrate, James, what with you coming home, and Abe's come back, and little Johnny," said Grandpa. "I imagine we'll be missing Lucy, but Matilda and her new husband brought our granddaughter to visit us in September."

James thought back on his good friend Jeremy—how his life was cut too short for a man with so much to give. Thought of Jeremy's pretty wife, Matilda, and their sweet daughter. And those thoughts took him straight back to the battlefield and all those lives cut short. Hundreds. Thousands. Fallen without any dignity for naught but a rich man's war. He remembered writing that letter to Watkin's wife, telling her that her husband Paul had been captured. Now Pete's gone. How many widows will this war leave?

"James. James." The voice of Grandma called him back. "Here's some apple cobbler right out of the oven."

"I imagine you seen too much death, boy," said Grandpa, "for any young man to have to see. I've read the papers. We're just glad you're back. You have to live full now, Son. For yourself and for all your lost friends. Don't you die with them. There's all kinds of ways to die."

"Grandpa, eat your cobbler," said Grandma.

Fidelia appreciated the quiet with James gone and Boyd out riding the land. She wanted solitude. Even Johnny seemed to understand, amusing himself with a spoon and pot on the floor. She pulled out her journal and carried it to the kitchen table. She would write again when the baby napped.

When she stepped on the porch to sweep, she looked out to the barn and beyond, where winter clouds skipped across the blue-gray sky above harvested fields, reminding her how much she loved the country. Most of the trees near the house had lost their leaves, stripped bare by fall's winds. Still, they were regal, their branches reaching high, some holding bird nests trusting spring will come. For all the years she'd dreaded coming to live in Pa's isolated cabin, she was filled with a sense of peace when she was startled by a bird abruptly flying off. She looked down, where the bird had come from, to see a fallen bird at the base of the oak tree. As she walked toward it, Johnny came out the door to follow her. She found a stilled mourning dove. She saw no injury, and it appeared dead.

"No, Johnny, don't touch it. It might just be stunned, so let's leave it be for a while."

After Johnny ate and went down for his nap, Fidelia opened her journal to the next blank page. She sat and waited, but nothing came in those moments, nothing but a sadness that she knew was grief—a peculiar grief for a man she had given up on and whose death did not seem real to her. Maybe it was her own weakness that uneased her. *Had her love for him not been strong enough to wait?* She remembered her love for Miles being strong, but it was she who'd been weak. Now, it seemed the war had broken everyone.

She walked outside to the fallen bird and found it still there, but the bird she'd seen fly away earlier was lying beside the dead bird. Cooing. A mournful coo. And she realized what she saw was the very origin of its name. The ache of loss and grief, as sad as she herself. She did not go near but sat on the step and watched, kept the bird company, though the mourning dove saw nothing but its loss. She sat there until her young son came to her on the porch, pulling his blanket with him, and then they sat there together until she had to start cooking supper.

CHAPTER 40

Cypress Creek

When quiet moments came, Fidelia would take the letter from Miles, often going out under the tree where she'd first read it, and she would reread his words. Searching for more. Maybe it was his presence she looked for. She went back to all the losses she'd had as a child and recalled how Gray Feather had told her everyone that she'd loved was still with her. In her eyes. In how she saw the world. But she could not find the presence of Miles. She'd read the letter again and again, but the air around her was still empty.

After three days, the dead mourning dove still lay where it had died, and its partner had flown off at dusk the day before, so she buried the dead bird. Though she had knitted a blanket for her grandparents, she had no gifts for the children at Christmas. She had seen the swing in the barn, and memories of her own swing made clear that Johnny had received a wonderful gift. She had said nothing to James about it but knew she should.

That evening, when the chores were done and James had gone to bed, Fidelia lit the oil lamp and brought it to her desk. She pulled the journal out again and opened it to the blank page, dipped her pen into the ink, and let the image of the last few days drift onto paper.

Mourning Dove

Oh, dear dove, why do you weep?

Your loved one is stilled

yet your vigil you keep,

your pleas unrequited,

you soar to the sky

and leave me here to cry.

Do you still hear her cooing,

feel the warmth of your past?

Are you searching to see if

she still flies in blue skies?

When you sailed away

was she with you still?

Soaring nearby?

Did you lift her spirit

from stilled feathers

to fly in clouds high?

Tell me, please. I want to know

the secret of your sorrow.

She slipped Miles' letter into the pages of her closed journal and returned it to the drawer, went upstairs, and quietly slid into bed. She awoke in the morning, before sunrise, to find James' arm was around her, the weight and warmth of him comforting on a cold morning. As he slept, she lay there a bit longer before rising to fix breakfast for the men.

CHAPTER 41

On the way to Pond Springs

When Christmas Eve came, James wished he had brought the Hughes' buggy from the small barn at the Austin house, but the family gladly bundled up and piled into the wagon. Fidelia had made two pies and a bowl of cherry-lemon relish from the black cherry tree near the creek, and James placed them in a wooden box in the wagon before he and Boyd started arguing over who would lead the horses. Boyd wouldn't give up, and James sat beside Boyd on the wagon seat.

As expected, Grandma had a tree decorated with ornaments, many of which Fidelia remembered from her youth. Fidelia recalled the year so long ago when her pa wouldn't allow a tree inside, but Grandma had finally gotten her way. Now with the children, Johnny and Abe and Reka's two children, a celebration was imminent. They had arrived early enough to attend the Christmas Eve service, and having grown up in that church, Fidelia felt right at home and spoke with friends she'd known in school. Even Boyd agreed to go, but he and James stuck close together. There were prayers for the country and for the soldiers, but, in his heart, James knew they would need much more than prayers.

After Johnny was put to bed, Fidelia sat with her grandparents in the sitting room while Boyd and James carried firewood into the house.

"Delia, I want to tell you that I've torn up and burned the papers giving Abe and Reka their freedom," said Grandpa. "I know we've discussed this, but after the state impressed Abe, I knew they were safer as our property with no inquiry to our breaking the law. With no chance he be taken away and sold to another. My will has been rewritten and notarized passing ownership to you. I hope at the end of this war they will gain freedom, but I know you will ensure that when possible. I have explained it to Abe, and he understands, though it took a while to assure Reka about the children. And protecting them is another reason I had to do this."

"I believe that to be best, Grandpa. The President says they are free, but they are not. James thinks the war will end soon. He said the losses are too great and support for war is waning. Tomorrow is not soon enough for it to end."

Before Fidelia went upstairs to bed, Grandma pulled her aside.

"Is everything right with James?" The chilled civility between Fidelia and James had not escaped Grandma's notice. "I sense some distance between the two of you."

Fidelia stood silent, not expecting this question, but she should have known as her grandma misses nothing.

"Grandma, we are working through some things. I will tell you when I can. Now is not the time," said Fidelia. Grandma squeezed her granddaughter's hand tight.

"Well, I love you both. And I'm delighted to see that James looks much improved from when he arrived home."

As she walked up the stairs, Fidelia gathered how unwitting she'd been, how she'd been buried in her own miseries and failed to notice how her husband's health had gently returned. How the hollows in his face had filled and how he carried more weight of the work at the ranch.

When Fidelia walked into her old bedroom, the snug room

beside the room where Matilda and Jeremy had once resided, where Johnny now slept, she found the light of candles wavered about the walls. The smallness of the room glowed in the light, and James sat on the bed, waiting for her.

"Delia, I have a gift for you and it's something I want to be private. Can you sit here, next to me?"

She didn't answer him but felt uneasy as she sat on the bed.

"I have a lot to say, so forgive me, and I have this gift for you. I don't want it to upset you, and I give it in love, but I will tell you what it is before you see it."

He paused at the vision of his wife, luminous in the veiled dimness of candlelight, reminding him of dreams he'd had back in Tennessee, and he took a deep breath.

"When I found Miles, I also found what the scoundrels had left of his journal."

Fidelia gasped audibly, and James took her hand.

"I know that this journal was important to him. I have not kept it from you but wanted to clean it up and rebind the loose pages. It is yours because I know you loved him. I cannot say I wasn't jealous of him, of your feelings for him, but I accept that you loved him. I accept that you might have chosen him had he not died. I accept that he will always be a part of your life."

She squeezed James' hand as she thought of the words she'd written about the doves.

"So, I want you to have this," and he handed her the journal.

She held it in her hands, looked at the unopened leather book that was worn from time and tragedy. She felt the weight of it and then, looked up at James. *Who was this man? It was not the man she remembered from before, the businessman, always unruffled and wheeling and dealing.*

She looked hard into his eyes and saw they'd begun to tear up as she looked at him. There, in his eyes, she saw a sadness not there before the war.

"I love you more than anything. I know you deserve more than this half a man that's come home to you, but you are all I wanted to come home to, Delia."

She suddenly saw him flawed, with his nightmares and his doubts and this new softness. He was broken, like her, yet he'd remained steadfast through her sorrow and indecision, present to comfort her. He needed her. He'd never needed her before, but now, she felt drawn to him.

She laid the unopened journal on the bed and reached for her husband, tentative like a rendezvous between two new lovers. She took him in her arms as he returned her embrace, holding each other together—for, she realized in the moment, together they were whole.

They slept little that night but talked away the night hours. James had never seen his wife more beautiful than in the ether of the lambent candlelight, as if she were the essence he'd been seeking. For she was, and James told Fidelia about his trip to San Saba, and she said the young man who'd guided him sounded like the white Indian and she told her husband all about the boy who'd been captured once by Comanche. And then, he told her that Miles' horse, Marco, was in the barn at home, and her eyes grew wide at the providence of such a gift. She told James that he should have Miles' gelding since she had Trapper, and she told him how much she missed her mother and shared all the disappointments she had in her father. She told James that he was not half a man. He told her all about Clark and his friend Pete and that he had nightmares of the war but refused to say more about it, and she kissed him.

They made love as if it were the first time. They slept, and then they talked about the ranch and how much each of them loved it near the river, how Johnny ran free and joyous, how they loved it more than their lives in the city, and as their words fell back and forth, Fidelia saw a reflection of herself and all the moments that led her to this night. To this man who sat before her so vulnerable and, at once, big-hearted.

And she could not think these thoughts without remembering Miles who'd made different choices. Too full of exuberance to know his heart. Too full of love to be patient and steady. He, too, brought her here, to this day.

CHAPTER 42

Christmas Day, Pond Springs

After breakfast, Abe's family joined the McCord and the Hughes family in the sitting room, while Johnny followed Abe's young children around, intrigued by the company of people nearer his size, and the family shared their gifts while knowing full well that the gifts were truly each other. There was a new toy for each child, and Fidelia had stitched a blanket of down for Boyd.

"Quite timely," said Boyd, and he raised a cup of cider.

The holiday dinner was raucous and delicious, and as Fidelia watch the joy in the room, she thought about how much had changed since they'd arrived in Pond Springs in 1847. Through loss and time, how the family was smaller, yet still complete. And, at that moment, Fidelia felt the presence of all of them that were gone. A vision of Miles' easy laughter crossed her mind, and she looked across the table to find James's eyes resting on her and, there behind him, stood the faint presence of her old friend, Gray Feather, smiling at her, always reminding her that loved ones are never gone. That Christmas morning had never felt more like home, and in the midst of a horrible war, she was filled with gratitude.

Grandma smiled at Fidelia, for her granddaughter's glow had not gone unnoticed as Johnny sat in Grandpa's lap.

"I want to share with everyone here that Delia and I have decided to stay and work the homestead, with the help of Boyd. I going to contract its purchase from John and likely herd more cattle and plant fewer crops when the war ends. With all of that, I can pay Boyd more than the empty promises he now receives."

There was laughter and praise around the table at the news.

"Son, that farm should be Fidelia's and yours free and clear, what with the way my son walked away from it, leaving the work to my granddaughter. If you need any help getting a good deal, you just tell me and I'll be writing a long letter to my son, John."

"Who would like a cup of coffee? Real coffee," asked Grandma, and the children watched in bewilderment as the adults all cheered at once.

Discussion Questions

1. Discuss the factors that may have led Fidelia to choose to marry the "other man" instead of Miles.

2. Did Fidelia always feel the need to be the problem solver and caretaker? Why? Discuss the impact Fidelia's mother, father, and grandparents had on the kind of woman Fidelia grew to be.

3. Describe Fidelia's relationship with Leona? How did it grow over time? How did Leona change with the passage of time? How do you believe James' absence likely impacted them?

4. What motivated Miles to leave the place and people he loved in Texas to go north as war approached? How was Miles Maloney conflicted; what steered his choices?

5. James knew his wife had loved another man. How did this affect him as he was away from home? How did these feelings change because of the war, and how did the war change him?

6. Compare and contrast the two men who loved Fidelia.

7. Discuss Tony Norton and his impact on Miles' choices? How are Miles and Tony Norton alike? How are the two men different?

8. In what scene did the full consequences of Miles' choice to leave Texas become clear to him? Discuss.

9. How important is Clark to this story? What was the weight of fate and of the camaraderie between Clark and James?

10. Was Miles adept at lying? What traits made him good at information gathering and storytelling?

11. What was the impact on James at finding Miles in Tennessee? How did it change James? How did it change James' relationship with his wife?

12. How did Fidelia's discovery of the mourning doves bring comfort and clarity?

13. Did Fidelia choose the right path, or did destiny choose? What do you believe she would have done if both men had returned from the war?

14. How did perseverance reveal itself in the journeys of these characters? Consider the dangers of being abolitionists in a southern state. How did weakness influence the decisions of the characters?

Acknowledgments

For the Fidelia McCord Series, I always must start off acknowledging a young girl named Fidelia R. who traveled to Pond Springs from Illinois in 1847 in covered wagons—a girl whose story of loss broke my heart and inspired me. It was her story that created the fictional Fidelia McCord ... both young girls who suffered great losses as children, who persevered. The more I research and study the history of Texas, the more I am awed by the strength of this state's early settlers. They were courageous, stubborn, often lawless, and more persistent in the face of adversity than a mule headed home through the west Texas desert mountains.

As for research, I cannot remember all the rabbit holes I've delved into, online and in person, all the books, websites, and documentaries I've traveled to. Here, I shall name a few of my resources that were instrumental in revealing details of the time and places of this story: *Terry Texas Ranger Trilogy* (the personal accounts of J.K.P. Blackburn, L.B. Giles, and Ephraim S. Dodd); *The Lone Star and State Gazette*, by Marilyn McAdams Sibley; the *Weekly Star Gazette; None But Texians*, by Jeffrey D. Murrah; *Soap Suds Row*, by Jennifer J. Lawrence; *Texas and the Texans in the Civil War*, by Ralph A. Wooster; *Lonestar, Blue and Gray*, by Ralph A. Wooster; *The Call of the San Saba*, by Alma Ward Hamrick; and *The Spy of the Rebellion*, by Allan Pinkerton.

In getting this novel to print, I am so grateful for the

support of my peers who gave critical feedback and to my readers who, through a pandemic, kept asking for the rest of Fidelia's story. I am grateful to Atmosphere Press and their staff for their consistent encouragement and assistance in finalizing my work throughout this series. The words of *The Mourning of the Dove* would not have come together as seamlessly as they have without the guidance and patience of my editor, BE Allatt—always asking pertinent questions! And, of course, through my historical novels, the amazing Jenny Quinlan of Historical Editorial never disappoints on book cover design. I can assure you that Ms. Quinlan can take the stock photos I glean from wherever and magically create impeccable art that is a lovely reflection of a story.

Over the years, I have come to love writing about Texas. I was not born here in Texas but came, over time and circumstance, from the mid-Atlantic state of Delaware. I grew up in many places, including Amarillo, Texas, as my dad was a military man, but in almost fifty years, I have not been able to make my home elsewhere (though I admit I've tried a couple of times). The more I learn of Texas history and the more small Texas towns I visit in the prairies and hills, the more I find the draw of Texas grows stronger and my roots deeper.

IF YOU ENJOYED THIS NOVEL, PLEASE CONSIDER WRITING A REVIEW ON AMAZON OR GOODREADS. THANK YOU.

About Atmosphere Press

Atmosphere Press is an independent, full-service publisher for excellent books in all genres and for all audiences. Learn more about what we do at atmospherepress.com.

We encourage you to check out some of Atmosphere's latest releases, which are available at Amazon.com and via order from your local bookstore:

Dancing with David, a novel by Siegfried Johnson
The Friendship Quilts, a novel by June Calender
My Significant Nobody, a novel by Stevie D. Parker
Nine Days, a novel by Judy Lannon
Shining New Testament: The Cloning of Jay Christ, a novel by Cliff Williamson
Shadows of Robyst, a novel by K. E. Maroudas
Home Within a Landscape, a novel by Alexey L. Kovalev
Motherhood, a novel by Siamak Vakili
Death, The Pharmacist, a novel by D. Ike Horst
Mystery of the Lost Years, a novel by Bobby J. Bixler
Bone Deep Bonds, a novel by B. G. Arnold
Terriers in the Jungle, a novel by Georja Umano
Into the Emerald Dream, a novel by Autumn Allen
His Name Was Ellis, a novel by Joseph Libonati
The Cup, a novel by D. P. Hardwick
The Empathy Academy, a novel by Dustin Grinnell
Tholocco's Wake, a novel by W. W. VanOverbeke
Dying to Live, a novel by Barbara Macpherson Reyelts

Looking for Lawson, a novel by Mark Kirby
Yosef's Path: Lessons from my Father, a novel by Jane Leclere
    Doyle
Surrogate Colony, a novel by Boshra Rasti
Orleans Parish, a novel by Chad Pentler

About the Author

Sandra Fox Murphy wrote her first novel in 2015 after retiring from the U.S. Geological Survey. She is intrigued by the journeys of our ancestors, and before writing *Let the Little Birds Sing* and *On a Lark* of the Fidelia McCord Series, she published *A Thousand Stars*, set in Rhode Island, and a Civil War tale called *That Beautiful Season*. Sandra finds that the history of early America begs for the stories of the characters, both real and imagined, to be told.

Born in Delaware and growing up as a USAF "brat," she eventually found her way to Texas where she graduated from The University of Texas at Austin. She has lived throughout the USA and on islands in both the Atlantic and the Pacific. She now resides in central Texas and dreams of living in Marfa.

Learn more at www.sandrafoxmurphy.com.